THE
SUM
OF
YOUR
FLESH

BEVERLEY LEE

Published by Ink Raven Press
Copyright © 2023 Beverley Lee

ISBN - 13 978-0-9935490-6-9

Cover design by
ELDERLEMON DESIGN
Interior design by
PLATFORM HOUSE PUBLISHING

For those who play in the sandbox of words.
Dream on.

There are more things in heaven and earth, Horatio,
than are dreamt of in your philosophy.

Hamlet (1.5.167-8)

CHAPTER ONE

The train sped deep into the November night, slicing through the fog-shrouded bleakness like a scythe. Condensation ran down the windows, and the occasional lonely light swept past in the hungry dark. Inside, people stood, rammed up against each other, every precious inch of space a luxury for whoever managed to grab it.

Haven sat next to the aisle, his holdall stuffed under his seat with his jacket. He tried not to think about what might be on the grimy floor, and for the third time in his journey he wondered if he had made the right decision. He didn't like crowds, even though his line of work—if you could call it that—frequently put him amongst a throng of gyrating bodies.

That was a necessary evil. This was simply his own decision.

The train lurched slightly as it changed tracks, and the man standing in the aisle next to him reeled. His bag slipped from his shoulder and the corner caught Haven across the cheek.

'I am so sorry,' the man began, but when his gaze fell upon Haven, his words came to an abrupt stop.

Haven saw the usual prejudice shadow in the man's eyes, saw the intolerance behind it. It happened a lot.

'Not a problem,' Haven said, his voice emotionless. The man looked away quickly.

For someone who would have much rather blended in, Haven Ford stuck out like a street mutt at Crufts. He was tall but had mastered the ability to fold his limbs into cramped spaces, much like the one he was in now.

The voicemail had come just as he was about to go out of the door for the evening, which was probably why the man stared when Haven's black, heavily made-up eyes met his. Haven could work a mean winged eyeliner.

Or maybe it was the barbed wire ink that crawled across his throat, barely visible above his skull-print bandana. Or his dark hair, which he wore long. Tonight it was loosely braided over one shoulder.

Yes, of all the people in the carriage that night, Haven would be the one people remembered if questioned.

He took his phone from his jacket pocket and listened to the voicemail again.

I need you to help him, Ven. That name had knocked all the air from his lungs. No one else but Sebastian ever called him that. *I can't do it anymore. I'm so fucking sorry.* Here the message paused, and Haven could hear hitched breathing in the gap. *Remember I told you about Rafferty? Of course you do, you never forget anything.* A small laugh. *Please help him. And if you can't you'll know what to do. Don't think badly of me. I need to go now. You were always my place to hide.*

That was it, the message ended. Haven had replayed it a dozen times already.

He hadn't heard from Sebastian in months—How many? Four, five?—and Haven had almost got to thinking that he had smoothed it all out with his weird family, that things were finally working out for him.

And now this, right out of the blue.

Haven didn't like it. He didn't like the note of desperation he heard in the spaces between the words.

Which is why he'd shoved a few things into a bag and left the house, his steps not leading him into the city, where the rain shone like glass on the roads and pavements, but to the railway station.

He had first met Sebastian in a small bookshop, the kind that had barely any space between the rows, the kind Haven liked best. It had old-fashioned shelving, with no back partitions, so books nestled together, story against story. Cocooned in the dusty section labelled OCCULT AND SUPERNATURAL, Haven pulled out a book he hadn't seen before—and met Sebastian's harried gaze in the adjacent aisle.

No one else was ever in this section. Haven had got used to the solitary joy of leafing through old books, his eyes scanning for words that might explain what had happened on the night that had changed his life. Some might call that over dramatic, but there were no real words for when you see a dead body get up and walk away.

Maybe it was the fact Sebastian had the same interests—kindred spirits and all that. Or maybe it was the desperate look in his eyes, one Haven had seen many times staring back at him from a mirror. Whatever it was, they got talking and an hour later were in a side-street bar, bottles of cold beer on the table in front of them.

How old had they been? Haven did a little mental maths. Twenty? Twenty-one? It had been a few years into Haven's new life and he was still trying to get his head around all of it, still hovering on the jagged edges before it swallowed him whole.

He remembered condensation running down the bottle onto his fingers, the garish glow of a pink neon sign reflected in the mirrors under the optics.

'How much do you believe in it?' Sebastian said, his shoulders hunched, as though that might protect him from Haven's reply. 'The supernatural.'

Haven took a drink, felt the chilled beer slide down his throat as he studied Sebastian's face. He'd been played with before. 'Enough.' He waited, watched Sebastian chew the edge of his thumb nail.

'I have a very fucked-up family,' Sebastian finally said. 'Stuff you wouldn't believe.'

Haven didn't push for any more details, although part of him screamed *just try me!* It was as though this simple exchange of words had forged a tentative bond between them. They got blindingly drunk, and when Haven opened one bloodshot eye the next morning and stumbled to the kitchen, he found a note stuck on the fridge with a magnetic tag.

Thanks for the couch and the beer. A mobile number scrawled underneath.

Two months after, Sebastian appeared at his door, this time holding up a six-pack. This was how their relationship went. Sebastian came and he left, usually after a day, maybe two.

Haven came to understand he only did this when things at home became too much.

'It's like everything comes together, like a volcano wanting to blow, you know?'

Haven was his safe space, the place where Sebastian could rest until the lava in his mind settled back down again.

Rafferty was the reason Sebastian never stayed long. He didn't want to leave his younger brother by himself for too long, was always worried Rafferty would *wander into something he shouldn't.*

One thing was for sure, Sebastian adored Rafferty. Which was why the voicemail had set all Haven's alarm bells screaming out like an air raid siren.

I can't do it anymore.

Haven sat back in his seat and willed the train to hurry.

He wasn't sure what he could do to help Rafferty, but Sebastian had asked and part of Haven was curious about this side of Sebastian he'd never seen. His home side. The weird family. The house at the fringe of the village.

But where was Sebastian if he wasn't going to Haven's?

There were too many questions and the air in the carriage was too hot, too full of disillusionment, for Haven to even contemplate picking them apart.

The announcement ticker at the front of the carriage burst into life and the train began to slow.

Haven gathered up his bag, slung his jacket over his shoulder, and squeezed through the throng blocking the exit door.

The train slowly juddered to a halt, the doors opening in a pneumatic blast of air. Haven stepped down onto a deserted platform, a single light piercing the foggy darkness at the side of a locked ticket booth. He took a deep breath, welcoming the chill of the night into his lungs.

Haven watched as the train snaked into the distance and the crimson glow from its rear lights winked out.

Only one other person got off the train, a woman with a small, wheeled suitcase. She had her phone to her ear as Haven made for the exit.

He stopped at the gate, his gaze sweeping over the empty car park, the name of the station displayed above the payment machine. Mortimer West. It was a proud admission for a speck on the map, as though it was large enough to have an East or a North or a South.

Headlights sliced through the dark on the road in front, then turned in at the entrance. A taxi drove slowly down the small incline leading to the car park, pulling up at the gate.

Haven began to walk. The edge of the station was lit, but beyond that an unpleasant darkness yawned. No street lamps. No houses. He swore under his breath at his lack of planning.

Maybe this spur-of-the-moment decision to come here had royally fucked him over. He pulled his jacket collar up against the chill.

Two beams of brightness lit his way as the taxi slowly cruised alongside him. The rear window slid down.

'I'm guessing you haven't been here before?' The question came from the woman in the back seat. The woman who had got off the train. She quirked an eyebrow in his direction, her phone still clutched in her hand.

'No. First time,' he answered. 'Is that obvious?'

'Pretty much so.' A smile tugged at her lips and she studied him. But it wasn't the kind of look he usually got, where people were working out how aggressive he might be. 'The village is a couple of miles away and there's no pavement for much of it, unless things have changed. I'd hate for you to meet a horrible end.'

It was a joke, delivered with a laugh that crinkled the skin around her eyes, but Haven felt it like a blow. *Her choice of words.* He dredged up a smile, tried for an air of nonchalance.

'Get in,' she said. Not *would you like a lift?* The latter gave him the option of stepping back, of saying no.

Haven got in.

CHAPTER TWO

'I assumed you were heading to the village? There's not much else around here,' the woman said as the taxi pulled out of the station and swung onto a country lane. The driver dipped his main beam as drifts of thick fog swirled towards them.

'Yeah. I've come to look up an old friend.' It wasn't exactly a lie. Part of him hoped he'd knock on Sebastian's door and find him standing there, that his voicemail had been simply a low point in a bad day.

'Can we drop you there?'

This was a perfectly normal question, but one Haven didn't have an answer for. He made a play of fastening the strap on his holdall whilst his brain tried to come up with something that sounded plausible.

'It's a surprise visit,' he said, 'but it's too late now. I'll go round in the morning.'

It sounded lame, even to Haven's ears. But something stopped him from asking to be dropped at the Henderson house, something that made him curl his fingers into his palm.

'Well, I'm staying at The Cross Keys. You could always ask if they have a room for a night?' She offered him a smile, which made him feel bad. He didn't like lying. Lies had a nasty habit of coming back to bite you.

When he didn't respond she filled the awkward silence with an introduction, without missing a beat. 'Meredith Evans.' She unwound the scarf from around her neck. 'I'm here for work.'

She glanced away then, her hand touching her throat.

So he wasn't the only one not being wholly honest. Most people would have missed it, but Haven had made a point of studying people, their subtle nuances and gestures. Often they said far more than any words.

The taxi slowed and the driver muttered something under his breath. The fog was thick here, and the headlights drowned in its embrace. Haven glanced out of the window but there was nothing but persisting white. It obliterated everything.

'It won't be long now,' Meredith said. 'It's very open here, just fields on both sides, too much green.'

He wondered how she knew.

The driver changed down a gear and the taxi began to climb a steep hill. Soon the fog became more of a shifting ghost than a blanket. Hedgerows appeared out of the murk, silhouettes of winter trees, the occasional small cottage nestling by the roadside.

They passed an old church with an overgrown graveyard, a Victorian primary school with a clock tower, and a lonely play park where the headlights picked out the shining eyes of a prowling cat in the grass.

It all seemed so very rural. So very ordinary.

The taxi rounded a bend and the village sign flashed by. A few hundred yards of picturesque terraced cottages and then streetlights punctured the darkness.

'And here we are.' Meredith's voice dragged him out of his scrutiny.

He glanced left and saw a whitewashed pub set back off the road, a few trestle-type tables outside. Golden light illuminated the windows.

Haven reached for his wallet as Meredith gathered her things. This was another problem. His cash flow was what most people would call minimal.

'Don't worry about that.' She waved a hand dismissively. 'My boss is paying. I usually drive but my car is in the garage, brake problems. So I struck a bargain. I'd take the train if Cameron— that's my boss—would get all my work stuff sent here and arrange to get a hire car to me in the morning.'

All this as they both climbed out into the chill of the night. Haven listened; it felt good to be a part of an actual conversation, even if he wasn't adding to it. So much of his life now was spent watching. Calculating. Being invisible unless he wanted to be seen.

'You really didn't need to hear me prattle on.' She steepled her fingers by her mouth. 'None of this means anything to you.'

Haven lifted her suitcase from the boot and slammed it closed.

'It's fine, really.' He wheeled the case over to her, wanted to add, *Actually, it's more than fine. Most people give me a wide berth, judge me on how I look. I appreciate you treating me kindly, without that judgement.*

He wasn't asking for pity. He'd chosen this life for himself, but occasionally people swept by and reminded him that not everyone was spiteful and narrow-minded. Some people were just good people.

He didn't count himself as one.

'Are you coming in?' She was by the pub door now, the entrance lantern bathing her in a soft glow. Now he could see her hair wasn't blonde like he'd first thought, it was silver, and her eyes were wrinkled with smile lines, her mascara smudged beneath them.

'Maybe in a bit,' he said, hoisting his bag onto his shoulder. 'Thanks for the ride.'

They both knew that was a lie, just as they both knew there was more to say.

Haven watched as Meredith wheeled her suitcase into the pub. He caught a glimpse of a roaring log fire in an old hearth, of people laughing and chattering, huddled around beaten-brass-topped tables.

The door closed and he shrugged his shoulders, zipping up his jacket against the biting cold. He was here, for better or worse, but what he would find was still cloaked in mystery.

The hair rose on the nape of his neck and he glanced back over his shoulder, saw a face quickly disappearing from the pub window. His lips narrowed. No doubt he'd been tarred and feathered already. His sort did not belong in quaint country villages.

A sudden gust of wind took up, scattering the dried autumn leaves across the road. They danced away, skittering over the pavement, vanishing under the gate that led to the church yard. His gaze settled there.

The lychgate. The timber-framed gateway with the pitched tile roof where the coffins would rest on their way to burial.

Haven knew a lot about death. About the traditions surrounding it.

About the dead who wouldn't stay that way.

He lifted his gaze to the church tower, shrouded in drifting fog, the circular timepiece on its wall nearly obscured behind the lofty reaching boughs of a majestic yew tree.

Haven crossed the road and opened the gate. It squeaked softly. He caught the scent of moss and damp from the rafters, let his focus drift up the path as it meandered into the dark.

Something was off-kilter here. He couldn't have put his finger on what it was but logged the sensation anyway.

Things happened for a reason.

CHAPTER THREE

Meredith unpacked the clothes from her suitcase and laid them on the bed.

Her room was at the front of the pub, reached by a set of rickety stairs that led from a door at the right-hand side of the bar. The floor sloped slightly, which made the furniture seem like it had had one drink too many, but it was clean. Or as clean as she needed it to be for the few days she was here.

Three days. Four days max, she had told Cameron when he asked how long the job would take.

She had read the preliminary report so knew how many items were in the various rooms—although the precise number of books in the library wasn't stated—estimated how long it would take her, and then she'd added a couple more days because Cameron never checked. . . . She stopped, her gaze flicking to the window as a tanker rumbled past on the road. The glass vibrated in the old frames.

She wondered when it had become so easy to lie, or possibly it was just a way of bending the truth?

So maybe she'd said four because that would give her an extra day to look around? It wasn't that big a deal, and she hardly took any time off.

No one would remember her here. She'd been thirteen when she left and looked nothing like the slip of a girl who'd been more than happy to leave this place behind.

If she was honest with herself, she'd taken this job purely because of its location.

Meredith folded a couple of jumpers and placed them in a drawer, went across to the window, and stared out at the darkened street, the thickness of the night interrupted by the fog-drenched glow from a couple of streetlights opposite. She thought about the young man in the taxi and scratched the side of her neck.

He hadn't told her his name, and his reasons for being here didn't add up. Visiting a friend? That sounded genuine. But not calling because it was late?

She checked her watch. 8.10 p.m. Hardly the middle of the night.

Why was she letting a stranger's caginess get under her skin? A surge of annoyance flared, and she unfastened the catch on the sash window and dragged it up. Cold air rushed in and she knelt, her knees protesting slightly.

Meredith laid her cheek on the narrow sill and closed her eyes.

Laughter roared from the bar below. The creak of a door, the sound of footsteps running across the cobbled street.

She was tired. Travelling always made her tired now, as though being away from home was a disease that sapped all her strength. But it was only advancing age. Although fifty-five wasn't particularly ancient.

But close enough to becoming invisible.

Meredith had no intention of disappearing into the ether but she was well aware that her best years were behind her.

A laugh came from her lips. Trying to turn back the clock wasn't on her agenda, and whilst a lot of her friends relied on injectable fillers, she was happy enough in her own skin. Unless a photograph caught her at a precisely cruel angle.

The harshest judge is behind our own eyes.

She closed the window and stood, frustrated that her thoughts had turned so maudlin. Her stomach rumbled, reminding her she hadn't eaten anything since lunch.

Meredith grabbed her phone and headed downstairs.

The bar was packed with people but she navigated her way through to a small alcove where a table sat empty.

A young woman, wearing an apron with the pub's name embroidered on the front, came across.

Meredith ordered chicken pie, as it was the first thing on the menu, and a large glass of red wine. She didn't specify. This wasn't the sort of place to offer choices from the wine list.

One positive thing about getting older and becoming more invisible is it allows you to people watch without any personal scrutiny. Meredith let her gaze wander about the bar. She wondered if any of the people drinking and chatting together were children she had known, still stuck in the place they'd been born, like whirring cogs, always moving but never going anywhere.

But most of all she wondered if Amelia and Grace were still here.

They'd been older than her, and were more her sister's friends, but Meredith had tagged on behind, especially during *that* summer, because her parents were always working.

Some days Amelia and Grace included her properly, and those were the days when she daydreamed about gaining their trust. Daydreamed about them taking her aside, speaking in hushed tones, making her blood-promise never to tell anyone. And hadn't she done enough to earn that trust on the first day?

13

But Amelia and Grace Henderson had secrets. The Hendersons always had secrets. Always kept to the fringes. Because people here had long memories.

'Here you go.'

Meredith was forced out of her thoughts by the plate clattering onto the table, followed by cutlery wrapped in a napkin and a generous measure of red wine in a balloon glass.

The pub door opened and a man entered, unbuttoning his coat as he went to the bar. The barmaid exchanged a few words with him, then pointed across to Meredith.

'Glad I found you,' said the man. He took something from his coat pocket, slid it across the table towards her. 'Found it in the back of the cab when I clocked off. Knew it had to be you or that bloke you were with. You've been my only fare today.'

The salacious grin he gave her suggested he thought he knew more than he did. He ambled back to the bar where his pint stood waiting.

Meredith picked up the phone. It looked like a million other phones with its black screen, surrounded by a black rubber case, the kind you could drop from a mountain and not worry about it.

She took a large mouthful of wine, let it slide down her throat before pressing a button at the side.

The lock screen lit up with a photo.

Not a person or some downloaded screensaver.

A photo of what looked like an abandoned warehouse, stripped down to its shell, with concrete pillars and old wiring hanging from the ceiling. Puddles of dark water lay on the floor and a thin light oozed through broken windows.

If ever there was a place of despair, this was it.

Why would anyone have this as the first thing they see every time they used their phone?

But now she had a problem. She had to locate the young man she'd shared the taxi with and return it, and she didn't even know his name.

Maybe he didn't want her to know, had come here with his own intentions and needed to fly under the radar.

When it came down to it, this place was steeped in secrets, of untruths told to keep the seeds of those secrets buried and dormant. It was the kind of place that called to those with their own.

Like calls to like.

Which is why you're here, yes?

She took another gulp of wine.

The question scorched across her mind. She shivered at the tracks it left behind.

CHAPTER FOUR

Rafferty Henderson sat by the fire in the gatehouse cottage, his fingers clasped between his knees, his lips pressed firmly together as though he was scared of the words that might erupt.

His grandmother—although he never called her that—and aunt were in the kitchen. The clatter of crockery and the sound of a wooden spoon beating the contents of a bowl into submission. Amelia Henderson always turned to baking when things were out of her control.

'He'll come back.' Amelia's sister, Grace, voiced the words they all were holding on to. All were praying. Although Godly intervention was in short supply in the Henderson house.

'I will flay the skin from his hide.'

The spoon quickened, and Rafferty knew the batter was taking the beating meant for Sebastian. But it was all figurative. Theirs was not a family that resorted to violence. There had been enough of it in their past.

Grace's voice lowered. 'How is he?'

Rafferty's ears pricked up. Now he was under discussion.

'Quiet.'

A heavy sigh.

'I feel like every time Sebastian leaves, a little piece of Rafferty ebbs away.' Amelia's voice was barely a whisper, but Rafferty caught it. His sense of hearing was sharp, something they sometimes forgot.

He leaned forward and picked up the poker, stabbed at an ash-covered log. It collapsed and the flames soared. Instant heat warmed his face.

Rafferty understood why Sebastian felt the need to leave, why he needed pockets of time away from the cottage, time where he could maybe pretend to be someone else.

Because being a Henderson wasn't easy.

Scratch that. Being a male Henderson wasn't easy.

Families are forged from the cinders of those who came before, be it a facial resemblance or a weird trait that resurfaces three generations down the line.

There's always the fear that something not quite pleasant will rear its head too.

And nothing could match what Irving Walsh had wrought on his male lineage.

The sins of the fathers . . .

Rafferty shook his head, then wandered to the window. He pulled back the curtain, longing for a light, longing for the gate to creak and bang back against the post.

But there was only the thick, fog-drenched darkness.

He wanted to run too. But at fifteen years of age there was nowhere else to go.

'Are you hungry, Rafferty?' Grace's voice interrupted his thoughts.

'Not yet.'

He didn't want to tell her he'd taken a snack into the woods earlier. Mealtimes were sacrosanct in the Henderson household, but eating outside always made him feel more alive.

He turned and found her frowning in the kitchen doorway, dirt from the garden smearing her denim dungarees. Grace found

17

her solace in the earth whilst Amelia drowned her sorrows in sugar and flour. That part of their make-up was, at least, fairly normal.

'You need to eat,' Grace said, a little too firmly.

'Leave him be.' Amelia's immediate response, as though she had been waiting for her sister's words, knowing what they were before she had spoken. They had a connection that verged on the uncanny, but given what they knew, that wasn't much of a surprise.

Grace huffed and went to the chair Rafferty had vacated, picking up her knitting from the side table. The click-clack of the needles fell into the silence.

Rafferty wandered into the kitchen, found Amelia pouring cake mixture into a blackened tin.

He wrinkled his nose at the scent of fat and sugar.

'I know.' She nodded, a smear of flour on her cheek. 'I made you something earlier, though. It's in the fridge.'

'I'll have it later,' he said, looking down at his bare feet. The warmth from the range stove bled from the old quarry tiles. A worm of guilt wriggled in his gut.

He wondered how hard it was for both of them, living with him, putting up with Sebastian's disappearances whilst the legacy of Irving Walsh refused to die.

He'd asked Amelia once why they couldn't all simply move away.

'We have responsibilities, Rafferty. Our roots are here, and we can't just leave and pretend the past didn't happen.' Her tone had softened then, her fingers reaching out to touch his cheek. 'I know it's hard for you, but believe me, Grace and I have done everything we can to make your life better. To protect you. One day you'll understand.'

All he knew was that Irving Walsh had been the captain of a ship that had been marooned in the Arctic ice during the late

1800s. He was found, close to death, in the spring of the following year, the only survivor. There was no sign of his crew, a crew furnished from the able-bodied men who had lived in this area.

Rafferty guessed that's why they were shunned if they ever went into the village. Families need someone to blame. Especially when there's nothing left to bury.

Especially when the family responsible has a crypt in the village churchyard, containing all the bones of their ancestors.

The first time he went to the village he'd been about six, and he had a firm memory of Sebastian's hand in his and the excitement of seeing somewhere that wasn't the cottage or the woodland surrounding it.

He'd worn a black wool suit, the collar turned up against the cold. It had made his neck itch and he fiddled with it until Amelia told him not to fidget.

They had stood, Sebastian and himself, Amelia and Grace, as the awful sound of ruptured stone engraved with Henderson names filled the air. The stone windows, behind which the coffins slept, decimated. The coffins themselves were dragged from the crypt and placed on the ground in front of it.

He didn't know why. Nobody told him.

And there were no villagers paying their respects as the late afternoon sun slanted down through the bare trees and the clouds gathered in a skulking mass.

It began to rain as the line of long black hearses drove in along the side road. Rafferty watched as men he didn't know loaded the coffins, one by one, Amelia and Grace overseeing the operations.

Something else had happened afterwards, but it was only a hazy blur in Rafferty's mind.

Then Sebastian had taken him to a tea shop and Rafferty had sat with a huge slab of chocolate cake in front of him on a china plate—just to appear normal. He poked it with a fork, brought a few crumbs to his mouth, then had to spit them into a napkin.

The staff watched them from behind a counter, their eyes filled with judgement.

That was the first day he realised other people despised them. It had only gone downhill from then.

Rafferty crossed to the back door and reached for his jacket hanging from a peg on the wall.

'No.' Amelia placed her hand on his shoulder. He turned his head from the smell of butter on her fingers. 'No going out tonight. Not with Sebastian away.'

He wanted to argue, launch the rebellious side of him he knew was inside but which never fully surfaced.

But all he did was back away from the door, grabbing a snack from the fridge as he passed—he wasn't really hungry but he needed something to comfort the hollowness in the pit of his stomach.

Then he padded up the narrow, wooden staircase to his room.

His curtains were open and he didn't switch on a light. The fog had settled to a shifting, ghostly blanket above the fields. Through the woodland, sparse and winter-thin, he could see the church tower a few miles to the east. The moon, three days from full, cloaked in cloud, nestled above it. He rested his brow against the window, felt the cold glass separating him from what lay beyond.

The dish he'd taken from the fridge contained two things. They gleamed slightly in the diffused moonlight. He picked one and held it up. It was slightly sticky in his fingers. He lapped at the end, felt the beaten raw egg coat his tongue.

His saliva glands flared and he bit into it. Not absolutely perfect. A little too cold. That always masked the true flavour.

But Amelia said she couldn't leave food lying around, even in winter.

Rafferty chewed slowly, his gaze fixed on the church tower. Didn't let his thoughts dwell on what else lay in the dark to the west.

He licked his fingers. A sudden image crossed his mind of someone watching him from afar, their expression one of unsurpassed disgust.

Because Rafferty could only eat raw foods. As a child, Amelia had tried to balance his cravings with vegetables and the odd piece of fruit, but now Rafferty would only consume one thing.

The final piece of his snack lay in the dish. The juices from it had pooled in the bottom.

He took the shredded raw steak, held it in his fingers whilst he tipped the dish to his lips.

The bloody meat juice ran down his throat, and all too soon it was gone.

CHAPTER FIVE

Amelia Henderson had long since considered herself the matriarch of her family even though Grace was three years older. Grace was happy enough to let her slide into the role, especially after Sebastian and Rafferty had been left on their doorstep by Grace's son, Rafferty a sleeping babe in his brother's arms. Most people would have insisted that the parents step up, that whatever it was that was bothering them could be worked out with family love and support. But they weren't most families.

And maybe Grace's son had known what was going to happen, because six months later a policeman knocked on their door. Aaron Henderson was dead. A freak climbing accident.

But nothing about the Henderson deaths was ever an accident.

The irony that keeping the family secrets fell to the women, when all the misdeeds of the past had been committed by one man, was never far from her thoughts.

Amelia dried the last plate on the drainer and stacked it in the cupboard, the strain of recalling the memories ratcheting up the tension in her neck. She wouldn't settle tonight. Not until she checked.

'I'm going for a walk,' she yelled through the doorway as she pulled on thick boots and a coat that had seen nearly as many winters as Rafferty.

There was no answer from the living room, only the constant click-clack of the needles, although she knew Grace had heard her. Heaven forbid she go out without saying so, though; now that would start a war.

She opened the door and went out into the November night. Rafferty was safe inside. This thought warmed her against the biting chill.

Her boots crunched on the swathe of dried leaves over the path and she could smell the scent of wood smoke from their chimney. Comforting sounds. Comforting smells.

But there was less comfort in her heart.

If only Sebastian were here . . .

She shouldn't be worried. He'd disappeared before, many times, but always came home. This time, though? This time it felt different.

And she was angry too. Angry that he had gone again, because he knew what this did to Rafferty.

Life would be so much simpler with girls. But there hadn't been a girl born to the Henderson line in decades.

Only boys. Boys who had all been not completely normal.

There wasn't an inherent family gene defect, nothing any medical person could document. But they were all marred, sometimes since birth. Tainted with the poison Irving Walsh brought back from that fated expedition.

The surname wasn't the same. Years ago someone had changed it to Henderson, probably to try to rid the stigma, but it didn't alter the past or the bloodline, nor people's memories, passed down as they were.

The darkness thickened as Amelia veered off into the woods. A startled rabbit darted across in front of her and disappeared into the undergrowth. She turned and could just see the cottage through the trees. Rafferty stood by his bedroom window.

A pang of regret knifed through her. *What kind of life is this for him?* Living with two old women and a brother he couldn't rely on.

Living with the burden of what he was descended from.

Oh, sweet boy, she thought, *you don't know the half of it.*

The things she had done would never be written down, but they were carved into her bones.

She turned back to the path, and despite the hazy moonlight the darkness seemed more concentrated now, as though her thoughts had bled out and coagulated within it.

Amelia shoved her hands into her coat pockets and strode on, her steps leading along a pathway barely marked by footfall, but she could find her way here with her eyes shut.

Did Grace know about her wanderings? That they always led here?

She suspected so, but Grace wouldn't ask. Amelia had always been the one to double check the locks at night, to make sure the stove was turned down before they went out.

It made sense that she would check for this too.

An owl screamed deep in the woods, the piercing sound reaching her ears too loud, as though something else had ridden in on the back of the scream.

Stop it, she told herself. *There's nothing here now.*

She tramped through a tangle of blackberry vines, barbed stems snagging at her clothes. A thick cane bounced back and scored her cheek.

First blood.

Wisps of fog curled around the slender, bone-white trunks of the silver birch trees. She could smell rotting vegetation and the dank stench of standing water.

And then she was out into the small clearing where the birds never sang and where insects never ventured, even in the sweltering evenings of full summer.

The well sat there, as it had always done, squat and solid and sleepy. It had long ago lost its roof containing the winding mechanism. The bucket that had drawn fresh water was a distant memory.

Just a round, stone-built structure covered in moss and thick lichen.

Just a hole in the earth that led down to an underground stream.

That's what everyone thought, and Amelia was in no hurry to change their minds.

She walked towards it and ran her fingers over the rough old stone, peered down into the black depths although it was far too dark to work out where the bottom really was.

For an instant she imagined that something lay there in the dark, watching. And waiting.

'You're a stupid old woman,' she muttered.

There was no reason to think anything had changed. Yet she felt *something* was awry, something that made her gut twist into knots.

The last time this had happened had been nine years ago.

She could still see the line of hearses driving in, the frigid cold clinging to everything, Rafferty's pale face, so curious and confused. Grace's hands clasped together, her fingernails gouging half-moons into her skin. Amelia knew her sister was petrified about pulling the corpses from the crypt.

'They're just bones,' Amelia remembered saying.

But then why did she think they wielded such power?

If the villagers thought they were strange before, the removal of the coffins amped that up a thousand degrees. She could only imagine the gossip that night.

They took the coffins to the well and, one by one, emptied the contents into its depths. Some were dry bone and dust, but others? Others still contained strips of withered flesh clinging to the remains. Insects that had made their home in skeletal cavities scurried out over their hands, the smell of decay covering them with a miasma that had taken weeks to subside.

It was a desperate attempt to quell the sensation that something terrible had turned its face towards them. An offering of Henderson bones to the water, a reparation in the hope that perhaps the *wrong* that she felt would melt away.

But it didn't. And then the something terrible came to play.

CHAPTER SIX

Haven slept on a church pew wrapped in a silver foil sleeping bag he kept for occasions such as this, although 'slept' was perhaps too hopeful a word. There was a reason pews were solid wood and uncomfortable. It stopped the congregation from dozing.

He was thinking about this, lying on his back with his holdall as a pillow, when steps sounded on the stone floor.

Fuck it. He thought he'd be out of here without coming under scrutiny.

'Good morning.'

A male voice came from the back of the church. A flick of metal switches and the lights blinked on above. Haven shielded his eyes and scrabbled for his phone.

It wasn't there.

He swore softly again.

He eased himself up from the pew, took the tie on his wrist, and gathered his hair into a ponytail. His stomach grumbled noisily.

The man came across. About sixty years of age with a square jaw and dark hair peppered with silver. He wore corduroy trousers and a turtleneck jumper, along with a tweed sports coat.

'I'm just passing through,' Haven said, holding up his hands. He suddenly realised that he must look like a wreck. A wreck that might steal church property. The last thing he needed was polite conversation, but he was willing to admit his guilt at using the church as an overnight stay. 'I didn't break in. The door was open.'

'As it is always open, my young friend,' the man answered with an affable smile. 'Peter Edwards. Reverend Peter Edwards.'

Haven's eyes flicked to the man's throat and Peter laughed.

'You're very astute. There's no dog collar. It's eight a.m. on a Monday morning. I only came in to grab the notes I left here after last night's service.'

Haven stood, one hand rubbing the back of his neck. It ached from lying awkwardly.

'I take it you wouldn't say no to a coffee? Come into the vestry. I've got a coffee machine there, although you'll have to take it black.'

Peter set off down the central aisle.

Haven shrugged. What did he have to lose? The draw of caffeine was too strong.

By the time he entered the small room tucked away by the left-hand side of the altar—ducking his head under the low lintel—the filter machine was already gurgling. Peter had his back to him, a sheaf of notes in his hand.

'So, Mr. . . . ?' Peter paused, then turned to face him. 'What brings you to our quiet and frankly uninteresting little village?'

'Haven,' he said. 'Just Haven.'

Just Haven was his default answer when people queried his use of the single name. No one knew whether it was a Christian name or a surname or something he'd adopted along the way. But in the end it didn't matter. Names were what other people called you. Not who you really were.

But now Haven had a problem. If he continued with his passing-through cover story, he couldn't ask questions.

He tossed a figurative coin in his mind. It came down heads.

'I'm actually here to look someone up. An old friend.' His mouth watered as Peter poured coffee into two mugs, each with an illustration of the church on one side.

'Ask away, I know just about everyone here. And if I don't I can find out for you.' Peter cleared his throat.

Haven took a gulp of coffee. It burned his tongue but he didn't care. He looked around the room at the scattering of objects: stacks of worn bibles on an old bookcase, a painting of the church from an unusual angle—the building itself was in the background, the foreground showcasing the ancient stones of the graveyard—the alms plate on a desk with a pile of church booklets.

'I apologise for the mess, Haven. I am, for my sins, an unorganised soul.'

'Hey, I'm not judging,' Haven said with a smile. He reached forwards to put his mug on the table—he really needed to search for his phone—and caught sight of his reflection in the mirror hanging by the vestment cupboard.

Smeared mascara and eyeliner, which made the blue of his eyes seem cold and clear, a smattering of dark stubble, a red crease in his left cheek from the buckle on his holdall strap.

He wasn't sure whether he would have been as gracious as Peter if the tables were turned.

But not everyone was out for what they could get. He should remember that. The people he'd met here so far had been nothing but courteous.

Peter's voice cut into his thoughts. 'This old friend. Does he have a name?'

'Sebastian. Sebastian Henderson.'

The name echoed around the small room like a moth that couldn't settle.

Peter turned away briefly and topped up his mug. He flipped the sheaf of papers over, placed them on the desk on top of a small leather journal.

'Well, you are in luck, Haven. The Hendersons are well known in these parts. Although, I'm sad to say, not very well loved. May I ask how you came to know Sebastian?'

Haven's inner mental guard rattled.

He knew all about how the Hendersons were ostracised by the locals, that there was bad blood going back generations. There was no way Haven would let anyone know that Sebastian stayed with him on occasion.

'I knew him from school,' he said. 'And then I relocated.' The lie tripped from his tongue like a song. 'I was coming this way and wondered if he was still around.'

Peter took a pair of horn-rimmed glasses from his jacket pocket and cleaned them on a handkerchief. He appeared to be deep in thought.

'The Hendersons live up by the crossroads,' he said. 'But they're very private people. I'm not sure whether they would even open the door to a stranger.'

Haven mulled this over for a moment. Sebastian had said much the same thing.

'Tell me, Haven, are you in need of a small job whilst you're here? I can pay cash, but please don't tell the churchwarden.' A sheepish smile settled on Peter's lips.

'What kind of work?'

To be fair, he would take just about anything now. His bank balance was hovering dangerously close to zero.

'In the churchyard. I need the ivy and the undergrowth cleared out from around the old graves. No one comes to tend them now, and I can only do so much. There are tools and winter jackets in the outhouse.' Peter paused, perched the glasses on his nose as he picked up the sheaf of papers. 'You really would be doing me a favour.'

Haven considered the offer. It was actually pretty perfect. Cash in hand whilst he poked around and got to know more about the Hendersons. About Sebastian. *About Rafferty.*

As if to sweeten the deal, Peter added more.

'There's a room you can use in the church annexe.' He waved his hand behind him. 'Just over there. The bed is a bit basic, but it is private and there's a small shower room.'

And there it was, an opportunity waiting for him to grab it before it danced away.

Fate seemed to want to keep him here, and despite the strange feeling he'd had last night, Haven found himself nodding as Peter reached out to shake his hand.

CHAPTER SEVEN

Early morning sun slanted through the winter-bare branches of the oaks lining the drive to the house. The iron gates had been open when Meredith Evans turned off the narrow country lane, and for that she'd been grateful.

She drove slowly, as the overgrown drive was littered with potholes and windfall branches from the trees. No one had visited this place for a very long time, or if they had it was on foot.

Weird dreams had plagued her slumber. She couldn't remember exactly what, but everything had been tinted with an undulating blue light and she'd woken at 4 a.m. with her heart hammering in her chest. Then she'd fallen into a deep sleep and almost missed breakfast, but at least the hire car was waiting for her outside the pub.

The displaced phone sat in her bag. She still didn't know what she was going to do with it.

As the façade of the sprawling Victorian house came into view, she felt a momentary flash of remembrance. It tugged her back to her childhood and she was suddenly nine years old again, the house looming above her, her hair sticking to the back of her neck with sweat, Amelia whispering into her ear.

Meredith climbed out of her car and surveyed the building. Built in 1876, it was a red brick house with a porched entrance at the front. To the right of the door was a bay window, peeling paint hanging from the frame. Rotted gutters hung at an angle from a slate roof covered in tree debris and coated in thick moss.

She stood in front of the house as pale sunlight glinted from the filthy glass of its upper floors, and wondered why out of all the companies who dealt with discreet contents transference, this one had appeared on their books.

Meredith wasn't even supposed to be available, but her booked client had cancelled and suddenly she was free, and there it was, in her inbox, listed amongst half a dozen others. Her reply to Cameron saying yes to number 1267 was immediate.

She'd spent the rest of the day pacing the floor, her thoughts as scattered as dandelion seeds, feeling the magnetic pull of this place deep in her chest.

Now she stood before it again, with overgrown rhododendron bushes crowded against the outer walls at both sides and the skeletal limbs of a dead tree towering over the roof.

Time to go in, Mere. Time to put the ghosts to rest.

Of course, there hadn't been real ghosts. Only a panicked young mind fed by whispers and an overactive imagination.

She didn't have a key. The door would be open, she'd been told.

Her hand closed over the round metal handle. She twisted and pushed the door. It moved a little, the warped wood scraping on the threshold. Meredith put her shoulder against it until it finally gave and the door swung open.

Gloom crept to meet her. A dark wood staircase, bereft of carpet, led up to the left, rising from a long hallway with dusty ornate tiles covering the floor. A grandfather clock stood against the back wall, the glass case over the clock face riddled in cobwebs. Pale patches showed on the staircase walls, where paintings or photographs had once hung.

Bubbles of damp blistered the wallpaper below the dado rail, and the air had the same dank tang. The house was beginning to rot from the inside out.

It was tired and unloved, as though it was wearing a jumper that had seen better days and needed a good night's sleep.

No one had lived here since the original occupant.

She tried out the toggle on the metal light switch in the hall. A single lightbulb hanging from a twisted cord on the ceiling flickered to life slowly, begrudgingly bestowing a thin, wan light that barely broke the shadows.

So there was some life in the old house still.

If friends ever asked what she did, Meredith used the term 'cataloguer.' Most were happy with that description, although she suspected she was the source of much gossip when her back was turned. I mean, who would actually choose to spend their working days in run-down places in the middle of nowhere, some without plumbing or services?

Truth be told, she found it difficult to come up with a proper name. 'I pack away contents of old houses' was a bit of a mouthful. And not entirely true. Added to that should be the addendum 'weird old houses.' She loathed the term 'house clearance,' bringing to mind furniture shoved into a van with no care for it or the memories it held.

When she'd first started she often wondered why the families who owned the houses didn't do it, but as the years went on she discovered that the houses all had something in common. There was no family left to do it, or if there was they didn't want to get their hands dirty.

So she dragged packing cases into dusty rooms, wrapped objects and paintings, carefully itemising each one. Then a quick phone call to say the job was done, and she was on her way.

Meredith checked out the ground floor, looking in each room to make sure nothing had been left off her schedule of work. Sometimes families forgot little things hidden in corners. She pushed away the thought that she was only putting off the inevitable. She was here to pack books and personal items.

And in this house the latter made her mouth run dry.

She stood and listened, heard the wind rattling the loose tiles on the roof, and—she cocked her head to one side—the distant trickling of running water.

The sun disappeared behind a bank of clouds and the shadows thickened around her.

The outside door creaked open.

'Meredith Evans?'

Meredith wheeled around, her eyes widening.

A delivery driver in a brown uniform stood in the hallway, an electronic signing device in his hand.

Her heart hammered in her throat, but she nodded and tried to display a modicum of professional calm.

'Sorry, the door was open. I've got some items for you,' he said, his gaze taking in the ramshackle nature of the house. 'Where shall I put them?'

She edged past him, carrying down the hallway to a room to the left of the front door.

'You can put them in here.'

It was the room with the most light.

It felt odd to stand back and watch him bring in the packing cases and rolls of bubble wrap. Normally she brought these and the other supplies in the back of her car.

She hung around in the hallway, scrolling through her delivered emails until he finished. The signal here barely had a heartbeat.

He handed her the device to sign and she scrawled her signature across the screen.

'Wouldn't catch me working somewhere like this,' he said.

She fixed him with a cool stare. 'I like old houses. Better than people.'

He clipped the stylus onto the device and headed for the door, pausing to glance back. His gaze lifted to the top of the staircase.

She watched him reverse his van, exhaust fumes ghosting into the freezing air.

For some reason he had ruffled her feathers, and she set to work with her jaw clenched. She sometimes made up stories about the people who had lived in the houses where she worked. It whiled away the hours, made her feel closer to them as she wrapped once-loved possessions in tissue and placed them in packing crates.

But this time she knew who had lived in the house. It was the reason she'd leapt on it as soon as the email pinged into her inbox

Irving Walsh. The man who had disappeared in the frozen Arctic wastes. The man who had come home when all the others hadn't.

The house Amelia had whispered about, sowing seeds in Meredith's young mind that had germinated and bloomed. And still bloomed to this day.

She wondered why the house had never been on the market. It stood on a large plot and was very private: a country lane on one side, open fields on the other, and dense woodland to its rear.

Prime redeveloping material for someone with a bucketload of money.

It's none of your concern, Mere.

She worked steadily, carefully wrapping and cataloguing the books and packing them into the cases. Most were dry old texts with titles such as *Economics of the Victorian World* or *A Guide to Forest Management.* But there were a few nautical-themed books, both fiction and non-fiction.

It was odd how Walsh had made his home here and not on the coast, but she guessed that after the ordeal he went through, being close to the ocean had lost its appeal.

She stopped only briefly to eat a sandwich bought at the coffee shop opposite the pub and to drink a flask of coffee, Rosa, the bar maid, had thrust into her hands as she left.

Just as she'd finished up in the library a light rain began to fall. A glance out of the window showed a mass of dark cloud building to the west over the tarn. The gloom inside the house deepened.

Maybe she'd stop for today, come back tomorrow?

As soon as the thought entered her head Meredith gathered up her bag and scrambled in it for her car keys.

A sound met her ears as she stood by the front door, one hand outstretched to open it.

She strained to hear, inclining her head to one side. It was the unmistakable slow tick of a clock, sharp and monotonous.

Her gaze flew to the grandfather clock, the pendulum hidden within its wooden case like a secret heart.

The tick stopped. Silence took its place.

She twisted her mouth in confusion, thought that maybe the sudden movement in the house had coaxed the clock to wake.

Relief washed over her as she stepped outside. Meredith lifted her face to the sky, let the cold drizzle settle on her flushed skin.

A glance back as she climbed into her car. A glance to reassure herself that everything was okay. Everything was perfectly normal.

CHAPTER EIGHT

The annexe was attached to the side of the main church by a narrow hall, although it had its own glass-fronted entrance.

A set of stairs led to an upper floor, and this is where Haven stood, on a small landing, a key in his hand.

He opened the door and surveyed the lodging that had miraculously come his way. A single bed sat under a sloping roof, a chest of drawers at its side. Opposite the bed, a console-type desk with an Anglepoise lamp and a wooden chair. The walls were a non-descript neutral and the wooden floor was partly covered with a brightly coloured, tasselled rug.

The only adornment on the walls was a crucifix above the bed.

But the thing which dominated the room and looked out over the graveyard was the floor-to-ceiling glass window, etched with a huge cross.

There were no curtains or blinds on the window.

Nothing like reminding the occupants of the room that life is fleeting.

Haven pushed the thought away and peered around the only other door in the room. A tiny bathroom with a corner shower lay beyond it.

In short, everything he'd need for his stay here.

It was as if the place had been quietly dozing, waiting for him. He snorted at the ridiculous imagery, grabbed a few toiletries, and scrubbed away the smeared eyeliner in the bathroom, splashing cold water on his face and cleaning his teeth. A shower would be a treat after finishing a day's work.

He emptied his bag completely, looking for his phone, sure it had snuck into a pocket or got caught in a tangle of clothes, but came up empty.

'Fuck.' The expletive slipped from his lips.

It wasn't only the loss of communication, it was the loss of the photos stored on it. The loss of the screensaver. Not that he really needed it. The image was seared onto his brain.

As he went back down the stairs, Peter met him by the door. He thrust an envelope into Haven's hand.

'Just a small advance. You do need to eat.'

He patted Haven on the upper arm and disappeared into a room opposite the glass doors.

In the envelope were two crisp twenty-pound notes.

Haven wasn't used to things running smoothly. A nudging inner voice told him everything was too good, everything was falling into place too easily.

But as he went out into the winter morning, a watery sun climbing in the sky over the fields, he shrugged it off.

By the law of averages, he had to get some breaks, surely?

He really wanted to visit Sebastian's house, really wanted to find him there, but Peter had paid him to do a job, so that would have to wait till later.

Haven pulled open a weathered door set into the side of the church by an outside tap, looked up at the stained-glass window—a benevolent saint gazed down. He shook his head.

What kind of God are you to allow what I saw?

A blast of cold wind hurtled across the churchyard, scattering dried leaves around his feet. Some people might have said it was a sign of divine displeasure.

Haven was not one of those people.

Behind the door was a narrow room. The air was damp and musty. A waxed jacket hung on a peg on the wall. Uneven shelves held old plant pots, bundles of twine and soil-caked hand tools. A wooden wheelbarrow was propped up against the side with an array of gardening implements behind it.

After bringing out the tools he thought he'd need and cleaning dried mud from the fork and spade, he decided to go for a walk around the gravestones to see which ones needed his attention most.

Bright splashes of colour showed the graves that were still tended, but these were dwarfed by the ones that stood worn and neglected.

A clump of yew trees sat in the centre of the graveyard. Their needle-heavy boughs almost touched the ground in some places, their trunks thick and covered with papery bark. Blood-red berries dotted the rich earth beneath.

The tree of death. The tree of resurrection.

Haven felt his pocket for his phone, felt its absence like a missing limb.

Now was not the time to remember.

He focussed his thoughts and followed the pathway, making a mental note of the stones that were leaning at dangerous angles and the ones where ivy had nearly obliterated the names of the dead.

As he walked, the pathway began to climb slightly. He passed the yew trees. Passed an old man sitting on a bench feeding crumbs to the birds. Passed a few ancient graves with moss-clad Celtic crosses as their markers.

The boundary of the graveyard ran along to his left, the old stone wall following the rise in the land. Now he could see what looked like a small building standing sentinel at the crest of the hill, slightly hidden by a younger yew. The off-kilter feeling from last night flared again. It brushed its fingers against his skin and he shivered. There was only the whisper of the wind in the long grass to keep him company.

Haven stopped and stared as the building came fully into view. If a child had constructed a church in miniature, this was it. It had a grey tiled roof with two stone crosses at either end of the roof's apexes. Built from large blocks of grey stone, with an arched window on the side closest to him that was bricked up.

He left the path and strode through the tall grass to the front of the building. Two double doors with peeling green paint, three steps leading up to them.

Above the door was an inscription carved into the stone. Haven peered up at it, tried to decipher the crumbled lettering.

The crypt, for that's what it was, overlooked the whole valley. Swathes of dark forest clung to the rolling hills. The roofs of houses mingled with patches of farmland. Haven shielded his eyes from the watery sun and tried to get his bearings.

To his left rose a large hill, set at the end of a sloping meadow. Spindly trees clung to the hillside. Haven found his gaze fixed there momentarily.

In the far distance, smoke curled up from a house lost in the trees.

Haven tore his eyes away from the landscape and tentatively tried one of the crypt doors. It opened slowly. Easily.

He stood on the threshold and peered inside. Absolute black beyond the sliver of light from the door. The kind of cold that would snap a bone. The space felt odd. Lonely. Very wrong.

'You won't find anyone in there.'

Haven's heart shot into his throat as he wheeled, one hand on the door.

Peter stood on the grass bundled up in a quilted jacket and a black-and-white striped scarf. In his hands he clutched a paper bag and a disposable coffee cup.

'I was just getting the feel of the place,' Haven said, stepping back out into the winter sunlight. A strange kind of relief fizzed through his veins. 'There's no one buried inside here?'

A cloud passed over the sun and Peter's face darkened. 'Nobody at all, I'm sorry to say.'

Haven felt his eyebrows shoot up. It was a pretty impressive place to be empty.

'There used to be, of course. That's why it was built. But then the family removed all the coffins.'

The hairs on the nape of Haven's neck prickled as he waited for Peter to continue. When he didn't, Haven prompted him. 'Did the family move away?'

Peter gazed out into the valley for a moment as though he was carefully constructing his next words.

'Oh no, the family are still here. In fact, oddly enough, it's the family we were discussing earlier.' Peter thrust the coffee cup and bag into Haven's hands. 'I'm glad you've found the tools, Haven. If I was you I'd begin at the other side of the yews. There's some dreadful creeping ivy there that has swamped a lot of the stones.' He re-tied his scarf and set off down the pathway.

Haven called after him, Peter's abrupt change of conversation a jarring rattle in his head.

'The family who were buried here. You did mean the Hendersons?' It was suddenly important to Haven that Peter reaffirmed.

For a few moments Peter didn't answer, and Haven thought his words must have been taken by the wind. But then Peter paused and turned to face him, his shoulders hunched.

'I did.'

Sebastian's family has a crypt?

Another question punched its way into Haven's mind.

'Why did they remove the coffins?'

Peter rubbed his gloved hands together, his expression reserved.

'Personal family reasons.'

With that, Peter set off back towards the church, his steps quick and urgent.

Haven opened the paper bag and found a bacon roll. He sat on the crypt steps and devoured it quickly, licking his fingers when he finished. It barely touched the corners of his appetite, but it would have to do for now.

As he sipped the coffee, he looked over his shoulder and stared into the darkened crypt. From here it was simply an empty space, a mausoleum of the forgotten.

A chill crept over him, despite the warmth of the coffee. His breath ghosted in the cold air.

What weren't you telling me, Sebastian?

And why did everyone seem to want him to stay?

CHAPTER NINE

It was early morning when Rafferty awoke, and darkness still painted his window. His eyes flicked to the alarm clock by his bedside. 6.10 a.m.

The shroud of a dream clung to the space behind his eyes.

He threw back the covers, felt the cold press of an unheated house settle on his skin, and padded across to his door, peeking out along the gloom-drenched hallway.

Sebastian's door stood slightly open.

Rafferty's heart sank. That meant he wasn't home yet.

But still, Rafferty crept along the hallway, avoiding the floorboard that always creaked as the door to Amelia and Grace's room was closed.

He had to check.

But there was nothing in Sebastian's room. Only aching darkness.

The crushing weight of his brother's absence enfolded him, and for an instant, Rafferty found it hard to breathe.

This time it felt too final.

He ran his fingers through his hair, tugging at the tangle of waves, reprimanding himself for letting negativity open its eye into his thoughts.

Sebastian deserved some time away. He rarely left the gatehouse. Worked from a tiny space carved out of the attic—one part an office, the other a makeshift darkroom.

Rafferty slipped into the bathroom, emptied his bladder, then hung his head over the sink and splashed cold water on his face. There was a crack in the bowl, a dark spider's web of tiny lines, the result of a dropped bottle from long ago.

He let his fingers play over it, felt the slightly roughened edges under his fingertips. In his mind he heard the sharp clatter of glass meeting porcelain and he winced as his hand jerked back, his fingers tingling with static electricity.

Had he lost his grip on the bottle, or did he simply remember hearing it fall?

Rafferty lifted his head, slight lines forming between his eyebrows. In the mirror the soulless hallway leered beyond the open bathroom door.

A floorboard creaked in the dark.

The thud of his heartbeat vibrated in his throat as he crept to the door, thought he caught the edge of something moving in his peripheral vision, but when his gaze wheeled to the spot, nothing was there.

I need to get out.

The thought loomed, larger than the prickle of fear dancing over his skin. He ran to his room, dragged on a thick jumper over his T-shirt and sweatpants, then edged down the drab staircase, pulling on boots and shrugging into a jacket as his fingers unlocked the door.

Rafferty broke into a run, jogging into the woodland surrounding the gatehouse. The bite of early morning seared his lungs but it felt good to move, to be on the road to somewhere.

Maybe that's why Sebastian left, to be somewhere else. To peel away the suffocating presence of this place. To stuff his anxieties in a hole far away. Rafferty just kept his close, like a second skin. He wasn't sure what he would feel like without them.

The Henderson family curse. It sounded like something from a low-budget movie, something to spook you in the dark, the stuff of an overactive imagination.

He had grown up knowing it. Had been shocked when he realised, around the age of eight, that not all families lived in a similar shadow.

Maybe he should have known, because all the other kids gave him the widest of berths no matter how hard he tried to fit in. Maybe they thought it was catching.

Amelia had pulled him out of school then, and taught him at home.

It's easier for everyone that way.

He never questioned why. Just lived with the knowledge that the male line of his family was never happy. Never whole. Never able to escape the taint that ran down through the decades.

Sebastian suffered bouts of pure terror that left him locked inside his room for days. Rafferty heard him muttering to himself in the dark, and sometimes the screams would start, the awful blood-curdling screams that pierced the bedroom wall as if it were made of paper.

I think I'm losing my mind. Something's out there, Raff.

Those were the words Sebastian had told him a few days before he disappeared. The words that had drilled a hole in Rafferty's skull and made themselves comfortable.

Dawn peeled a layer from the night and the sky lightened. Rafferty stopped running and hunched over, his hands on his thighs, letting his heartbeat slow.

The silver birch copse loomed, ghostly pale in the waking day.

Rafferty pushed his way through the tangle of waist-high wild blackberry canes and winter bracken. Thorns snagged his clothes, grabbed strands of his hair and yanked them out. But something made him continue. Something he needed to see again.

Sweat coated his skin by the time he arrived at the well. A place he'd been warned not to visit.

He hadn't been here for a very long time, yet it felt familiar, like an old pair of shoes, moulded to his feet.

Where've you been? You took your time.

Rafferty wheeled around but there was no one with him in the quiet of the bone-white trees.

His gaze drifted towards the well.

This. This was where . . .

He shook his head.

Are we too old for games now?

The voice again. The very familiar voice.

He took two more steps, splayed his hands on the rough stones of the well and stared down into the fathomless black eye.

His tongue delved behind his teeth, searching for that warm, copper-edged pocket where a milk tooth had once sat, found the hard enamel of another in its place.

You do remember.

Rafferty pushed himself away and sank to the ground, cold leaching into his hips. He'd spent time here as a young boy. Thrown stones down the well. Played tag around it.

But that was impossible.

He'd been alone.

Alone?

The voice mocked him from a place that didn't seem to be inside his head.

He closed his eyes, pressing his lids together so tightly that it made his ears ache.

We played here. Truth or dare, and I won. I asked for your loose tooth, made you pull it out. Made you put it in my hand as the blood ran down your chin. Watched as you licked it off. Watched as you cried when it stopped bleeding.

Without warning, a spear of hunger knifed through Rafferty, turning his guts inside out. Saliva pooled in his mouth as his stomach twisted itself into corded knots. He went to all fours and lowered his head, let the spittle dribble to the ground as he rode the ebb and the flow of the violent pain.

A high-pitched ringing vibrated in his ears.

And then, silence. A sudden and acute silence as though all sound had been sucked from the world.

The hunger vanished. The pain vanished. He held his breath, waited for it to begin again.

And from out of the silence came a sound he would never forget, a sound that tore through his flesh and seared against his bones.

The sound of Amelia's scream.

Rafferty raced back through the woods. Low-hanging branches whipped his face but he felt nothing. Nothing, apart from the rapid, heavy beat of his heart. It drummed against his ribcage. Hammered in his ears.

Amelia was plain-spoken and forthright. She wasn't one to indulge in what she called unnecessary hysterics.

He listened for another scream but there was nothing. That made the first one seem so much worse.

His feet slipped on a wet patch of fallen leaves and he stumbled, hitting the trunk of a gnarled oak. It knocked all the air from his lungs and for a moment he wanted to sink into the thick carpet of moss at its base, because something awful was waiting and he wasn't sure if he could take it.

Necessity pushed him on.

The voice and what had happened at the well tumbled away, leaving only the anguish of the here and now.

He scrabbled down a banking, crossed a thin stream, freezing water splashing onto his sweatpants. Up the other side, his hands reaching for loose roots, soil compacting beneath his fingernails, chest burning with exertion.

How had he run so far away?

Now he could see the early morning smoke from the gatehouse chimney curling into the wan light of a new day.

The comforting scent warred with the panic lodged against every nerve ending.

Out onto the pathway that led to the gatehouse.

Rafferty stopped dead in his tracks, small stones flying up from his boots.

Two people were climbing into a car. Two official-looking people.

Somehow his legs got him to the front door.

He burst through.

Amelia sat in one of the wingback chairs. Grace knelt on the floor with her hands holding Amelia's.

They turned to him as one. Silent tears streaked their faces.

He stepped back, felt the solid frame of the door against his spine.

'No.'

He shook his head, the ice of disbelief crashing against him like a storm wave.

Amelia held out her hand.

He ignored the plea, numbness creeping through his limbs, wanting to run away, to hide.

They stood and came to him. Slow, shuffling steps.

Amelia's hands taking his, holding them to her chest, as all the while he shook his head. Pushed away the horror of what he knew was coming.

The flames roared in the hearth, dry wood splitting under their touch. Rafferty felt like he was burning too.

Grace's hands holding his face, the rough texture of her fingers, the skin worn from digging in the earth.

And then Amelia's words as a log collapsed into ash.

'He's gone, Rafferty.'

CHAPTER TEN

Meredith sat in a corner alcove, engrossed in a book. She'd come back to the pub after leaving the house, grabbed a long, hot shower, and ordered an early glass of wine. It mellowed the uneasy edge the house had left on her skin.

She raised her head as the door opened, felt the cold draught as the winter air blasted in.

'Ah!' The exclamation fell from her lips.

The young man from the taxi turned and met her gaze, raised his hand in greeting.

Now everyone in the bar was watching the two people who didn't belong here.

The man took a seat on a tall stool by the bar, his eyes flicking to a small television where some news programme droned on in the background. A few locals looked across as he scraped his loose hair into a ponytail and tied it back.

One of them nudged another, and they laughed.

A flush of anger rose in Meredith's chest at their judgement.

Before she knew what she was doing, she slammed her book on the table and marched over. She inched in beside the man, caught the barmaid's eye.

'Another glass of red, please, Rosa, and whatever this gentleman wants.'

She turned and smiled. He looked different without the heavy eye make-up. Different in the warm glow of the bar lights. Her gaze fell to the ink on his throat. She looked away quickly, felt her cheeks burn at her own scrutiny, had an almost overwhelming desire to tell him to catch the next train out of here.

She wondered where he had slept last night.

'I don't think anyone has ever called me a gentleman before.' He laughed and pointed to a beer in the cooler under the optics.

Rosa snapped the cap off and slid the bottle across.

Eyes bore into Meredith's back. She wheeled and gave them what she hoped was a withering look.

'I'm glad I found you,' she said. 'I believe you might be missing something?'

He paused with the bottle halfway to his lips.

'My phone?'

'The taxi driver dropped it off here, but I didn't know where you were. Shall we go over there?' She inclined her head. 'Away from wagging ears.' She raised her voice for the last part. The men had the good grace to look guilty.

They went over to the alcove and Meredith took the phone out of her bag and handed it over. The screen was dead now, the battery done.

'Thank you.' He turned the phone over in his hands as though he couldn't quite believe it was there. 'You're a lifesaver. Again.'

'We do seem to be in each other's orbits.' Meredith paused and took a sip of her wine. 'I don't even know your name.'

He slid the phone inside his jacket pocket and rested his elbows on the table, his clasped hands under his chin.

'Haven. Just Haven.'

'Well, Haven, I'll probably regret this but I have to ask.' The words rushed to the tip of her tongue, horrifying her normally restrained nature. 'Your lock screen. Where's it from?'

Haven sat back and folded his arms across his chest. He watched her for a moment, his tongue playing over his teeth.

'What if I told you that photo was the point at which my life changed? That everything I'd known before ceased to have meaning.'

She watched him over the top of her glass, trying to work out if he was teasing her.

He wasn't. His expression remained deadly serious, and there was something in his eyes, something haunted.

'I'd say that those moments define us even if we don't understand why.'

She could write a book on her own moments, remembered the day by the well and the stench of dark water, her own fear coating her throat with acid. The sound of something wet and nameless moving beneath her . . .

'Are you okay?' Haven's voice cut through her memories.

'And I'd say we had more in common than you think.' She laughed softly and took a gulp of wine.

Steady, Mere. Alcohol loosens your tongue.

Someone turned the volume up on the television. It attracted attention like a honey smear in a garden of wasps.

A newsreader in a pink jumper began to speak, her expression solemn.

'News just in. Police are investigating the discovery of the body of a man in the River Avon this morning. Identification was found by the scene. Anyone with information that may assist in this incident should contact the following number.'

The newsreader continued for a few moments more, but Meredith didn't hear a word. She was watching Haven's face, saw every ounce of colour drain from it as though something had sucked him dry.

'Haven?' She reached across and tugged at his sleeve.

He brought his hand up to his mouth and Meredith saw him bite down on his forefinger. He closed his eyes. 'I know who it is.'

Rosa flipped the screen over to a football match, although no one turned to watch it.

Meredith waited for him to say more.

'It's Sebastian.' He shook his head. His jaw slackened. 'How the fuck did I miss it?'

'Sebastian?'

She felt his arm go rigid, then it loosened. His posture crumpled.

'He's the reason I'm here.' Haven pressed his fingers to his temples. 'I was going to go over tonight. But figured I needed a beer before knocking on that door.'

'Whose door?'

Balanced on the knife edge of shock, Haven wasn't making much sense. He laughed, a harsh, dry sound that hardened his eyes.

'The door that leads to hell, if you believe the stories he told me.'

Meredith gripped the edge of the table.

'Sebastian Henderson?'

Haven nodded, his pain-drenched eyes fixed on her face.

'I know the family,' she said. The words queued up in her throat felt like splinters. Words that if spoken, she'd never be able to take them back. 'I lived here as a young girl. My sister was friends with Amelia and Grace.'

She watched as her words settled upon him.

'Fuck it.' Haven took a long draught of his beer. His throat rippled as he swallowed. 'He sent me a voicemail, that's why I'm here. Asked me to look after his younger brother.'

'You know about the family burden?' Meredith didn't like to call it a curse. That was like calling upon it to show itself.

'He told me a lot of stuff that didn't really make sense, but I never pushed him for more. We didn't have that kind of a relationship. He just turned up when he needed to get away.'

Meredith caught Rosa's eye and nodded.

This was going to be a long night. She was here and Haven was here. And Sebastian Henderson was dead.

Walk away, a little voice whispered. *You don't need to know why this is happening. Go back to your safe, little life.*

She retreated inside herself for a few seconds and tried to pull the tattered threads of her emotions together.

'They took the corpses out of the crypt,' Haven murmured, still shell-shocked.

Her brow furrowed.

'The Hendersons. They took the coffins, all the coffins, from the crypt. Why would they do that?'

Meredith took Haven's hands in hers and they sat in their own bubble of anguish as life went on around them.

An old man sat in a corner alcove by the fire, building a house of cards. He placed the last one on the top, his gnarled fingers shaking.

And the house collapsed in on itself.

CHAPTER ELEVEN

Haven walked back through the graveyard. The cold night air after the warmth of the pub had helped to clear his thoughts a little but his head felt so full. So heavy. Like it was a balloon with too much air and any moment now it would explode and his brain matter would spatter over the nearby graves.

Sebastian was dead. He didn't know why he was so sure, apart from the awful fist of dread that had opened in his gut at the newsreader's words.

Dead.

The realisation hammered again and again against the inside of his skull.

He took out his phone. Someone had lent him a charging cable, but he didn't remember who. Maybe Meredith had got it for him.

He pressed the phone against his ear and listened to the voicemail again.

I can't do it anymore. I'm so fucking sorry.

Please help him. And if you can't you'll know what to do. Don't think badly of me. You were always my place to hide.

It was there, as plain as fucking day. The goodbye hidden in his words. And Haven had failed to see it.

He doubled over and retched into a bush by the church wall.

No matter how hard he tried, people around him died.

Don't go there, an inner voice cautioned.

But he did, because he deserved to suffer.

The catalyst for all of this had happened ten years ago, on Halloween, and if he thought about it too much he could still see the events spiralling past his mind's eye as sharp as cut glass. Could still see the crumpled body lying in the dirt on the deserted warehouse floor. Could see the ruin of a throat no longer there, dark blood pooling in the filthy dust.

Why hadn't I gone to the police?

But that had never been an option. He had been too worried about being implicated, which was crazy, as all he had done was put into motion the wheels of hurt—*sent the text, hidden in the shadows as the boy waited and waited, basked in the dejection rolling from him*—hardly a criminal offence. Yet some part of him knew if he hadn't been so arrogant and thoughtless, so filled with the desire to show those he allowed into his inner circle how domineering he could be, this wouldn't have happened.

Someone else would come across the body. Someone else would clear away his sin.

But he had gone back the following night, draped in black, his hood pulled down over his face, at one with the darkness as he stood on the bridge overlooking the derelict warehouse.

The body was still there.

Squealing rats circled around it, running through the congealed pool of blood, rodent tongues feeding from the clotted mess.

And then he had seen the impossible. The slight curling of a hand. A foot stretching. A body that had been most definitely dead, reanimated.

But it was the sound that came from the throat that was no longer ruined that made his muscles quake and his vision spin.

It was the sound of acute distress. A sound that still haunted his nightmares.

What had I seen?

Even now he wasn't sure. Although the word *vampire* had always felt right.

And the knowledge that what he had set in motion had led to someone suffering this plight, perhaps for hundreds of years, was like a knife in his gut, digging out his juicy organs, one by one.

A sensible person would have processed all of this and come to the conclusion that there was nothing they could do. It had all been an unfortunate mistake on his part.

Total crap, Haven. You were a fucking bully. You knew how much he wanted to fit in.

It was the night that changed his life. Haven knew he could never live with himself if he didn't try to atone for what he'd done. It was an impossibility that he would ever come across the boy he had wronged, but there had to be others like him, living on the edges of humanity or inserting themselves into it. People went missing all the time. Haven had a gut feeling some of these disappearances were vampire related.

But he had no proof.

It was why he put on the Goth persona, why he frequented all-night clubs. Why he himself lived on the fringes of society in the vain hope he would find a lead, maybe even track down something that shouldn't exist.

If he could rid the world of even one of these creatures, put it out of its misery, his own life would be worthwhile.

Of course, there was always the possibility that Haven had a death wish and this was his mind's way of making it seem relevant, a way of balancing the scales he had so hideously upset.

He steadied himself on the wall of the church, grimaced at the foul taste on his tongue. As he lifted his head a light caught his eye in the middle of the graveyard. It moved slowly to and fro.

Someone walking with a torch.

Haven pressed his back against the church wall, slunk along until he was nearly at the door to the annexe.

The security light flared to life and he shrank back, craving the anonymity of the darkness.

He went inside and stole up the stairs, entering his room without turning on the light. He crept to the floor-to-ceiling window, the one with the huge etched cross in the middle, and pressed himself into the left-hand corner by the wall, his knees drawn into his chest. From here he could see the whole graveyard, or he would be able to if it was daylight.

The torchlight was still now.

His phone rang, the sudden sound jarring through the silent gloom.

It was Meredith.

'I didn't disturb you, did I?' Her voice was strung out like a tight wire.

'Hell, no. I keep nocturnal hours.' Haven tried to lighten the mood. He stretched out one leg. Vomit spatters dotted his jeans.

'I just wanted to check you were okay.'

Haven could imagine her sitting in her room as the pub emptied below. Sounds of gathered glasses clinking and people shouting farewells as they made their way home.

'I'm not okay,' he said, after a minute of silence. 'He more or less told me in his voicemail, told me what he was going to do. And I fucking missed it.'

He hung his head, his hair falling over his face. Somewhere along the way he'd lost the band that tied it back.

'It's not your fault,' she said gently. A pause. 'Look, meet me in the bar after work tomorrow, yes? We can go over all this again. See what the best option is going forward.'

He didn't answer, just waited for the line to go dead.

There was something she wasn't telling him. But he couldn't blame her. There were things he hadn't told her either. They were virtually strangers, thrown together by some ill-omened meltdown.

Why had she really come back?

And what about Rafferty?

It was the last thing Sebastian had asked of him. Haven couldn't let him down on this.

Please help him. And if you can't you'll know what to do.

What the hell did that even mean?

Haven sat in the dark for a long time.

At some point he fell asleep, woke in the middle of the night, half-frozen, and crawled into bed fully clothed.

Just before sleep claimed him again, he looked at his phone.

At the screensaver.

There was no crumpled body in the dirt.

But Haven could still see it imprinted at the back of his eyes.

SHIP'S LOG (DECEMBER 1874)
CAPTAIN IRVING WALSH

Ice and darkness. That is all there is.

I know there is a hell and it does not contain fire and brimstone. It contains this crushing nothing surrounding me.

I have lost track of what day it is, and time has no meaning because there is no dawn. Only an eternal midnight.

The creak of the ice haunts my dreams. And the ship answers its call with her own groans. We are marooned here on the frozen sea, and I fear I will not see England's shore again.

The fact that our predicament is because of my own miscalculations lies heavy in my heart. Greed took my senses, the promise of acclaim too tempting to resist.

Take us all the way, McDonald urged. Take us and on our return I will mention your name to Her Majesty.

McDonald was always so sure of his expedition's success. His Etonian nurturing did not have failure listed as an option. His swagger irritated me, as did the way he looked at the crew. As if they were merely there to cater to his whims.

We sailed past the spur of land marked on my map as the northernmost point of our journey. We sailed on despite the misgivings from my first mate. Despite the shortening of the daylight. The crew were surly, prone to fighting at the slightest provocation. They are frightened, he told me.

I did not heed him.

I believe now the moment we passed through the Arctic Circle was when this all began. Or it is possible that was simply the point of no return.

The following day we finally reached the bay McDonald and his team were destined for. There was already a makeshift huddle of a camp present, another expedition with the same urge—the same madness—to explore the Arctic wastes, but illness had decimated their group, and only two fur-clad men waited on that godforsaken shore.

I will say now that leaving McDonald in that desolate place filled me with nothing but relief. The sun rose only briefly now, and it would be a race against time and climate to sail south.

It would be remiss of me not to mention that McDonald and his crew and provisions were bundled into row boats and transported to the shoreline by my men. This took many trips, and the oarsmen were changed frequently, tiring easily in the extreme cold and arduous conditions. The crew helped drag the crates and other equipment up to the huts. I saw a couple of my men enter, and, when questioned, they said they'd been offered a measure of rum for their assistance. I could not fault them for that.

I believe now something came back with them from the shoreline and I condemn my own inadequacies for not checking the hull on our departure. If this sounds like the ramblings of an unhinged mind, it is not. I am of sound mind, or as sound as I can be, given what has happened.

Falling to the oblivion of lunacy would be a blessing.

The first death occurred that night. Perkins became violent, lashing out at his fellow crew members. He began to scream that we all would die and had to be manhandled into the brig to cool off. He was dead when Mitchell went to check on him.

We buried him at sea the day after. Already great chunks of ice were forming, rattling against the hull with a sound like thunder. The ship floundered and Cartwright had a hard job keeping her on course. He knew her limitations.

We did not beat the ice. Every morning it appeared thicker, stretching out as far as we could see in the sparse blue-hued daylight.

Two more men died. Of what, I am not sure.

The crew roamed the deck. They clustered and whispered in corners and I have heard talk of curses and dark magic. This was only strengthened as the dead men were given to the ocean. A polar bear with a head as big as a bull came out of the sea from under the ice. It fastened its jaws around the wrapped skull of one of the corpses. We heard the crunch of crushed bone as we stared in horror. The sea turned crimson.

By then the first mate and I had all but lost control of the men. They were becoming as wild and as ungodly as the habitat around us.

Two days after, the polar night descended. Two days after that the sea froze completely.

The first mate rallied the men slightly, told them that when we did not dock at our agreed port on time a search party would set out. This placated the men for a short while until one of them realised nothing could reach us until the ice melted.

The crew were put on rations. There was enough food, we told them, but we had to be careful. This was a lie, but you do not tell men they are about to starve.

Fate came to the rescue with appalling consequences.

Illness swept through the crew, a sudden and graphic explosion of fever and loose bowels. In the matter of a few hours men became disorientated and wild-eyed. They were slick with sweat despite the freezing temperatures, their mouths opening and closing, nonsensical words spilling out.

We do not belong, they wailed, blood-flecked foam oozing from their nostrils. Their limbs spasmed and they struggled to breathe, as though their lungs were filling with water. After that point, death took them quickly.

We lost half of the crew within a week. The ones that remained received extra allowances gladly, but they were on edge and churlish. They asked for extra rum rations but I refused.

Drunkenness would not help them.

By now the bodies were piling up on deck. The extreme cold slowed down the rate of decomposition but no amount of constant sweeping could halt the flow of body fluid that marred the decks, and the stench became an ever-permanent miasma.

The first mate came to me with a solution, and I reluctantly agreed.

We ordered the remainder of the crew to cover the bodies in tar. This they did, grateful for a task to keep their hands busy, grateful that the corpses were not their own.

The tarred bodies were hauled out onto the ice and heaped in a pile. We set them alight whilst a prayer was uttered by the few men who still believed in the existence of a benevolent god.

The smell of burning human flesh is something I pray you will never have to endure.

This was only the beginning, and I need to focus my thoughts before my next entry.

I do not know if I have the strength to put the horror into words.

CHAPTER TWELVE

Meredith rose early. It was still dark, and when she looked out of her bedroom window the slick cobbles of the street were deserted save for a lonely milk float. The clink of bottles pierced the misty silence.

She took a quick shower, hoping it would help to settle the torrent of thoughts swamping her mind. Those thoughts had kept her awake most of the night.

The expression on Haven's face when the television delivered its sombre news.

Shock. Pain. And something else . . . the haunted shadow of guilt.

What were the chances that she would come across someone else with ties to the Hendersons? Someone else caught up in their secrets.

She'd half regretted letting it slip that she knew Amelia and Grace and had lived here as a child. It was something she kept tucked away, like a postcard from a once-familiar place that served no useful purpose but you kept it anyway. Haven hadn't batted an eyelid when she started talking about family curses—something else she regretted blurting out.

He was a strange one, this young man. But she felt an affinity with him she couldn't quite put into words.

As she pulled on a thick jumper she went over what she had found out.

Haven and Sebastian had crossed paths. Something about Sebastian visiting him when things got too much?

Sebastian had asked Haven to look after a younger brother. Rafferty. A memory carved itself from the past—Amelia's matter-of-fact admission. *Boys. It only affects boys, so Grace and me are okay . . .*

The remains of the Henderson dead had been removed from the crypt.

The last point went around and around in her head, like swirling water in a drain.

Damn it, Mere. Get a hold of yourself.

She squared her jaw, pulled on her boots, and went downstairs.

Despite the early hour, Rosa was behind the bar, polishing glasses as she took them from the dishwasher. Dark circles marred the pale skin under her eyes. She tucked a strand of hair behind her ear as Meredith came in.

'I'll get you some coffee,' Rosa said, and disappeared through the swing door into the kitchen.

Meredith looked around the empty bar. Chairs stacked upside down on the tables. A mop bucket leaning against the door.

Dents and scratches covered the old floorboards, and she found herself wondering if Irving Walsh had ever walked across them, ever drank at the bar she was leaning against.

Rosa came back through carrying a mug and a filter jug filled with coffee. As she poured, her fingers shook.

'Are you okay?' Meredith asked.

'Sorry. Not quite with it this morning. I didn't sleep well.'

Meredith was about to murmur solidarity when Rosa's eyes met hers.

'The man you were with last night. Haven. Tell him to leave. Getting caught up in anything to do with that family always brings heartache.'

She sniffed and fumbled in her pocket for a tissue.

The penny dropped for Meredith. She curled two hands around the mug.

'Were you and Sebastian seeing each other?'

'It was a friends–with–benefits thing. This place can get really lonely.' Rosa's throat rippled.

'You don't have to say anything else.'

Meredith didn't want to cause Rosa any more distress.

Someone called Rosa's name from the kitchen. She paused before she went through the door. 'The last night I was with him he had an awful nightmare. He kept screaming Rafferty's name. And when I shook him awake he grabbed my hand, looked right into my eyes, and said, "Rafferty isn't what he seems." How's that for sounding messed up?'

After breakfast Meredith set out for the house. She had a flask of coffee and a sandwich from the kitchen. The early morning sun shone low through the bare branches of the trees as she drove, blinding her vision as she negotiated the winding turns in the rural lane.

As she neared the house the lane narrowed and she slowed to a crawl. Now she was driving directly into the sun and her visor was as useless as a snowball in hell.

A flash of yellow caught her peripheral vision and she braked, the car skidding slightly on the frost-laced road.

Through the haze of piercing sunlight she saw a boy vaulting over a gate into a field. He was wearing jeans and a yellow sweatshirt but no coat. The temperature gauge on her car said minus one.

She tapped her fingers on the steering wheel. The hairs on the nape of her neck prickled.

She shook her head to clear her thoughts and carried on down the lane to the house.

It took three hours for Meredith to repack the contents of the library. Mice—or rats—had made a meal of the corners of all the boxes and she had to bring out the packing crates with reinforced edges. She worked methodically, slightly irritated by her own idiocy at not using them in the first place.

After taping up the final box she poured a cup of coffee, grabbed an energy bar, and stood by the window in a puddle of wan sunlight. Her plan lay open on the sill.

Library. Done.

Next room, upstairs. Master bedroom.

Draining the last dregs of coffee, she grabbed an armful of packing supplies and lugged them up the staircase. As she met the staircase turn she glanced down at the grandfather clock. It stood silent as a tomb, and she pushed away the thought of the time it had marked here.

She carried on to the landing. Felt the gloom of the house deepen. *Third room on the left.* She clasped the boxes under her arm so she could free one hand to open the door. As soon as her fingers touched the door handle, a surge of static electricity bolted up her arm. Her hand recoiled so quickly her wrist clicked in protest, her elbow tingling with shock. Bubble wrap slipped from her grasp and pooled onto the floor.

Gingerly, she reached out again, curled her fingers around the handle. An intense cold seeped into her palm.

Of course it's freezing, Mere. It's the middle of winter and this place has stood empty for years.

Meredith opened the door. The bedroom lay at the north side of the house and the room basked in shadow. An austere and inhospitable space with an iron-framed double bed central on the wall opposite the door, a wooden chair with a high back by the window, and a narrow vanity unit containing a white porcelain wash bowl and a white jug. An oval mirror sat at the back of the unit, shrouded in dust.

The bed had been stripped of all linen, leaving only a stained horsehair mattress upon it. The lone adornment on the walls hung above the bed: an oil painting of a tall ship upon a vast blue ocean, its sails filled with wind.

She shivered as she entered the room, dropping her supplies by the door to keep it open, to try to clear the musty, damp-drenched smell.

Okay, this was a bit odd. There was hardly anything here to pack or catalogue.

She ran her fingers over the metal on the bed frame, felt another wave of cold burning through her skin.

The frame was definitely Victorian, and when she wandered across to the vanity unit, it, too, bore all the hallmarks of the era. Not that she was an expert, but after working for so long with old objects she had developed a feel for what was genuine or not.

These would fetch a hefty price at auction.

A loose floorboard creaked in the hallway as she constructed another box, and the sound spun out into the silence. At any other time she would have popped her ear buds in and lost herself in a podcast as she worked, but there was something about the feel of the air since she'd come upstairs, something she couldn't pinpoint, something that made her want to listen intently.

She carefully packed the jug in reams of tissue, letting her fingers play over the smooth porcelain of the wash bowl before that, too, was safely wrapped and stashed away. Opening the small drawer at the front of the vanity, she checked for what she expected to find there. A comb or a shaving brush, perhaps.

What met her eyes was something completely different. It was a slightly curved blade, about seven inches long, with a bone-inlay handle. An aged red leather sheath lay to one side.

The nerves in the small of her back tingled.

Item from Master vanity, she wrote on a label. *Flensing knife?*

Pulling a sheet of bubble wrap across, she reached into the drawer. Something scuttled from the edges. A fat, brown mottled beetle scurried over her fingers. A deathwatch beetle.

A yelp left her lips and she yanked her hand away, disgust wrinkling her nose. This was the part of old houses she didn't like. The bugs that nested in the dark. Nested in the forgotten memories of abandoned places.

Gritting her teeth, she dropped a piece of bubble wrap around the knife and scooped it out, the plastic a barrier between her and things with many legs.

She licked her lips, a nervous gesture. Then licked them again.

Salt on her tongue.

She pushed the oddness away. Placed the blade into its sheath then packed it into the box. She checked her list.

Her gaze flicked up to the painting above the bed.

That was the next item to wrap. It had its own bullet point on her list.

Laying a sheet of protective tissue on the bed, she tried to apply logic to the strange tang on her lips. Scents have a way of hanging around, especially in closed-off rooms. It could be from the mattress, but there was no way she was sticking her nose closer to its soiled surface.

She crossed to the window, meaning to drag the chair to the bed to use as a makeshift ladder, and her gaze fell on the overgrown garden at the rear of the house. Wild grass had claimed what was once a lawn. Overgrown bushes vied for space in the crowded border. A gnarled apple tree stood by a well.

A gasp of shock left her lips. She rubbed the sleeve of her jumper on the grimy window, felt a chill creeping into her marrow.

The well.

She hugged her arms across her chest. Leaned against the windowsill. Gazed out into the distance.

And there, in a clearing amongst the trees, smoke curled from a hidden chimney.

The gatehouse.

She'd been so close and never realised, hazy childhood memories of distance and road orientation clouding her perception.

An awareness unfurled itself in her gut. An awareness that made a sharp, inhaled breath stick in her throat.

The boy she had seen by the gate was Rafferty Henderson.

The floorboard in the hallway creaked again. And there was another sound. One that stripped away the years and left her as a shivering girl in the dark. An impossible sound, given her whereabouts.

A faint dragging. Something corporeal.

Something saturated with water, crawling across the floor.

CHAPTER THIRTEEN

Rafferty awoke with a pounding headache. He was curled up on the sofa, a handknitted blanket covering him.

He pushed himself up onto one elbow and his world tipped sideways. The awful events of the previous day came tumbling down around him like a house of cards.

A small cry left his lips. Something sharp and urgent. Something so filled with pain it seemed impossible that it should sound so meaningless.

Sebastian is dead.

The hard, cold fact of it lay in his stomach like the remains of a meal he would never be able to digest.

He eased himself up and put his head in his hands.

Soft footsteps sounded on the floor.

Someone touched the back of his neck and gently pressed a mug of something hot into his hands.

He looked up and found Grace, her eyes red-rimmed.

'Amelia?' His fingers trembled and tea sloshed over the side of the mug.

'She's gone for a little while. But she'll be home soon.'

The way Grace said it, it almost sounded like Amelia had gone for a walk, had even maybe decided to go shopping.

But Rafferty saw the true meaning behind Grace's haunted eyes. Amelia had gone to do the unthinkable: identify Sebastian's body.

The sheer, terrifying horror of that thought wrapped itself around him, crushing his chest. Numbness owned his limbs. He felt like a shell, as if Sebastian had taken everything Rafferty was with him.

There was nothing. No anger. No tears.

I must be a monster.

The thought reared its head and the accuracy of it wore fangs.

Grace nudged his hand and urged him to drink. He took a mouthful of the brew, something herbal and slightly bitter.

'Drink it. It will make you feel better.'

Rafferty didn't think anything could make him feel better ever again, but he took another mouthful.

Grace sat with him as he sipped, her hand on his arm.

'How did it happen?' he said. The words hurt his throat. He'd been too wrung out with grief yesterday to even ask. He knew it was because if he didn't he could pretend it wasn't true.

Grace paused and studied his face as though she was trying to work out how much to tell him. Her mouth opened, but the words hung on her lips before she spoke them.

'He drowned.'

Rafferty closed his eyes. His brow furrowed in pain. Sebastian was always careful around water. He'd been the one to drag Rafferty out from the tarn when Rafferty decided to wade in a little too far, when he thought he saw something floating just beneath its surface, when he'd lost his footing and gone under and the water had gushed down his throat. Sebastian yelled at him and shook him by the shoulders, told him that the water here was dangerous. . . .

The memory snapped through Rafferty's head in quick motion slides. The searing pain in his sinuses. The anger carved on Sebastian's face. And the terror.

Why would his brother drown?

'But how? I don't understand.'

Grace glanced away, her fingers playing with a loose thread on her dungaree pocket.

'It won't help to know the details, pet.'

That term of endearment she rarely used now ran a jagged edge along Rafferty's frayed nerves.

He didn't often go into confrontation mode, but he felt it now burning up his gullet, harsh words like bile at the back of his throat.

His head felt groggy and his stomach churned, and he couldn't work out if he was starving or wanted to throw up.

'Why won't you tell me the truth?'

His words were clipped, sharp at the edges.

Grace reached across and patted him on the shoulder, then eased herself to her feet, and his rage took flight.

He stood, up in her face now, his fists clenched. It wasn't her fault but the resentment in his veins was at its boiling point and the unfairness of it all was like a savage beast looking for a way out of its cage.

'What's in this?' He brought the mug up to his chest, not caring that it slopped over the sides onto the rug. 'I know you give me things that suppress my appetite. That make me sleep.'

His accusations came thick and fast and he gave her no opening to answer. Now his anger had found a portal, and he had no control over its ferocity. Part of him was afraid he would say something terrible, something he couldn't take back.

Grace tried to reach for his hand but he jerked away. A moment of guilt at the pain in her eyes.

He suddenly knew, with incredible clarity, why Sebastian needed to get away.

'You go on and on about this great family burden.' He air-punctuated the last word. 'About how we have to suck up what happened in the past. Endure its legacy. But what can be worse than what I am? I'm fucked up enough as it is.' Grace cringed. She hated vulgarity. 'If you won't tell me I'll find out for myself.'

He sliced his hand through the air as though he was cutting himself away and stormed out of the door, slamming it behind him. It was childish behaviour but for once he hadn't accepted what was happening. He had raged against it, and it made him feel better.

He paused as he went out of the gate, sure that she would be following, but the door remained closed.

The cold air chilled his flushed cheeks. He wished he'd grabbed a jacket before leaving but there was no way he was going back in to find one. Rafferty stuffed his hands in his sweatshirt pockets and headed down the lane towards the village.

He was angry at Sebastian for going away and leaving him.

For dying.

He was angry at Amelia and Grace for constantly keeping things from him. For pretending that everything would always go on as it had. For never talking about his future.

His expelled breath created clouds of white vapour. It dissipated into the freezing air as he walked with his shoulders hunched. A car moved slowly towards him, the sound of tyres on frozen tarmac. His gaze flicked sideways and found a gap in the hedgerow branched by a five-bar gate. A sloping field lay beyond.

Rafferty ran at it and scrambled over the top, his fingers slipping on the frost-laced wood, then he sprinted up the hill, through the ankle-deep grass, stumbling over frozen cow pats and hidden rabbit holes. He ran until his muscles burned and he couldn't run anymore.

At the top of the slope he put his hands on his thighs and doubled over, his heartbeat drumming in his ears. When the drum became a dull beat he raised his head. The winter wind screamed against his face, numbing his nose and lips. But he stood there until his eyes watered. Because from there he could see the village laid out in the valley below, the houses like tiny models set upon ribbon roads. Smoke curled from chimneys, cars moved slowly from place to place, taking people to do normal things.

All he ever wanted was to do normal things.

But somehow he had managed to be born into a family of pariahs. As a child he'd never really noticed it. He'd thought he was normal then. And when you have the run of the woods and a big brother to play with, and an imagination that never lets you down, well, what else do you need?

Only me.

Rafferty wheeled at the voice but there was no one there.

He gnawed at the inside of his cheek where a lesion had only recently healed. That's what he did when he was starving, when the urge for something raw and bloody descended like a scarlet veil. He found comfort in his own flesh.

You don't have to do that.

Rafferty closed his eyes. Told himself the voice wasn't real.

A scent drifted in on the back of the wind, something which made all the hairs stand up on his arms. He inhaled, a sharp intake of breath that pinpointed the scent with razor-edged accuracy. It was coming from just beyond the low drystone wall to his left. He ran towards it and vaulted over, his feet sinking into the wet, deep grass. An old tractor attachment lay rusting close to the wall's base—a harrow with the tines pointing towards the sky.

A crow fluttered its wings at his approach. A crow with its neck impaled on one of the tines. Blood coated its silky feathers but its round, brown eyes still had a flicker of life.

Rafferty couldn't take his eyes off the slow trickle of red where tine met flesh. It called to him. Made drool run from his lips and his stomach ache with need.

He reached out one hand and trailed his finger along the crow's wing. It fluttered again, this time languidly. As though it knew a predator looked on. The blood was warm, sticky. His stomach clenched but then a wave of revulsion speared through him.

No. He wouldn't. This was one step too far.

But it was here and accessible.

And no one would know.

He could just have a little taste. He brought his finger to his mouth and dabbed the blood onto his tongue. The taste sent shock waves through his body and he jerked away, stumbling to the wall.

He cowered by it for a few minutes, his knuckles rammed against his teeth.

Another crow flew onto the tractor attachment. It cocked its head and watched him, occasionally hopping closer to its mutilated kin.

He imagined it thinking *this is mine, go away.*

Rafferty edged back towards the harrow. He waved his arms and the other crow took flight, cawing its indignation.

His hands closed over the hapless bird. One sharp tug and he yanked it free of the tine. Two trembling heartbeats against his palms. Then it stilled.

Now all his senses were hyperfocused. His eyes roamed over the hole where the tine had punctured its neck. His fingers clawed into the soft feathers. And the scent. Oh God, the scent. It was everything he had ever wanted and more. The raw, commercialised meat and the watered-down juices were nothing now, merely a journey on his way to this.

He brought the crow to his mouth, fastened his lips around the puncture hole, and let his tongue delve into the sweet, copper-tinged goodness.

Rafferty smiled against the open wound. Blood filled his throat, dripped down his chin onto his sweatshirt.

There was so much wrong in what he was doing, but in that moment, he knew that this is what he was made to do.

CHAPTER FOURTEEN

A village graveyard wasn't normally a place associated with drama. But as Haven laced up his boots the sounds of raised voices filtered through the open window.

He was still groggy from a disturbed night's sleep and too much alcohol, the ache in his chest like a black hole, carved by a friend whose demons had driven him to take his own life.

Drowned. Haven shivered.

He grabbed his jacket and ran down the stairs, out into the frigid morning. The sky was bright blue today but an overnight frost still veined the gravestones. It sparkled in the weak sunlight.

As he trundled the wheelbarrow along the pathway to the crypt his gaze flitted to a group of people standing around a grave. He narrowed his eyes. One of them was Peter.

But this wasn't a sombre meeting over a lost loved one; the erratic gestures and highly charged voices suggested something confrontational. Haven kept his ears tuned into the conversation, kept the group in his peripheral vision. He wasn't in a sociable mood.

'What are you suggesting caused this, Peter?'

A man in a waxed jacket stood with his hand outstretched towards the ground.

'I'm sure there's a reasonable explanation, Nick.' Peter's voice was calm, his hands raised in supplication.

'Graves do not simply collapse without a reason.' This from a small woman in a mustard anorak. Her arms were folded, as though she was trying to ward off any perceived threat.

'Haven, help me out here.' Peter's gaze flicked towards him, followed by those of the group. Haven felt their scrutiny like a scalpel blade against his skin. This morning he'd left his hair loose. It hung over his shoulders, marked him as Someone Different. He knew what they were thinking as he walked across.

The grave in question was marked by a stone engraved with the skull and crossbones of memento mori—*remember you must die*. He pressed his lips together. Haven didn't appreciate the timing of this reminder. Ivy clung to the weathered slab as it leaned at an acute angle, long grasses reaching to swallow it whole. The name on the stone had long since disappeared.

A large, deep hole scarred the ground. Haven peered inside it. The crumbling remains of the gravestone base lay in the pit of earth.

'Erosion,' he said. 'Could be from the yews over there.' He nodded towards the trees, felt their meaning prickle against his scalp. 'The root systems are shallow but they spread out extensively.'

After the warehouse horror he had thrown himself into the study of death and resurrection, as if knowing more would help him come to terms with his part in it. It didn't.

Don't go there. Not now.

Someone muttered under their breath.

'A perfectly reasonable explanation.' Peter's smile was directed towards him. 'Can you tape this off please, Haven? To be safe. We don't want anyone falling in.'

Haven nodded. He went back to the wheelbarrow.

'What kind of a name is Haven anyway?'

The pointed accusation followed him.

He could have retaliated but he let it slide, trundling the wheelbarrow to where he had finished yesterday. He set to work with the rake, taking his irritation out on a pile of fallen leaves. His hair blew over his face and he stopped to braid it into a loose plait.

The group dispersed slowly, grim faces occasionally glancing back at the grave. Peter made his way across to him.

'Thank you for coming to my rescue,' he said. His smile crinkled the corners of his eyes.

Haven shrugged. 'It was a lucky guess.'

'Maybe so, but you saved me from a situation that could have turned a little ugly.'

'How can an old grave collapsing be your fault?' Haven asked, leaning on the rake.

'I'm sure you're well aware by now that this village will leap on anything out of the ordinary.' Peter paused and Haven saw the words coming, wanted to shrink back out of their range. 'I'm so very sorry about Sebastian. Such a terrible thing.'

'Is it true? About the male Hendersons all meeting fucked-up ends?'

Peter didn't recoil at the profanity.

'They do seem to be very unlucky in the scheme of things, but people here will always tarnish, always elaborate. Small village syndrome, I'm afraid.'

'What can you tell me about Rafferty?'

Haven knew his tone was less than polite but this place was rapidly trying his patience.

Peter inclined his head for a moment. A robin hopped from a nearby branch and perched on the edge of the wheelbarrow.

'We rarely see him. He doesn't go to the local schools. But I do know that he's the last male descendant, unless there are some hidden away in the woodwork.'

Haven raised an eyebrow. The robin pulled a grub from a clump of leaves.

'The Hendersons are, shall we say, a family who don't follow the societal norm. Rafferty isn't a prisoner. I've seen him wandering alone on the fields between the gatehouse and the village. But I fear he is a very isolated boy. Amelia and Grace have taught him not to trust, so that is his default. I sometimes think that's one reason why the male line withers. They live too much within their own heads . . .' Peter placed his hand on Haven's shoulder. 'Look at me, rambling like an old woman. I've got a meeting to attend and you must carry on, my young friend.'

Haven watched as Peter made his way back along the pathway towards the church.

I can't be who they want me to be. Sebastian's words came back to him. *The weight of it, you know, it drags me down.*

Sebastian had shrugged it off when Haven nudged for more information and Haven let it ride, happy to be the shoulder Sebastian leant on.

What kind of secrets was this family keeping, locked away in their little gatehouse?

He thought about Rafferty and what Sebastian had asked him to do.

Please help him. And if you can't you'll know what to do.

What the hell did that mean?

Haven wracked his brains for any conversations they'd had that made Sebastian think that Haven was a capable person. He came up empty.

The robin flew across to the collapsed grave and Haven followed. He'd better find something to tape this off before he continued with his other work. He knelt by it and took a closer look. The sides had all caved in as though something beneath had shifted. There were no predominant root systems. He went back for the rake and cleared away some of the earth in the bottom of the hole.

Now he could see the edge of the degraded coffin. He raked again. Exposed the lid. Or what was left of it. Very gently he lifted the coffin lid with the prongs of the rake, expecting to see old bones.

A shroud lay crumpled in the coffin base. He moved it aside. His jaw fell open.

The coffin was empty.

CHAPTER FIFTEEN

By the time Rafferty reached the meadow behind the church, sweat coated his body. Shivers wracked his slim frame, but when he ran his fingers over his skin it felt hot and clammy. It hurt to touch.

Pain pounded in his temple and his stomach was a writhing mass of corded knots.

Is this what it's like to be sick?

The thought drifted hazily past his mind's eye.

He'd never been sick before, not even the trace of a cold. It was the only positive to being a Henderson, short-term illness didn't touch them.

You deserve it. Shame flared on his cheeks. He'd drunk the crow dry, torn into its soft flesh, savoured every mouthful until his teeth met its breastbone.

The drystone wall around the church loomed at the edge of his vision. He stumbled towards it, heaved himself over, scraping his wrist on a jagged edge. His limbs didn't seem to want to behave as they should.

And he had no idea where he was going.

His foot slipped on some loose earth on the banking and he fell to his hands and knees. He stayed there for a few moments, head bowed, his breathing laboured.

Somehow he managed to climb to his feet.

Rafferty stood in the churchyard, a place he hadn't visited for nine years. There were no other people around. The only sign of life was a discarded wheelbarrow filled with leaves by the pathway.

He could hear traffic moving on the road. A car horn blared. Someone shouted. Children's laughter came from behind a low building next to the church.

The dour bulk of the crypt loomed in front of him, the doors closed.

Was this where he'd been heading?

He chewed the edge of his lip and walked towards it, swaying slightly.

Dried leaves skittered across the steps leading to the crypt. He found he was fascinated by their erratic movement, the sunlight on their curled surfaces.

Three steps from the doors, he stopped.

He was suddenly six years old again, his small hand in Sebastian's, watching the coffins as they were pulled from their resting place. Even then he had felt the wrongness of it. The dead do not like to be disturbed.

He reached out towards the peeling green paint, let his fingertips rest on the worn wood.

His vision tunnelled and he felt himself drawn towards it. He was both outside and inside the crypt, but the latter felt more physical. He could smell the damp moss on the walls, feel the intense cold on his heated skin.

Where the coffins had rested were deep, dark holes, and each one seemed to whisper his name. This place knew him even though he had never been inside. It knew his blood.

'What you doing, boy?' A voice dragged him back into the present. An old man stood on the pathway, his hands clasped in front of his chest.

Adrenaline spiked through Rafferty's veins. He bolted around the side of the crypt, through a mass of tangled ivy. It wound around his legs, made each forward step a struggle, but he pressed through and stumbled onto the path, his heartbeat thundering in his ears.

Panic overrode how rough he felt. He glanced down at his sweatshirt, saw the patches of blood, and a frenzied fear took hold.

He was a cornered rabbit with a hound on his tail.

'Stop. It's okay!'

Rafferty wasn't stopping. It wasn't okay.

He ran, spooked and disorientated, his racing steps leading him to the lychgate. People moved on the street: a woman pushing a buggy with a toddler holding her hand, an old woman with a walking stick, two teenage boys in school uniform, their ties loosened and hanging like nooses.

All turned to stare and Rafferty saw the shock written on their faces. Despite keeping to the gatehouse and hiding his existence, they knew who he was.

A Henderson. He might as well have had a target painted on his chest.

A wave of dizziness overcame him and he clutched the top of the gate. He glanced down at his blood-caked fingers. Saw the dried gore under his fingernails.

And he knew it was smeared on his face. His sin plain for all to see.

The woman with the buggy backed away. The old woman stared, rheumy eyes judging him silently. The two teenage boys, smug grins plastered on their faces, looked at him as though he was a smashed bug on the ground. One had pulled out a phone, was videoing the whole thing.

Rafferty hid his face in the crook of his arm.

His stomach clenched tight, then a surge of bitter liquid flooded his throat. He doubled over in pain. Warm vomit spattered the flagstones. Warm, crimson vomit.

'Jesus!' one of the boys exclaimed. He turned to his friend holding the phone. 'Are you getting this?'

Another voice reached his ears.

'Can't you see he's sick? Fuck off out of here!'

A hand on his shoulder, another around his waist, leading him away from the lychgate and people and cruelty. He stopped once to throw up again but this time it was mainly bile. It burned his throat. Brought hot tears to his eyes.

Someone covered his shoulders with a jacket.

Every muscle in his body ached, every bone felt like it had been ripped out and rearranged.

Amelia and Grace would be furious. Their first rule: Do Not Attract Attention. And now he'd done that royally.

He'd never be able to explain the blood. He remembered how he'd felt whilst drinking it. Whilst tearing into the raw flesh. The invincibility surging through his veins. The irresistible thought he could own that feeling, make people fear him.

He didn't have to do that. They feared him already. Because he was different. Because he was a Henderson.

'I need to go home.' He tried to pull away from the hands that held him.

'You need to lie down right now, Rafferty.'

How does this man know my name? The thought flickered through Rafferty's mind like ash on the wind.

A door opened. The scent of beeswax and cold stone. The church. He was in the church. Panic flared again. The grip around him became firmer. Now there were steps to negotiate. He let himself be led.

They pushed through a doorway and his legs gave out. He felt himself lifted. Hair tickled his face.

A bed. A blanket. Someone tugging off his trainers.

The sound of water running. A warm cloth on his mouth, wiping away what clung there.

A glass to his lips. Cold water dribbled down his aching throat.

'Easy, not too much.'

He wanted to get up, to say he was fine now. But the bed was so comfortable and his body hurt, and he just wanted to sleep and forget about everything.

He struggled to open his heavy eyelids, found the man sitting on the edge of the bed watching him. Concern furrowed his brow.

Light flooded from a huge window at the other side of the room, a cross etched into it. The man didn't look like he belonged here.

A fever-laced smile tugged at Rafferty's lips.

Belonging. Only a word.

But Rafferty didn't feel like he belonged anywhere.

Exhaustion dragged him down into a dreamless sleep.

Chapter Sixteen

Haven waited until Rafferty's breathing had settled before leaving his side.

He contemplated calling a doctor but something stayed his hand from reaching for his phone.

Terrified. That was the word he'd use to describe how he'd found the boy cowering at the lychgate.

But of what? The people? That didn't seem to add up.

Haven had seen Rafferty careering down the pathway as he tightened a screw on an ancient spade, his mind still firmly mulling over what he'd found—or hadn't found—in the grave. Had known it was Rafferty the instant he laid eyes upon him.

He watched the boy sleeping. Watched the way his eyelids flickered as though even in dreams something was nipping at his heels. His gaze flicked down to the sweatshirt, the front and cuffs soaked in blood, the edges of the stains crusting.

Haven went into the bathroom and shoved a towel into the sink, running hot water over it, one ear listening for any movement from the bed.

Gently, he pulled down the blanket and lifted the bottom of Rafferty's sweatshirt. A white T-shirt underneath but not quite as bloodstained. This was good. It meant the source of the blood wasn't Rafferty.

But he had to check.

Rafferty's skin was clear, apart from a few smudges that had soaked through. Haven wiped them away with the warm towel. Then he sat with Rafferty's hands on his thigh, cleaning his blood-caked fingers as best he could.

He wondered what the villagers would say if they knew he had a boy in his room.

In his bed.

But he knew exactly what they'd think.

People were so fucking quick to judge, convinced that what they thought was the only right option.

But what to do now?

He pulled at his bottom lip with his thumb and forefinger.

Rafferty stirred and muttered something in his sleep. Sweat beaded on his upper lip. He reached out a hand. It flopped languidly onto Haven's knee. A smile tugged at the edges of the boy's lips. 'Sebastian.' The whispered name was like an arrow notched in Haven's heart.

If Rafferty woke fully, what would Haven even say to him? *I knew your brother and he asked me to look out for you.* That would only raise a whole heap of other questions, none of which Haven was sure he should answer because . . . because what? He wanted to protect Sebastian? It was too late for that now.

He closed his eyes for a moment, the ache of his own grief hollowing out his chest.

Think, Haven, think.

He crossed to the window and looked out at the churchyard. Winter sunlight glinted from the strips of aluminium foil he had strung on twine around the collapsed grave. He'd found both in the tool room.

Haven paused and inclined his head, measured the distance in his mind's eye between the grave and the pathway around the church.

It was where he'd seen the torch light last night.

A gentle knock on the door tore him away from his pondering.

An old man stood in the hallway. Liver spots dotted his brow, his face deeply lined with age. Wisps of white hair clung to his scalp. But it was his dark grey eyes, half-hidden in folds of flesh, that held Haven's attention.

It was the old man Haven had seen in the bar. The one who sat on the graveyard bench and threw breadcrumbs to the birds.

'I need to look at the boy,' the old man said. He rubbed his fingers over his chin. Calluses lined his palm.

'He's not something to gawk at.' Annoyance pinpricked its way over Haven's skin. 'And you are?' He arched an eyebrow, resting his frame against the door.

'Jack Tucker,' the man said. 'But everyone calls me Tucker and that sits all right with me.'

Haven fell into his club persona—a reserved but steadfast silence, guaranteed to make people drift away or back down.

Tucker did neither. He simply met Haven's gaze, both men assessing each other.

It was Tucker who broke the quiet.

'I'm not going to hurt him or spread any gossip. Heaven knows this place thrives on that, especially when it concerns the Hendersons.' He reached out a gnarled hand and placed it on Haven's forearm. 'But for everyone's safety I have to take a look at him.'

Something about the sincerity in Tucker's voice made Haven step back and let him into the room.

The old man crossed to the bed, pulled the blanket away from Rafferty. In a matter of seconds he delved under the boy's sweatshirt, his hands working over Rafferty's chest.

He turned to Haven. 'It's okay, thank God, or whatever looks down upon this miserable place.'

91

'I'd already checked that the blood wasn't his,' Haven said, but Tucker hadn't looked at Rafferty's skin, only felt.

'There's things here that can't be explained rationally,' Tucker said, patting the blanket back into place. 'But I think you know that, Haven. I see things, even though everyone tars me as a senile old fool. I see the knowing in you.'

His grey eyes raked over Haven, and Haven felt the scrutiny shredding away his carefully applied layers.

'The knowing?' He threw the ball back into Tucker's court.

'Aye, boy. The knowing. And don't try to bullshit me. You've seen things. Dark things. Things that leave a stain.'

There was nothing Haven could say to that. It was all true.

Tucker sighed. His whiskery chin trembled briefly.

'There are things unravelling here. I feel it in my marrow, makes my old bones ache. Take it with a pinch of salt, but be careful, boy. See with your heart not your sight.'

Footsteps sounded on the stairs. Someone called Haven's name.

He opened the door to find Peter standing there, his hair mussed by the wind.

'I believe we have a young visitor?'

Haven stepped aside. Peter stole across to the bed, laid a hand on Rafferty's brow. He nodded towards Tucker.

'Word travelled fast, then,' Haven said. His words dripped with irritation.

'In a village such as ours nothing is a secret for long, especially when it does something to relieve the monotony of the day.' Peter's eyes fell to the bloodstained towel.

'He's not injured.' Haven's reply was swift.

'That's a good thing. But we need to get this young man home.' Peter began to pull down the blanket.

'Wouldn't it be better to wait until he wakes up?' Haven had only just found Rafferty. He was in no rush to change that.

Something passed over Peter's face, like a cloud skimming over the sun.

'Amelia and Grace will be worried.'

'Can you ring them?' Haven felt like he was stating the obvious.

'Best to just get the boy back where he belongs. I'll bring my car around to the rear of the church.'

Peter glanced over his shoulder at Rafferty before leaving.

His words jarred against Haven's nerve endings. He ran his tongue over his upper teeth. There seemed to be too much of a rush to get Rafferty home.

'You feeling the wrongness?' Tucker asked, his hands folded in his lap as he sat on the edge of the bed.

The wrongness was neon-bright, but Haven didn't reply.

His gaze fell to the chest of drawers. On it was a Bible and a blank notepad and pencil. He scribbled something on the top sheet, tore it off, and stuffed it in his pocket. A plan formed in his mind.

Haven slipped an arm around Rafferty's shoulders and hoisted him to a sitting position.

'Come on, Rafferty, time to go home.' The name that had lived inside his head for so long felt odd on his lips.

Rafferty murmured and laid his head against Haven's chest, his body limp and vulnerable. A surge of protectiveness spiked through Haven's veins. The crunch of car tyres on gravel outside filtered through the window.

Haven wrapped his arm more firmly around Rafferty, let his other hand scoop under the boy's knees.

He stood with Rafferty in his arms. The etched cross watched him from a window that overlooked a graveyard where someone had been walking in the dark. Where a grave had caved in. Where the bones were missing.

He took a moment to grab a reality check before he carried Rafferty downstairs.

Peter waited in the car, the engine running.

'Put him on the back seat. I'll drive slowly.'

'He can rest against me,' Haven said. 'You'll need someone to yell if it looks like he's going to throw up again.' His gaze flicked over the shining cream interior. 'You don't want him to do that in here.'

'No.' Peter's curt reply was at odds with his usual genial manner. 'Amelia and Grace don't take well to strangers. And you understand, especially now, with Sebastian's tragic death, they need time to grieve.'

Peter leant across and flicked the catch on the rear passenger door. Haven tugged it open with his foot, trying to come up with something else to persuade Peter. He got nothing. He laid Rafferty on the back seat, then pulled off his jacket and covered him up. Peter watched him through the rear-view mirror.

'Thank you for caring for him, Haven. You have a good heart.'

Haven watched as Peter reversed the car then drove out towards the main street.

The wrongness.

That was how Tucker had explained it. That was what Haven felt. A wrongness building, layer upon layer, threatening to suffocate anything that dared to cross its path.

It was possible he was delusional.

But one thing was certain. Rafferty Henderson was going home, and he had Haven's phone number in his pocket.

CHAPTER SEVENTEEN

Grace peered down into the well. A small disc of darkness looked back, like a socket missing an eye. The brackish stench of water. Of a world beneath the earth. A world where unimaginable horrors lurked.

It was all starting to fall apart. This impenetrable wall Amelia had carefully built, crumbling. She closed her eyes, saw Rafferty's anger burning bright. She didn't think she would ever forget it. And who could blame him?

She sighed, felt age settling against her bones, felt the weight of the terrible secret they had kept for so long.

It was possible the decisions they had made in the past were wrong, but they had been made with only one thing at the forefront of their minds: Protect Sebastian. Protect Rafferty.

Feed what needed to be fed.

Grace had always been the quiet one. More than happy to let Amelia take the lead. Be the voice for both of them.

Apart from . . . Grace's lips silently mouthed the words. *Apart from that night when they tore it away.*

Nine years since they had severed the rot and left it to die.

Grace had wanted to wait. To see if Rafferty would settle.

Can't you see what it's doing to him, Gracie?

And Grace could see. Back then they had taken turns sitting by Rafferty's bedside, holding his small hand as he thrashed, his nightmares taking him to a place where neither she nor Amelia could protect him.

By day he had been an even-tempered and gracious child, content to live in his own imaginary world. With his own imaginary friend.

But the black-and-white photo Grace kept in her dungarees bib pocket told its own story.

A squirrel darted up the slender trunk of a silver birch, the movement bringing her thoughts back to the present.

A single drop of blood fell onto the weathered stone.

Wetness coated her upper lip.

She raised her fingers, found the source.

Only a nosebleed.

But she hadn't had one since the night they'd done the unthinkable. A stiff breeze stirred the dried leaves and high in the trees two crows took flight, their cries piercing the winter chill.

Her skin started to crawl, as though a beetle was scurrying along her spine, navigating each vertebra, unfazed by the curve and fall of bone.

She turned slowly, her gaze flitting through the trees, looking for . . . looking for what?

An impossibility, her brain whispered.

And Grace Henderson laughed at the meaning behind that word.

Because everything was possible.

A voice called her name, the sound carried on the wind. A flash of blue through the trees.

Grace hurried to meet it, anxious to be away from the well in case the visitor should set curious eyes on the stone structure.

'There you are.' Peter Edwards's genial face came into view. 'I have Rafferty in my car. I'm afraid he had a little incident.'

'Incident?' Her mind spiralled off into the awful realm of probability.

'Oh, he's fine now, I think.' Peter's face settled into lines of concern. 'Just a bout of sickness.'

Sickness?

Rafferty was never sick. It was the yin to the yang of the plague Irving Walsh had thrust upon them.

Grace pushed past Peter and hurried along the pathway. Along the twists and turns, her heart thrown out before her, desperate to reach Rafferty.

She could hear Peter speaking but ignored his attempts at cordial speech, wishing she could turn back the clock a couple of decades and run. Wishing for too many things that would never come true.

At last the gatehouse roof came into view and she ran the final fifty yards to Peter's car, yanking open the rear passenger door. She sank to her knees, buried her head in the crook of Rafferty's neck, her arms holding him tight.

Her heartbeat quickened. She could smell blood on his breath.

Reluctantly, she let Peter guide her away, let him carry Rafferty into the gatehouse. Watched, wringing her hands together, as Peter lowered him onto the sofa.

'Grace . . .' Peter turned, his gaze flicking from Rafferty towards her. 'Should I be worried?'

'No.' Her reply was thorn-sharp. She lifted her chin defiantly, daring him to continue.

He lowered his eyes. Cleared his throat.

'Well, I'll be off then. Unless you need any—'

'It's fine.' She cut any further words, a tourniquet against his supply of questions. Hated the bitchy tone in her voice. But she didn't need him. Not anymore.

She wasn't worried that he would expose their secret. Peter Edwards wasn't stupid. His involvement in it would tar him with a miasma that would finish his career.

But seeing him here, in this house, standing over Rafferty, brought back too many horrors. She wanted him out. Right now.

Her fingers curled into fists. Bile burned up her gullet.

He shrank back against the door, his eyes widening, as though he could feel her thoughts worming through his skull.

Grace turned away until she heard the sound of the car engine. She let out a strangled gasp of air and knelt at Rafferty's side, her gaze taking in his stained sweatshirt.

It didn't take any deduction to work out what he'd done.

What barrier he had crossed.

The steel claws of inevitability sank into her shoulders as she pressed her lips to his brow. Salt on his skin. So much salt.

Her eyes filled with tears.

She entwined her fingers together, clasping them tightly, her knuckles pressing through her skin.

Please don't take him, she whispered. *Take me instead.*

A hollow prayer. Because that would never happen.

Henderson women were carved from iron because they were the ones who bore the agony of loss.

Warm tears stroked her cheeks, settling into the deep lines between her nose and mouth.

She closed her eyes.

Felt a pressure building behind them.

The pressure of a storm building. A storm that had begun in the frigid cold of a polar night.

A storm that would change her world.

CHAPTER EIGHTEEN

Meredith sat in her car to eat her lunch. The engine was running and the heater was turned up to maximum but still she felt frozen inside.

You're being irrational, a little voice said.

Irrational wasn't part of her make-up, though. She prided herself on always having a clear, calm head, for not letting the little things in life ruffle her edges. She had been doing this job for over twenty years and not once had she felt this—she stopped, mid-chew, tried to find the right word—*unglued*. Yes, that was it. All her logic was coming away at the seams, letting her past ooze through the gaps.

She glanced back towards the house again, at its quiet despondency. It was hardly the quintessential Gothic manor.

But that sound she'd heard in the hallway . . .

She shivered and tried to crank the heater up another notch.

It was the beginning of the school summer holidays.

Meredith was nine years old, the youngest daughter of Mary Evans, florist, and Douglas Evans, carpenter. One older sister by five years, Alice. One crazy, crossbred dog, Freddie.

A normal family living a normal family life. School was out and the prospect of seven halcyon weeks of freedom beckoned.

But this summer was different. Mary had decided Alice was old enough to look after Meredith. The florist shop wasn't doing too well and Mary had let her assistant go to save costs. She had no time to entertain two bored girls.

And besides, what trouble could they get into? It was a small village. Everyone knew them and there were plenty of people to help if one of them got into something.

It was the 1970s. Children had house keys tied around their necks on pieces of string. They were allowed to roam.

Alice wasn't amused. She pleaded and raged, pouted and cried, but Mary was adamant. Alice would take care of her sister, and that was the end of it.

Meredith heard their arguments as she played in her room. Part of her thrilled at the thought of going out with just Alice. She straightened her shoulders and made a pact with herself that she wouldn't be a pest.

'Come on! You're such a pain, Mere.'

Alice walked quickly along the lane, her bag on her shoulder, long suntanned legs in skimpy shorts, the kind Mary would never let her wear outside if she'd known.

Meredith ran to catch up, twirling a pink foxglove bell she had plucked from a hedgerow in her fingers. 'Where are we going?' she wailed. Her hair was stuck to the back of her neck with sweat, her tongue thickened with thirst. And they'd been walking for *hours*.

Alice made a noise of intense annoyance, lifting her face to the sky. She wheeled around, blonde ponytail whipping around her shoulder like a serpent.

'I told you to stay at home!'

Meredith's bottom lip trembled. 'Mum said you had to look after me.'

Alice threw up her hands in frustration and continued down the lane.

Sheep grazed in lush green fields. Cotton wool clouds basked in the sky. No cars passed them.

They rounded a corner and Meredith stopped dead.

'We're not going there, are we?' She wanted to shrink back inside her shadow.

'Look.' Alice sighed. 'You can stay here if you want. Go into that field.' She jerked her head to the right. 'Make daisy chains or tell yourself stories or something. You've got lunch in your backpack. I won't be long.'

There was a hopeful note in Alice's voice, as though what she was suggesting was the best idea ever.

'No.' The word poured out of Meredith's mouth before she could catch it. 'I'm coming with you.'

Alice narrowed her eyes and tossed her hair again. It was rapidly becoming her Thing.

'Fine. Just don't say you're bored. And don't'—she raised her forefinger and jabbed it in the air towards Meredith—'say anything to Amelia and Grace. It's bad enough having you here. They don't want to hear your childish prattle.'

Alice eased herself through a gap between two huge iron gates. She didn't look back. Meredith chewed her bottom lip for a moment and then followed her sister, her gaze flicking over the old gatehouse. It didn't look scary. It just looked normal.

From what the other girls at school had said she imagined that it was huge and hulking, with dark windows and a door that creaked inwards when someone answered.

She scuffed a toe in the dirt, heard the squawk of chickens from the other side of the garden.

The gatehouse door opened a little. It didn't creak. Alice went in.

Meredith walked over a patchy area of grass to look at the chickens. They strutted across to the wire mesh, cocking their heads to one side hopefully.

'Hello, chick-chicks,' she said, then felt stupid.

A bumble bee droned past her and landed on a yellow rose bush tumbling from the garden wall. Dust kicked up by the chickens tickled her nose. She flopped down on the grass, took off her backpack, and ate one of her jam sandwiches. The jam was warm and sweet on her tongue. She drank some orange squash from her Holly Hobbie flask. She didn't even like Holly Hobbie anymore but Mum said there was nothing wrong with the flask so she was stuck with it.

She seemed to be stuck with everything. Cast-off clothes and toys from Alice. A summer that was going nowhere fast.

I want something exciting to happen. The thought settled. She liked it, so she closed her eyes, clenched her fist, and held it against her lips, wished with all her heart.

'Why have you got a dead man's bell?'

The voice came out of nowhere.

Meredith's eyes flew open. Her brow wrinkled, then her gaze fell on the foxglove withering in the dust.

She was suddenly mute.

Alice rolled her eyes. 'She won't be a problem, I promise.'

The two other girls looked at Alice, then Meredith.

'She better not be,' said one. She was the shorter of the two with dark hair that curled in on itself like it was alive. Pale skin that looked like it was lit from within.

The taller girl hung back. She had the same dark, wavy hair. But not as glorious, like she was a shadow of her sister.

'I guess she could be useful, though,' said the Glorious Girl.

Amelia. This had to be Amelia. Meredith had heard lots about her.

Alice glanced across at Meredith. Her eyes darkened. *Do not mess this up.*

Meredith stood and brushed the dust from her legs.

'Hold on.' Amelia came closer, reached out one hand, and brushed a soft finger over Meredith's lips.

Meredith's eyes widened and she had the urgent need to pee.

Amelia held up her finger. Something glistened there. Something deep and red.

Like blood.

She licked it away, studied Meredith from under lowered lashes.

'It's a sign,' said the Shadow Girl. *Grace.*

Amelia nodded and reached for Alice's hand. They ran into the woods, leaving Grace and Meredith standing there.

Meredith poked her tongue between her lips, found the sweet taste of jam. Colour rose to her cheeks. For one moment there she'd thought she really was bleeding.

'Go on,' Grace said. 'Follow them. I need to get something from the house.'

Laughter filtered through the trees, through the dappled sunlight. Alice's squeal of excitement.

Meredith's heart pounded in her chest. Adrenaline tingled in her fingertips.

I want something exciting to happen.

Maybe wishes did come true. Joy fizzed through her veins, along with a quiver of apprehension.

She pushed the unease away and ran into the woods.

And now she was back. Decades later. Back to finally face the disquiet that had hummed under her skin all this time. Back to investigate, to put her own mind at rest because she couldn't live the remainder of her life not knowing. It would eat her alive.

CHAPTER NINETEEN

Haven worked steadily all afternoon. He took one break and walked along the high street to the bakery, bought a sandwich, and sat in the graveyard to eat it. People turned to stare as he walked by, and he felt the concentrated weight of their judgement boring into his back.

But how much of that judgement was because of how he looked, and how much was because he had taken care of Rafferty? He wasn't sure.

This was a weird-ass place. So quaint and rustic on the surface, but the underlying atmosphere bubbled with resentment and secrecy. Maybe all rural places were like this. He'd grown up in a town and didn't have much experience when it came to provincial backwaters. His playground had been made of concrete and attitude. And with that came the need to be the one everyone looked up to, lest the concrete swallowed who you were, made you into dog shit smeared on its surface. He'd been that leader, had basked in the power and the way other kids reacted to his presence. He had thought it was the best feeling in the world. Until that late October night when the idea he'd come up with went so horrifically wrong.

How could he have been so cruel? That version of himself still haunted his dreams, along with the name of the boy he had wronged.

Say his name.

Haven's jaw set tight. This wasn't the place.

He finished the last bite of his sandwich and looked around the graveyard. The wind caught the foil on the makeshift barrier he'd erected around the grave. Did graves collapse? They did, but he didn't think nature was the cause of this one.

He bent down to fasten his bootlace, and when he looked up he saw people coming out of the church. Eight in total, Peter appearing at the rear. There was none of the usual human interaction, no talking between them, no waved farewells as they walked towards the lychgate.

His mouth twisted to one side. It felt off. But then, everything here felt off.

He thought about Rafferty. About the blood staining his clothes. About Tucker and his weird insistence.

Haven lifted his head, inhaled slowly. There was a strange scent in the air. Something dank and almost rotted. He glanced up towards the crypt.

He didn't see Peter watching him from the church steps before disappearing inside.

When he went into the pub that evening it was more crowded than usual. Some kind of meeting was going on around the fireplace, tables and chairs pulled together like a barricade, hunched backs a deterrent against anyone who wanted to breach their ranks.

Tucker sat in the corner, lost in the throng, his head nodding onto his chest, but they paid him no attention.

Meredith was in the same alcove as the night before, nursing a brandy in a balloon glass.

He raised an eyebrow as he went across, hooking his foot into the rungs of a stool and pulling it in as he took a seat opposite her. 'Tough day, huh?'

Her lips curled into a weak smile. Dark hollows lay under her eyes.

'What's going on over there?' Haven jerked his thumb over his shoulder. She would tell him what was bothering her if she wanted him to know.

'No idea,' she said. 'They were all gathered there when I came back. Village parley. No strangers allowed.'

Haven went to the bar and ordered a beer and another brandy for Meredith. Rosa wasn't on duty. A young kid who didn't look old enough to drink snapped the top off Haven's beer. His black T-shirt sported a logo declaring *System Failure* with a hazed skull behind the words.

'Cool T-shirt.' Haven nodded with a smile. His own was plain black tonight. He didn't want to start a conflict with his more Fuck Authority offerings, although he still wore his skull-print bandana around his neck.

The kid slid the beer across the bar. He took a glass and slipped it under the brandy optic. 'You should go.' He kept his eyes lowered as he rang the drinks through the till.

'What?' Haven thought he'd heard wrong. He handed over a twenty-pound note.

'Go,' the kid whispered. His eyes darted nervously towards the gathering by the fireplace before dumping the change into Haven's hand, then turning to the next customer.

Haven brought the drinks back to the table. 'This is the place that keeps on giving.' He rolled his eyes, told Meredith what had happened, tried to keep the frustration out of his voice. It had been a long fucking day.

'I met Rafferty,' he said, the words spilling out of his mouth as he leaned forward on the table with his arms crossed.

Meredith met his gaze. Her fingers played with the edge of a torn beer mat. 'As in you were introduced?'

'No.' Haven took a drink, felt the welcome chill of the beer slide down his throat. 'He ran past me in the graveyard, threw up by the lychgate. Poor kid was sick and people were looking at him like he was some kind of zoo exhibit. I took him back to my room and cleaned him up, then Peter arrived and insisted he take Rafferty home.'

'Peter?' Meredith asked. Her brow creased.

'Peter Edwards, the reverend here. He's been good to me.' Haven took another drink. 'But I can't quite work him out.'

A blast of rain hit the window by their table and Meredith jumped. Outside, the night pressed close. The sound of a log collapsing to cinders in the hearth and the clink of glasses. A murmured hum of voices.

Haven traced a line of condensation on his beer bottle with one finger. 'And just to add to the fucked-up feel of this place, a grave collapsed in the churchyard and the locals were pretty cut up about it.'

Meredith's fingers curled around her glass. She met his level gaze then looked away. Her throat rippled.

Haven gave her space. He had a feeling she was leading up to what was bothering her.

The pub door burst open and a man rushed in. His coat glistened with raindrops, his wet hair stuck to his scalp. He went across to the group, joined in the huddle around the hearth. A woman, her gaze explicitly hostile, turned to stare at Haven and Meredith.

'Give me a minute,' Haven said, pushing back his stool. The washroom doors were at the other side of the bar, the same side as the fireplace, separated from the main area by an internal wall about ten feet in length. He walked across, ignoring the heads that raised to watch him pass. He pushed open the door that led to the washrooms, stepped back, let it close with a soft bang so others would think he had gone inside, then leaned against the internal wall, his gaze on his phone.

He listened intently, trying to make out a few words from the conversation going on behind him. But everything was too muffled.

Movement in his peripheral vision made him lift his gaze.

A woman stood by Meredith's table. The woman who had turned to stare. She'd been at the churchyard earlier. At the collapsed grave.

Meredith sat with her spine ramrod straight, her jaw clenched tight.

> 'We need to do something *now* before it all escalates.'
> A frustrated statement from behind the wall.

'I do not appreciate your tone.'

Meredith's voice cut through the air. Anger trembled on the edge of each word.

> 'We're going to do something. That's why we're here.'
> A man's unflinching reply.

Two scenes were playing out before Haven, like two different movies on opposing screens.

He walked back to the table as the woman stormed away. Her upper lip curled in disgust as she passed him. Haven bit back a retort. When he was staking out clubs he'd learned that conflict dragged him away from his prime objective, which was watching and listening. Absorbing information.

'What was that all about?' He pulled up the stool and took another drink. The bottle gleamed with condensation and it nearly slipped from his hand.

'She told me to quit meddling. That I shouldn't disturb things that wanted to rest.' Two high spots of colour flamed on her cheeks and a nerve twitched in her lower jaw.

'You're clearing an old house, right? Hardly meddling.'

She met his gaze and something shifted in her face.

'What I didn't tell you was who ordered the clear-out.'

He cocked his head to one side and waited, had a feeling that whatever she said would take him farther down this fucked-up rabbit hole.

'My client is Amelia Henderson.'

And there it was.

In his mind's eye Haven felt the earth shifting under his feet, felt the pull of something that sent an electric shock vibrating along his bones.

Go, the kid behind the bar had said.

Go, said the instinct that had kept him alive so far.

Stay, said a voice that sounded like Rafferty. *Please stay.*

CHAPTER TWENTY

The sound pulled Rafferty from a deep sleep. He'd been dreaming. Standing on the deck of a three-masted ship with the ocean all around him. But the ocean wasn't blue or grey, it was white and frozen and endless.

The creak of old timber followed him as he opened his eyes, his lashes crusted together. Shadows played on his bedroom wall, skeletal limbs of winter trees sweeping across like a painter's angry brush strokes.

His whole body felt like he'd been bounced off a wall at high speed, and then run over by a truck.

Fragments of the day slipped in and out of the mire clouding his thoughts. He'd been at the crypt . . . then the full force of what had happened rose up like a creature from the depths and took the breath from his lungs.

Rafferty reached across and flicked on the bedside lamp, screwing his eyes up at the sudden light. He held his hands out in front of him and saw the dried blood compacted under his fingernails. He hadn't imagined it. Hadn't imagined the crow and what he'd done.

He stuffed his hands under the blankets.

There'd been a man with long hair. He'd felt it against his face as the man carried him . . . *where?* Rafferty wasn't sure.

And then the rocking motion of a car, his head pressed into cold leather.

Before that . . . The mocking laughter of the two boys resounded in his ears and colour rushed to his cheeks. What had he been thinking going to the village? But that was it, he wasn't purposely going anywhere, his steps had just led him to the crypt, and then the sickness . . .

It was such a strange and disorientating feeling, but part of him welcomed it. This was what everyone else felt. This was normal.

He swung his legs out of bed. Movement from downstairs, the creak of floorboards, the chink of china.

Sebastian?

No, never again.

Loss forced a whimper from his lips. His brother's absence was an aching void he'd never be able to fill. An urgent need welled in his chest.

Rafferty dragged his aching body across his room and out into the narrow hallway. There were no windows here and no light from downstairs to breach it.

The door to Sebastian's room was shut. Rafferty closed his fingers around the cold latch and pushed it open.

It looked like it always did: The bed neatly made. The top of the chest of drawers empty apart from an antique globe. The nightstand with only the lamp and a single book. Rafferty understood his brother's neatness. It was the one thing in his life he had control over.

He'd had *control over.* A lump formed in Rafferty's throat.

He padded across to the globe and spun it with one finger. It rotated smoothly, a soft mechanical vibration spilling out into the silence. His eyes fell on the moving land masses and oceans, all the places he would never go. Yearning held his heart in its fist.

Something caught his eye as the globe slowed down. He spun it backwards. There, in the Arctic Ocean, was a tiny red mark. A scarlet pinprick amidst the blue. He rubbed his fingertip over it and felt the slight rise on the metal surface. Someone had painted it on.

He spun the globe gently and found another identical mark.

In the south of England. Possibly right where he was standing.

Hot tears welled in his eyes. He wanted Sebastian to burst through the door and give him hell for messing about with his things. He grabbed hold of the edge of the chest of drawers as his vision swam for a few moments.

Breathe, Rafferty.

A little punch-drunk, he walked to the window and looked out into the dark. Night clouds hung in the sky like wisps of trailing smoke. He traced the outline of one on the cold glass. Rain pattered softly onto fallen leaves.

A flicker of light caught his eye, like the tail end of a bolt of lightning. He curled his fingers around the sill and stared into the dark.

It came again. Two quick flashes, edged in blue. A crease formed between his eyes. He was almost sure the light came from above the tarn, the small deep-water basin nestled between the hills above the village.

His nose started to stream. He wiped his hand across it—blood smeared his fingers.

He fumbled in his jeans pocket for a tissue. Something hard crinkled under his touch. He pulled it out and stared at the piece of paper. Read it over a few times to let it sink in. On it was a phone number and a message—

Haven.

I knew your brother. Get in touch if you need anything.

Rafferty dabbed his nose on his arm. He couldn't remember the last time he'd had a nosebleed. It was just something else to add to the turmoil of his day. All he wanted to do was curl up in bed and forget everything.

But the note lay clutched in his fist.

He read the message again. Maybe Haven knew things Rafferty didn't? Sebastian had never mentioned him, but did that mean anything? If Haven was Sebastian's secret there must be more to it. It dawned on him, as he stood in the quiet of his dead brother's room, that the legacy of his family was all secrets, skeletons in the cupboard kept tucked away in case their discovery unleashed some form of fresh hell.

A spark of curiosity kindled in his chest. Here was someone offering to help him. Up until now Rafferty hadn't even realised he needed any help, but one thing was certain, Amelia and Grace were keeping something from him and he was determined to uncover what it was.

Rafferty couldn't settle. He'd tried to go back to sleep after standing at Sebastian's window, watching for another flash of light. Had watched until his eyes ached. When he finally returned to his room he'd convinced himself that he hadn't seen it at all.

But as he lay in bed all he could see behind his closed eyes was the blue-edged light, as though it had imprinted itself on his retinas.

CHAPTER TWENTY-ONE

Peter Edwards sat at his desk in the vestry as the rain-laden wind howled around the old church. Some would say this should be comforting—a man of the cloth safe inside the building where he worshipped—but there was no such feeling resting upon Peter's skin.

He shuffled the papers in front of him. His eyes drifted to the worn journal upon his desk. The pages of which always opened on a certain date.

The bulb in the ceiling light flickered and his gaze cast upwards to the arched stone ceiling. Damp patches darkened the surface where the rain had seeped through crumbling mortar. The diocese didn't have money for repairs, and fundraising in the village was a painful and long, drawn-out affair.

He sighed. The wind dropped. Silence hummed against his ears.

Peter tapped a pencil against his lips, the small eraser at its end now merely a nub. Uncertainty made his stomach churn. An uncertainty that had begun when he discovered the collapsed grave.

But if he was being truthful this state of mind had plagued him insidiously for years. He was an expert at portraying a calm and confident front, but underneath—and unusually, for a man of the cloth—Peter believed in fate. Of things happening for a reason.

Which was why finding a young man in his church, a man who had ties to Sebastian Henderson, didn't ruffle his feathers at all.

And what did you do, Peter? a small voice asked. *You gave him a job and a roof over his head because you knew he was meant to be here.* Peter's internal judgement never gave him time to come up with his own answers.

He never expected to still be in this rural parish at the age of sixty. It had seemed like a stroke of immense luck at the time, fresh from a curate's post in a nearby parish and the position here falling at his feet. Of course he said yes. Of course he didn't check if anything untoward had happened in the diocese. But why would he? Back then the notion of cursed families and the kind of evil that moved through generations never touched his thoughts. He yearned for that time with all of his heart.

Sure, he preached about wrongdoings and temptations to his meagre flock on a Sunday morning. But he was simply going through the motions, because if he ever confessed his sins he would be tainted beyond redemption.

He was tied to this place as surely as the Hendersons were tied to that plot of land at the very outskirts of the village. And they were tied together by what he had done. What Amelia Henderson had begged him to do.

Peter stood and walked stiffly through to the transept. The altar was to his left, behind which the great stained-glass window rested in the darkness. Only one candle was lit at the head of the nave. It sat atop a tall, wooden stand, wax dripping down its sides. The candle flame shifted as he passed and shadows danced over the old stone walls.

Some might call it outmoded but Peter saved money where he could. Lighting the main body of the church for his sole occupation was frivolous. But still, tonight he wished for modern lighting to chase away the hulking shadows.

A gust of wind rattled a loose slate on the roof and his heartbeat quickened.

Things come back, Peter. They are never truly gone.

But he had only done what he thought had to be done. And wasn't his life's calling all about helping those who had fallen by the wayside?

A truly devout man would always answer yes.

It had all started the day they moved the coffins from the crypt.

The drizzle turned to freezing rain as the last hearse drove out of the churchyard. Peter invited Amelia and Grace into the newly finished annexe to dry out a little and for tea. Tea always solves everything, although Peter wasn't sure if disinterring your family's remains fit under that banner.

For all of his polite questioning, a reason for the removal wasn't forthcoming.

The boys—Sebastian and Rafferty—had wandered into the church, but this didn't bother Peter. Part of him hoped they'd find a shred of divine enlightenment there.

A silence fell between him and the sisters, the normal run of polite conversation quickly exhausted. He imagined what his other parishioners would think if they could see him now, conversing with the women most people blamed for anything that went wrong in the parish. But from his observations the attacks ran from the sisters' shoulders like rain from a duck's back.

They kept a low profile, rarely venturing into the village, but each time they did the gossip wheel began to turn. It would be in full swing tonight after the disinterment.

The door between the church and the annexe opened and Sebastian hovered in the doorway. Peter put him at about sixteen years of age. A little gangly, not quite grown into his limbs. His eyes were wary as they fell upon Peter.

'Can I interest you in cake, young man?' Peter winced inwardly at his clumsy wording. His dealings with teenagers were few and far between. 'Maybe take some for your brother? I don't mind crumbs on the floor.'

Amelia shot Sebastian a pointed look. A warning look.

Peter was left with his arm outstretched, holding the plate like some kind of sugar-drenched inducement.

A peal of laughter erupted from the church.

Amelia slammed her cup down onto the table, tea sloshing into the saucer. Sebastian wheeled in the doorway, his face draining of colour.

Peter scratched his head. Why were they acting as though something was wrong?

He stepped in front of Amelia as she made for the door, the smile on his face as soothing as he could make it. 'God's house is made for the laughter of children. I'll just go make sure he's not up to any mischief.'

Gloom hulked in the main body of the church, the daylight outside thin and grey. He could hear water sloshing. And something else, a child talking.

The boy stood by the font at the end of the aisle. Above it was an elaborate metal candelabra of twisted poppies in remembrance of the war dead from the parish, but Peter always thought they looked like misshapen daggers.

His eyes narrowed. The font lid rested against a pew. Peter's brow furrowed. The lid was a hefty piece of wood carved from a local oak tree.

Rafferty's jacket lay discarded at his feet, his shirt sleeves rolled up to his elbows. Peter resisted the urge to shout.

'What do you think, huh?' An animated tone, ripe with delight.

The boy faced away from him, his hands playing in the water. Peter's jaw dropped at the sacrilegious act. He'd officiated at a christening yesterday and had run out of time to drain the font. His hurried steps echoed from the flagstones and he expected Rafferty to turn or to realise his misdemeanour.

But the boy kept on playing. Now his hands swept the water to the edges of the font, some splashing down onto the floor.

Peter's resolve snapped.

'Please don't do that, Rafferty.'

His gaze fell to the water as it swirled in the font. He'd always loved the simplicity of the structure, the almost Grecian lines and the white stone from which it was carved. The symbolism of purity wasn't lost to him.

But the water within wasn't clear anymore. It had a yellowish tinge.

'You've spoilt our game.' Rafferty looked at him, his chin tilting upwards.

'What did you do?' Peter almost spit out the words in his throat, a surge of anger drowning his self-control.

Rafferty bit his lower lip. He shook his head, brown curls falling onto his brow.

'It wasn't me. I told him not to but sometimes he doesn't listen.' His chin quivered.

Peter clamped his lips closed as Amelia came to stand at his side.

'It wasn't me,' Rafferty repeated, a shrill plea in his voice.

Amelia snatched the boy's jacket from the floor then grabbed his hand and pulled him towards the door. She pushed him through it, then stopped, turning back to Peter.

'I'm sorry. I want to explain, but I can't.'

With that she disappeared into the afternoon rain and Peter was left looking at the font.

The font Rafferty had urinated in.

CHAPTER TWENTY-TWO

Haven slept like the proverbial dead, too many restless nights finally catching up to him.

Then his phone alarm trilled in his ear. Over and over and over again.

'Fuck.' He slammed his hand down on the phone and dragged it towards him.

The warehouse photo met his eyes, the torment of it scratching away any scab that dared to heal on his guilt.

I'm sorry. The internal mantra was the first thought of his day. Every. Single. Day.

He threw back the covers and massaged the tight knot of muscles at the base of his neck.

There was something about Meredith's confession last night that didn't stack up.

Sebastian had always said they didn't have a lot of money for luxuries, so why was Amelia Henderson paying someone else to clear a few possessions from a house? It didn't make sense.

He ruminated over this as he pulled on his clothes and cleaned his teeth.

He'd half hoped Rafferty would have rung him by now, but even if he had, what would he say?

Maybe Rafferty didn't need any help. Maybe it was all in Sebastian's head. There were times when Haven wasn't sure of his friend's mental state.

If a perfect stranger had come up to Haven when he was Rafferty's age and said he wanted to help him, Haven's suspicion would have soared into overdrive. But then, when he was Rafferty's age he'd been a very different person.

I'm so sorry. So fucking sorry, Logan.

He lowered his head, his hair falling over his face. Felt the taut wire of tension strung across his shoulders.

He didn't voice the boy's name often. It made him all too real.

A long, exhaled breath left his lips and he raised his head. This wasn't helping anyone.

People say grief lessens as the years pass, but what about guilt? In Haven's case it only grew stronger as he searched for a way to recompense for his sins.

That's what all the Goth club visits were for, in the vain hope he might see something that didn't belong, that he might see Logan again, on the prowl this time, and somehow give him eternal rest.

It was a plan dripping with a death wish.

He grabbed a jacket and ran down the stairs into the freezing winter morning.

By early afternoon he'd cleared another swathe of land around the oldest gravestones, letting the methodical work soothe his thoughts. The sky darkened with each passing hour, storm clouds gathering over the hills to the east. Ozone laced the air.

A figure appeared on the pathway by the crypt.

Tucker.

Haven raised his hand but the old man didn't return the gesture.

Haven's gaze travelled to the collapsed grave. Strands of twine whipped back and forth in the wind. Only a few aluminium strips remained.

He took the rake and walked across to the brooding hole in the ground. The sides had caved in a little and he had to scrape the new earth in the grave's base to one corner. When fragments of the coffin surfaced he wiped the back of his hand across his mouth.

A glance at the sky told him the rain was imminent. If he didn't do what his gut was telling him the grave would soon be waterlogged. The thought of it made his skin crawl. He reached between his legs and pulled his jeans away from his balls. Physically, they weren't happy with his decision either.

Haven jumped down into the grave. He stood just shy of six feet tall but the sides towered over his head and from this angle all he could see was a rectangular slice of sky darkening by the moment.

He gathered up the remnants of the broken coffin and flung the pieces up onto the ground above. The absence of any bones taunted his thoughts.

Either the coffin had been buried empty . . .

Or something had crawled out of it.

He shook his head and gave himself a mental check. This wasn't a horror movie.

This is something much worse.

He grimaced at the unsolicited speculation and was glad he hadn't decided to do this at night with only a torch to light his way. But then, this is how it had started. Someone had been here in the dark, and the following morning the grave had collapsed.

He wiped a trickle of sweat from the side of his face. A deep boom of thunder rumbled from the heavens. Rain began to fall, not a hesitant drizzle but a deluge, as though someone had opened a floodgate in the sky. He was soaked through in a matter of minutes, the earth in the grave rapidly turning to sludge.

There was only one piece of the coffin left now. Part of the lid, which had embedded itself into the side of the grave. He pulled but it didn't give. He pulled harder, going to his knees in the mud to give his muscles more leverage.

A corner slid out and he wrapped his fingers behind it.

'Move, you bastard,' he grunted.

He could feel the ooze of the wet earth sliding inside his boots, and his hair hung in soaked ropes around his face.

Another corner gave, and now Haven used the full weight of his body as he yanked it again and again. A sharp crack of wood. He tumbled backwards into the grave. Lay there with the sodden earth encasing his body, his hands still holding a fragment of coffin to his chest like a prayer book.

Fear like he had never known before gripped him, froze his limbs into place, iced his gullet. If the sides of the grave collapsed again he'd be buried alive . . .

Another crack of thunder sounded overhead, so loud he felt the vibration behind his ribcage. It spurred him into action and he dragged himself out of the mire, lumps of wet earth dripping from his limbs, his hair heavy with filth.

Even through the fading light he knew what his eyes were seeing. Where the coffin piece had been embedded was something—or rather, was nothing. He reached out a hand and it disappeared; wrist, elbow, to his shoulder. A tunnel. It was a fucking tunnel.

He flung himself on his stomach, heard the rain batter down against his jacket. Now his head was level with the tunnel opening. He reached in again, trying to gauge its size, his fingers blindly clawing over the cold earth surface.

Something brushed against the back of his hand. Something cold and soft, like raw chicken. Haven recoiled, trying to tell himself it had been a mole. *Or . . . or . . . or . . .*

He didn't like the images his brain was coming up with. He skittered back, cradling his hand to his chest.

'Haven. Good Lord, boy.'

Haven cranked his head back and saw the underside of an umbrella. A face peered down at him. Tucker's face.

Haven tried to come up with an excuse, but really what kind of excuse would have any bearing on the fact that he was sitting in the mud in an open grave?

He dragged himself up onto his knees, then onto his feet, slipping and sliding in what was now a mud bath. Tucker disappeared for a moment. Then the rake handle lowered into the grave. Haven wrapped his filthy hands around it, digging the toes of his boots into the soft grave sides to create a foothold. Tucker held the rake steady up above. The old man was stronger than he looked.

Inch by inch, Haven dragged himself out of the grave. He spat out a wad of soil-crusted saliva. Before Tucker could say anything Haven fixed him with a stare that had just lost its last measure of patience.

'How about you tell me exactly what's going on here?'

He knew he had flung down the gauntlet and Tucker could well decide to bluff his way out of it, but Haven needed answers. And he needed to know who was on his side. His gut told him one thing for certain: Jack Tucker knew much more than he was saying.

CHAPTER TWENTY-THREE

It was late morning when Rafferty padded downstairs and opened the fridge door. His lip curled at the sight of the neatly packed bags of raw minced beef. He grabbed one and flicked off the plastic clip, tilted it so that any juices ran to the corner of the bag, then tipped it to his mouth. The bloody liquid hit his tongue. He waited for the moment of delight. For the moment his stomach growled in anticipation.

Nothing. Just a watery taste edged in iron.

Nothing like the crow. Nothing like its still-warm flesh sliding down his throat.

He tossed the bag onto the counter and went to the kitchen window. Grace was in the greenhouse. He could see her through the smeared glass, washing pots in a bucket. He didn't need to see her mouth to know her lips were moving too. Maybe a song. Maybe an invocation.

And where was Amelia? He didn't like not knowing.

He slipped his fingers into the back pocket of his jeans. Found Haven's message.

Rafferty made a split-second decision, dashed upstairs, and grabbed Haven's jacket, shrugging it on over his T-shirt as he reclipped the bag and stuffed it into a backpack.

Maybe later he'd be hungry.

He slipped out of the side door. Grace would only grill him as to where he was going or rope him into helping her.

His bike rested against the wall. He hadn't used it for a few days and spider webs criss-crossed its frame, dewdrops beaded on the strands. He brushed them away with his arm and wheeled the bike behind the house, pushing through the narrow gap in the hedge and onto the lane.

Dark clouds brimmed on the horizon as he pedalled towards the village but the wind was behind him, and as he sped down the hill he gave in to the thrill of acceleration and the feel of the cold air rushing past his face.

He let his imagination soar: He was on his way to meet friends. Friends he'd had since infant school. They told each other everything. Understood each other without the need for words.

Rafferty grimaced as the dream dissolved around him.

This wasn't a classmate get-together. He was going to see Haven on the pretence of returning his jacket. He took one hand off the handlebars and turned up the jacket collar. It smelled like Haven's hair. Smelled of earth.

The church spire came into view as he rounded the bend, jutting up towards the leaden sky like an ancient spearhead.

His thoughts turned inward. A flush of heat rose to his cheeks. Part of him was acutely embarrassed that Haven had mopped up his vomit. It wasn't exactly the best way to introduce yourself.

If his mind hadn't been too focussed on his awkwardness he might have seen the group of teenagers on bikes crossing the road ahead.

It was the long, low whistle that snapped him back into focus. Three of them sat astride their bikes on the grass, but two had stopped, their feet firmly planted on the road, blocking his exit.

He braked hard. His front tyre skidded sideways, nearly toppling him off.

'Well, if it isn't the freak from the churchyard.' The tallest boy looked him up and down, a grin on his lips. A malice-drenched grin. 'Where you heading to, puke boy?'

Rafferty crossed his hands in front of his stomach. It was one of the boys who had ridiculed him outside the lychgate.

'Just to see a friend.' His voice broke, came out in a squeak, and one of the boys on the grass nudged another. They both laughed.

'You lot don't have any friends. You're all fucked up. Crazy in the head.' His accuser twirled his forefinger around in the air.

Rafferty's fingers tightened on his handlebars. He looked away, towards the hill where the tarn lay hidden. Dark clouds hung over it and the wind blew from that direction. It smelled like the sea.

One of the boys on the grass set off and rode towards him, standing on his pedals. He began to circle Rafferty in ever-decreasing loops.

Sweat dampened Rafferty's shirt, his palms clammy as he gripped the handlebars. His tongue stuck to the roof of his mouth. There was no way he could take on all of them.

The boy began to nudge Rafferty's back wheel.

'How crazy are you? Why don't you show us, huh?'

The boy's acrid body odour enveloped him. He closed his eyes. Red shadows pulsed behind his eyelids. *How would it feel to pin him to the ground and tear into his flesh . . . ?*

'Lost your tongue, puke boy?'

A rough yank and his backpack was torn from his shoulder. The sound of a zip wrenched open.

'What the hell? What in fuck's name is this?'

Rafferty didn't have to turn around to know that the boy held the bag of raw meat. The only other thing in the pack was a bottle of water left over from the last time he'd used it, refilled so many times that the original label had long since disintegrated.

127

The bag sailed over his head and the tall boy caught it. And now the others began to circle him too, like hyenas around a cornered gazelle.

They tossed the bag between them, their taunts hammering against his ears.

Rafferty raised his head and a large, fat raindrop landed on his brow. It was followed by another and another, and in the space of a few heartbeats rain poured from the sky, bouncing off the road, the wind on its heels bowing the branches of the trees in the nearby park.

'Jesus Christ.' The tall boy pulled up the hood on his sweatshirt.

A smile crossed Rafferty's face at the boy's stupidity, despite the plight he was in.

The boy's eyes narrowed. 'You laughing at me?'

Rafferty didn't have time to say anything. They dragged him from his bike, rough hands tearing at his clothes. He tried to retaliate but his fists hit clean air and then his legs left the ground. Someone wound their fingers into his hair and yanked his head back. Pain blazed across his scalp. A moment where he felt like he was in freefall, and then his body hit the ground, his head cracking against the edge of the pavement.

Stars exploded behind his eyes.

A fist connected with his cheekbone. Another against his jaw and his head snapped back.

'Hold him.' The order came and his limbs were pinned to the ground, denim-clad knees on the inside of his elbows and thighs. His muscles screamed in pain.

Two hands grabbed hold of his face, grinding the back of his head into the ground. Fingers forced his lips open. The metallic tang of his own blood on his tongue as his lower lip split.

'Choke on this, puke boy.'

The eyes staring into his burned with cold, hard hatred, and then rain pounded down on Rafferty's face, blurring his vision, the sky above an angry pewter grey.

Raw meat stuffed into his mouth. Lips forced shut by strong fingers. He couldn't breathe, let alone chew. Fragments of the minced beef fell down his throat and he gagged, trying to turn his head to one side but it was held in a vicelike grip.

He could smell the deep petrichor musk of soaked soil, smell the rain as it pelted down against his face. He lost himself in the scent, wanted to fade away and become part of it . . .

A blast of pain as an open hand connected with his cheek.

'No one said you could pass out, puke boy.'

Were his eyes closed? Maybe if he didn't fight back they'd leave him alone.

He hoped he wasn't crying.

Time to open your eyes.

The voice passed through him.

Show them what you are.

The toe of a boot slammed into his ribs and he cried out, his eyes flying open.

The tall boy paused, his fingers coated in raw meat. He scrambled away and the others followed his lead, their faces creased with uncertainty.

'Look at his fucking eyes!'

Rafferty eased himself onto one elbow, spat out the clump of meat. He retched, and bile burned up his gullet. There wasn't a part of his body that didn't hurt.

He looked at the boys. Their bravado had dissolved into a wary scrutiny.

A wad of spittle hit his cheek.

'You're a fucking monster.'

Rain battered down on the sodden grass. Thunder rolled over the rooftops, its echoes running rampant along the streets.

One by one, the boys grabbed their bikes and set off along the road, leaving Rafferty with his hands around his knees and his head bowed, lapping at his split lip, trying to find some comfort.

CHAPTER TWENTY-FOUR

Meredith arrived at the house far later than she'd intended. She pulled up in front of it and peered through the windscreen, her gaze flicking from window to window. There were no ghostly figures watching, nothing to suggest that this wasn't simply an abandoned old house.

If there was anything here, it was only memories.

She clapped her hands together, determination making the muscles in her jaw quiver.

Get on with it, Mere.

Her inner voice sounded like her mother.

She climbed out of the car and walked around the side of the house. Sprawling rhododendron bushes spilled over the path and she had to push her way through the dense foliage to the back garden she'd seen from the bedroom window yesterday.

The canopy of a climbing rose hung over the gate, late blooms sending fluttering petals onto her shoulders as she ducked underneath. And now she was here, in this dense green place. A place where no one had been in decades.

It was familiar in a way she couldn't put her finger on.

A calcified mouse lay in the middle of a paving stone, its tail curled neatly around it. She sidestepped the remains, felt sweat gathering in the small of her back.

The shadow of the house loomed over her. The skin on the nape of her neck began to prickle, gooseflesh creeping along her arms beneath her jumper. Something cold and wet splashed onto her brow. Another drop hit her shoulder and she glanced up. A section of guttering swayed precariously in the breeze.

A nervous half laugh left her lips, but in the back of her mind a memory stirred.

She knew she'd been here before, in that long-ago summer. Not in the house, but here, outside.

Her gaze trailed around the garden. It fell on a wooden archway at the rear of the lawn, almost obscured by a gnarled apple tree.

Meredith pushed her way through the waist-high grass, trailing her fingers through its tips. Moisture soaked into her jeans, making them stick to her skin, but she was a woman on a mission now, and she felt what she was looking for was close.

She passed under the weathered archway, wild honeysuckle tangled in its slats. Passed a bench overgrown with weeds. Crossed through what was once a vegetable bed. An ancient hoe lay resting against the fence.

Her mouth felt dry as paper, her heart pounding behind her ribcage. It thudded in her ears, as though it wanted to make sure she knew she was still alive.

And then she saw what she was looking for.

The well with the pitched roof, and the bucket that hung on a thick rope.

But all that remained now was the stone wall, the wall that went around and around. And inside that wall, the deep black hole that fell and fell into darkness.

She remembered then. The village was dotted with wells. Remnants from before water was piped from the reservoir. The water table here ran high, fed by the aquifers beneath the ground, layers of rock and soil with water seeping through their small pores.

She'd grown up with them. Part of the fabric of the village. Never thought anything more, until . . .

Meredith forced her feet forwards, stumbled over a loose root and fell to her knees by the side of the well.

Fear seized her by the throat.

It was here. It had happened here.

The sisters had run off through the forest with Alice, and Meredith had followed, desperate to be included. The sticky heat of the late July day. The sunlight winking through the dense, green canopies of the tall trees. The peal of the church bell away in the distance.

It all came back to Meredith, a seam rupturing in her mind, reckless images spewing from the gap.

There was laughter and teasing, and at one point Grace had held out her hand and Meredith had taken it, their clammy palms joined together. Amelia showed them where early blackberries grew and they sat on the ground and stuffed their faces, dark juice staining their skin. Sunlight glinted from Amelia's dark hair, and Meredith thought it was the most beautiful thing she had ever seen.

She remembered saying she was thirsty. Remembered the glance Amelia and Grace shared.

'I know where there's water,' Amelia said, and she sped off through the trees, the others following her Pied Piper lead.

It had led them here, although they had come to it from the woodland at its rear, not by the lane.

Meredith hadn't wanted to go in. She'd heard the stories.

'Oh, that.' Amelia dismissed Meredith's fearful whisper. 'That's only to keep people out. The house is empty. No one wants squatters.'

She'd said it in such a confident voice, Meredith instantly believed her. They pushed through a gap in the crooked fence and stood by the well.

Amelia cranked the handle on the pulley but it didn't move. She peered down into the depths.

'The bucket's stuck.' She sighed, folded her hands across her stomach. 'Someone will have to go down and nudge it free.' She looked at Meredith. Alice and Grace looked at Meredith. 'It makes sense. You're the smallest. There's a ladder, see?' Amelia pointed to the makeshift rungs disappearing into the darkness.

'I don't want to.' Meredith remembered the hot burst of panic and the way her voice felt strangled in her throat.

'Oh, for God's sake, Mere, don't be such a wuss.' Alice glared at her, her hands on her hips.

So Meredith complied. Because she didn't want Alice to be mad at her, didn't want the sisters to think she was a baby.

Birds circled in the cornflower-blue sky. A tractor rumbled along a road. But they were distant things and Meredith's world had condensed to only this moment of fractured time.

The other girls fussed over her as she climbed over the side of the well. A dank stench came from its depths. The wooden rungs creaked under her weight and she didn't want to leave the daylight behind. Each step took her farther into the dark. Farther into the creeping chill.

But she could see the bucket below, its rim snagged on a wedge of stone. All she had to do was free it with her foot.

The water glistened beneath her like black oil. It shivered, slow ripples spreading across its surface.

One more rung and she could reach out for the bucket.

She stretched out her foot. Pointed her sandal-clad toes.

Water splashed onto her ankle and she glanced down.

Something floated just beneath the surface of the water. Something pale.

Her head tilted sideways, brow furrowing in concentration. She stirred the water with the tip of her toe.

The something pale opened its eyes, and Meredith screamed.

CHAPTER TWENTY-FIVE

Haven pulled on a spare set of clothes, a wet towel slung around his shoulders. The shower had been long and hot and he'd watched the remains of the soil swirl around in the bottom of the bath and disappear down the plughole.

Back into the earth, where it'd come from.

He had been so filthy and earth-caked that Tucker had to hose him down. Standing in the pouring rain with ice-cold water blasting against his skin was an experience he didn't want to repeat in a hurry. As he stood with his hands splayed against the church wall, his thoughts turned to Sebastian. Two days since his death. Two days since he had shattered Haven's world. He felt like this place was all he had ever known.

After Tucker declared that Haven was as clean as a hosepipe could get him, he was too frozen to carry on a conversation.

'Will you be in the pub later? I owe you a drink.'

The old man studied him intently then walked away, stopping for a moment to shoulder a pickaxe leaning against a tree.

Part of him wondered if this time lapse would give Tucker a chance to come up with a reasonable explanation—if anything sane could be made out of a collapsed grave with a tunnel leading away from it. But what he'd sensed, what he'd felt in that tunnel, was too real to be palmed off with pacifying words.

Towelling his hair dry, he walked to the window and stared out at the churchyard. Only the nearest graves were visible, the others lost behind the grey curtain of pouring rain. His eyes tracked from gravestone to gravestone, his thoughts inward and maudlin. *Where would they bury Sebastian?* The aching hollow in his chest expanded.

Movement caught his eye on the pathway that led around to the rear of the church annexe.

Someone was walking slowly. No, limping slowly, pushing a bike. They were making no attempt to rush in from the rain, their gaze on the gloom-drenched graveyard.

Haven's hands stopped of their own accord as he recognised the slight figure.

Rafferty.

Haven bolted out of the room and bounded down the steps, flinging open the annexe doors as Rafferty drew level with them.

The boy was soaked to the skin, his hair dripping down his face. An ugly bruise bloomed on his cheekbone, another on his jaw. A roadmap of grazed skin lay across his temples, his lip split and purpled, one eye almost swollen shut.

Anger clenched a fist in Haven's gut. *Who had done this? Amelia? Grace?* His mind crossed through their names. No. Sebastian had always said the Henderson women were mama bears, overprotective of their cubs.

'Come inside.' He didn't ask, just opened the door wider. Rafferty wheeled his bike in and propped it against a wall. Shivers wracked the boy's body.

Haven linked his fingers behind his neck, because his first instinct was to wrap his arms around Rafferty, tell him that he was here for him, offer comfort and a safe space to unload.

But he hardly knew him and Rafferty had the same don't-come-too-close aura that had radiated from Sebastian sometimes. Haven had to be careful. Had to take things slowly.

He reminded himself that Rafferty, like his brother, had been taught to distrust, because too many people were out to hurt them.

'Wait here,' Haven said. He ran back up the stairs and returned thirty seconds later with two towels. He pressed one into Rafferty's hands.

'I'm sorry about your jacket,' Rafferty said, twisting the towel in his fingers.

Haven hadn't even realised that it was his jacket. Sodden, caked in mud and blood. It dwarfed Rafferty's thin frame.

'Who did this to you?' Haven asked, as gently as he could. He curled his fingers into his palms, pressed his nails into the skin because his rage was alive and it was screaming for an outlet.

Rafferty shrugged, his gaze trailing to the graveyard again. He raised his hands to dry his hair and winced.

'Can I look at those bruises? I could get some ice.' Haven hadn't a clue where from, but he'd find some regardless.

'It's nothing, really.' A half smile stretched the torn skin on Rafferty's lower lip. It died as quickly as it appeared.

'It doesn't look like nothing. Are you protecting someone?'

Haven could see from the expression on Rafferty's face that he'd hit the nail on the head. 'Are you in trouble? *Any* kind of trouble?' He added the last part as an opener, just in case it could coax an explanation from the boy standing in front of him.

'They were just kids messing around.' Rafferty looked down at the floor, hunched his shoulders, hid behind the fall of his wet hair.

So there'd been more than one. Haven flexed his fingers and pushed away the tide of memories swelling in his mind. A group of kids picking on someone different, taunts and mockery, physical assault treading on the heels of hurtful words. He knew the scenario all too well. Guilt bloomed, hot and sour and deep, and he had to pause and collect his thoughts.

Things go full circle. They always have. Sebastian's words, from the last time they met. When Sebastian knew what he was going to do. The horror of it made Haven want to tear something apart, anything to be rid of the remorse driving its claws into his shoulders.

'You knew my brother.' Rafferty's quiet voice tugged Haven back into focus. 'Did he say anything about me?'

How the hell was he supposed to answer that? He threw caution to the wind and slid his arm around Rafferty's shoulder, glancing at the boy's profile and seeing Sebastian's in a younger form.

'He did. But first let's get you warm. Come into the church. Reverend Edwards is in the vestry. There's a heater in there and you can get a hot drink.'

'He won't like it that I've come back.' Rafferty's chin quivered.

Haven opened his mouth then closed it again. The boy was worried about Peter? About Peter's reaction?

'It'll be fine, I promise.' Haven dredged up a confident smile, let it travel to his eyes.

He opened the heavy door to the church and the musty scent of the aged building rolled towards them. Rafferty hung back in the doorway and Haven left him there reluctantly. He rounded one of the stone pillars and headed towards the vestry. The door was closed. He knocked. No answer. He knocked again, was sure he'd seen a light on when he'd come in for a shower. Haven opened the door and peered around it, swore softly under his breath and turned to make some excuse to Rafferty. But the boy wasn't there.

'Rafferty?' His voice rang out into the church. It seemed to bounce back from the walls, to rise to the roof and fall again, a scornful echo in the gloom.

His eyes traced the lines of empty pews. He turned and scanned the altar, the shadows in the apse a murky, concentrated mass. The skin on his scalp tightened.

He crossed to the annexe. Rafferty wasn't there. Haven called his name again, this time looking up towards his room.

There was a chance the boy had run through the church and slipped out through the front door, but his bike still rested against the wall.

Haven's heart started to pound and he'd no idea why. His gaze trailed to the glass of the annexe doors. To the harsh beam of the security light spearing through the winter dusk.

There, at the farthest reaches of its track, he found Rafferty, kneeling in the pouring rain by the open grave, his arms hugging his body, rocking to and fro.

CHAPTER TWENTY-SIX

Amelia Henderson was at war with herself, ever since she had returned from identifying Sebastian's body. She'd had to ram her knuckles against her teeth to stop herself screaming that this couldn't be him.

Afterwards there were endless questions in a grey-walled room with an overhead fluorescent light. The hum and flicker of it was like a small insect burrowing into her brain.

There would be a post-mortem, to rule out foul play. She didn't want to think about clinical medical instruments carving up Sebastian, his organs weighed like meat at a market.

A nurse brought her a cup of tea, but the milk had soured and globules of fat floated on its surface. A young man wearing a polo shirt and jeans pressed a plastic pouch into her hands. She stuffed it inside her bag, didn't open it until she got home.

The contents of the pouch lay beside her on the bed.

A letter from a firm of solicitors stating Sebastian's last wishes along with a simple will. A waterlogged leather wallet, empty apart from a photo booth snap of Sebastian and Rafferty taken five years previously, both of them caught on camera with their faces creased with laughter. A mobile phone that didn't work.

How could she have missed how much Sebastian was struggling? He knew what they were protecting. Understood how important it was to keep Rafferty unaware of the true horror of his bloodline until he was mature enough to understand it. To accept it.

She couldn't grasp how he could have left Rafferty alone at such a tender age. Or rather, she hadn't understood until she read the letter.

Amelia had wanted to tell Grace as soon as she got back but she needed to process it first. Another day wouldn't matter. And then Rafferty had been brought home and Grace had gone to pieces.

Amelia had avoided him this morning, her heart too full of grief to explain why his brother had torn himself from Rafferty's life so cruelly. And part of her wondered if she'd set this horror in motion by arranging to have Walsh's house cleared, a task best suited to someone without Henderson blood in their veins.

The bedroom door squeaked open and Grace stood in the hallway, her feet clad in knitted socks, rain droplets glistening on her jacket.

'I need to talk to you, Gracie.' Amelia patted the bed at her side.

Grace shook her head, her lips a thin line on a drawn face. 'Not here.'

Amelia sighed. *Of course not here.* She gathered the items from the bed and followed Grace downstairs.

Rain blasted against the window and Grace glanced towards it, her eyes wide and anxious.

Amelia took her sister's hand, the skin dry and papery and cold. 'It's only rain. He'll be sheltering somewhere.' She wanted it to be true.

Grace looked at the letter Amelia clutched in her other hand. 'What is it?'

Amelia took a shaky breath. 'Sebastian's final wishes. He instructed a solicitor to give it to us as soon as possible after his death.'

'When can we bring him home?'

There was a catch in Grace's voice as she spoke and Amelia didn't want to continue. Didn't want to say the words that would send Grace into a tailspin.

A silence ticked between them.

Amelia smoothed out the letter in her fingers, forced the words from her throat.

'He didn't want to come home, Gracie.'

She watched the anguish dawn across her sister's face. Read the words from the letter.

Mr. Henderson requests that his remains be cremated at Oxbridge Crematorium, his ashes to be scattered in the garden there. He does not wish for anyone to attend the cremation or send flowers. The fees for this are already paid.

Grace gasped, then raised her hands in front of her as though to block out the meaning behind the words.

'He can't do that. He knows what has to happen.' She shook her head again, this time with a stubborn ferocity that made Amelia's heart constrict.

'He did it for a reason, Gracie.' Amelia sat heavily on the arm of the sofa, her strength sapped by what she was about to say. 'Sebastian knew exactly what he was doing. By not letting us bring his body back here, by not letting us feed his remains into the well. He wanted to break the cycle.'

Oh, dear God, Sebastian, what have you done?

Grace clamped her hands over her ears, sank to the floor by Amelia's feet.

'Sebastian ended his life so Rafferty would be the last male Henderson.' Amelia cupped her palms around Grace's face. 'We have to tell him now, Gracie. We have to tell him what we know and what he did.'

CHAPTER TWENTY-SEVEN

Haven flew up the stairs. He dragged his boots on, his fingers fumbling with the laces.

That fucking grave. He knew he was right about it.

He raced back down and yanked open the door, a blast of rain hitting him full in the face. The wind added to the misery, lashing water against the church walls, bowing the treetops, bouncing from the ground, so Haven was soaked to the skin again in a matter of seconds.

He peered through the deluge, shielding his eyes with his arm, the beam of the security light hardly penetrating the dark. Tumbleweeds of foliage rolled past him, the same foliage he had cut away and stored at the side of the graveyard.

Undoing what I've done. It doesn't want me here.

It was an odd thought as he braced against the fury of the storm, and it came to him as a warning.

He called Rafferty's name as he trudged forwards even though he knew it was useless. The edges of the grave would be slick and deadly now. It wouldn't take much for them to cave in, taking Rafferty with them.

Something wet and thin whipped him across the cheek and he ducked away. In his peripheral vision, a flash of silver. He reached out blindly and caught the line of twine he had put up, now loosed from its moorings.

He looked down. The open maw of the grave stared back, a pool of dark water in its base.

Rafferty was gone. Lost to the night.

Desperate frustration tunnelled his vision. He wanted to run and find a torch, go out into the dark and search for Rafferty because all of his instincts were screaming that the boy was in danger. *But from what? Think, Haven, think.*

One thing he had learned in his years of hovering in the shadows of clubs and all-night bars, of following people who tripped the wire on his radar, was that sometimes there was more to something than what was visible on the outside.

He turned away from the grave, saw a small circle of light on the pathway. Someone holding an umbrella, its canopy buffeted by the wind.

The light tracked his way and he raised his hand.

It was Meredith.

He looked down at his sodden clothes, saw himself through her eyes. A man stood by an open grave in a storm. The same grave he had been pulled from earlier. Not a lot about that said he was in full control of his mental state.

Haven wiped the water running off his nose with the back of his hand, thought about what he'd felt in the tunnel. His brain dredged up logical explanations. Rotten roots or tubers. Moles or other burrowing creatures.

It was the latter that flashed neon in his mind. He pushed away the tingling in his fingertips, refused to entertain the thought that he could still feel it.

With one last look back at the grave he made his way across to Meredith. An angry gust of wind snatched the umbrella from her hand, sent it sailing over his head. It tumbled into the dark like a deranged acrobat.

They went into the annexe, the heavy glass door muting the sound of the rain as it closed.

She took off her coat and shook it, folded it neatly over her arm.

'I was worried about you,' she said. 'Lots of gossip in the pub about you and why you're here. About Rafferty.' Her gaze flicked back outside and then lifted to his face. 'What did you find out there?'

Despite everything, a smile quirked his lips. 'Not, what the hell were you doing by an open grave, Haven?'

She shrugged, reached out to touch his arm. There was something in her eyes he hadn't seen before.

'I know you wouldn't have been there without a valid reason. Want to go upstairs and tell me about it?'

He emerged from the bathroom wrapped in a towel and resolved that he didn't want to get wet again for at least twenty-four hours. He grabbed his only other spare set of clean clothes, was about to return to the bathroom, when Meredith rose from her seat on the bed and walked to the window. Her hand traced the line of the etched cross.

Haven hesitated for a moment, then dropped his towel, pulling on his jeans. A hard knot formed in his throat. The jacket he normally wore with these was on Rafferty's back.

'I saw Rafferty again,' he said. She was still staring into the churchyard, and from where he stood the weak light from the lamp didn't touch her. 'Some kids had beaten him up.' He paused, decided he might as well hit her with what else he'd discovered. 'And there's a fucking tunnel leading from that open grave.'

Meredith's shoulders tensed. She walked back across, her arms hugging her body. 'It's not the only one.'

Haven felt his eyes widening. 'How do you know?' He yanked a black T-shirt over his head.

'Because when I was a young girl, Amelia Henderson sent me down a well. A well fed from an underground stream.' She glanced down at the floor, sat on the edge of the bed. Tapped the toes of her boots together.

Haven sat next to her, their shoulders touching.

'The tunnels aren't empty, Haven. Something lives in them.'

She retreated inside herself and Haven didn't press for any more information. What he did know took up enough space in his mind. He went into the bathroom and shut the door, crouched down behind it with his head in his hands, the hard, dead stone of dread weighting his gut.

CHAPTER TWENTY-EIGHT

Rafferty watched Haven as he stood by the graveside. It was easy to hide in the dark. Easy to hide by the crypt wall.

He wanted to go to him, to ask for help. But his trust hung by a delicate cord.

Haven had tried to take him into the church. All of his instincts screamed how wrong that was.

One eye was swollen shut now and Rafferty shivered in the bitter onslaught of the storm.

He didn't want to go home, but where else could he go?

The weight of Sebastian's death, of the beating he'd taken, the hatred hurled at him, at the lifelong shackle of being different, felt like a noose around his neck. A noose that was slowly tightening.

Something had called to him at the graveside. Something he thought he knew.

He watched as a woman appeared. She went into the annexe with Haven. He could see them clearly, the lobby bathed in light, a golden square pasted against the dark.

His tongue flicked over his distended lip and he fought the urge to bite down, to suckle his own blood. To feel flesh surrender to his teeth. With a sigh he crept around to the back of the crypt, his hand trailing along the rough wall that used to house his dead ancestors before they were ripped away. His bike sat in the annexe, but it was too much of a risk to try to grab it, even after the woman and Haven disappeared upstairs.

A car horn blared out on the high street and he turned towards the sound. There wouldn't be many people out on a night like this. Maybe he could explore. The thought was a warm spark in his misery.

Carefully, he edged out onto the pathway. Rain pelted his skin and he covered his swollen eye with his hand. The mass of the church loomed over him and he turned away from its judgement.

There was no one sheltering under the lychgate porch, no one hurriedly walking along the street.

A car passed him, teeming rain sparkled in its beams. The driver didn't see him, or chose not to.

Rafferty pulled the soaked collar of Haven's jacket up and turned onto the high street. From there he could see the lights in the pub at the other side of the road. The door opened. A man exited, ran across to his car. The beep of it unlocking.

His stomach growled. He hadn't eaten in far too long. The back of his throat still burned from the food forced down it earlier but the hollow cavity in his gut demanded to be filled.

Amelia and Grace always said he must eat at regular intervals. Never let the hunger grow too wild. Because of the fucked-up nature of his appetite. Because of the fucked-up way his organs lay in his body. He'd never had any reason to doubt them.

From somewhere farther up the street he caught the smell of greasy food. It punched into him and he recoiled. The stench crawled into his lungs and he retched.

But this food, no matter how repellent, drew him on. It all had to start out in a raw state.

A couple came out of a terraced house, a black umbrella held high. The woman saw him and she nudged her partner. He pulled her close and they hurried across the street.

Rafferty caught sight of himself in the black glass of a shop window. Soaked to the skin with his face bruised and battered, his eye swollen shut, his lip split. He stood hunched, withdrawn into himself, like a serpent about to strike. Their suspicion was understandable.

Hunger gnawed at the lining of his stomach, a deep longing that rolled through him relentlessly. Maybe Amelia and Grace had been right.

An alleyway loomed between an Indian restaurant and a butcher's shop, the latter dark and empty. But it was the scent drifting from the alley that moved his limbs, the scent that came from the back of the shop.

He stumbled over an empty beer bottle. It careered into the wall and the sound echoed along the alley. Rafferty paused, but there was no one around to hear it.

He stole into the darkness at the rear of the shop. Saliva ran freely in his mouth. His gaze flicked towards the door. He tried the handle. Locked, of course. Bars ran across the glazed window.

He slammed his hand against the door, resentment burning through him like a lit fuse. Rafferty knew he had to eat something. Eat something fast.

A large industrial waste bin sat against the high wall of the back alley. Revulsion tried to pull him away, but then he was lifting the lid, his foot on one of the rubber wheels. In a matter of seconds he was crouched on the rim. The rancid stench of rotten flesh enveloped him. He began to search amongst the remains, his movements frantic, spurred on by a hunger that burned behind his eyes.

Rafferty's hand closed over a string of linked bones. He yanked them from their resting place, brought them to his mouth, his teeth tearing away the tatters of meat. The taste sang on his tongue and he closed his eyes, delving for any shreds he had missed.

151

But all this did was notch his hunger to the next level.

All his focus snapped into place. He combed through the bones, discarding stripped ribs and exposed joints. Something wrapped in plastic touched his fingers. He pulled it out and sat on the edge of the bin, his legs dangling over the side.

The contents were soft. Fluid. A parcel of delights.

He unwrapped it, the high stench of old blood making his gag reflex rise. Something dark and smooth and slippery lay in a bed of its own gore. He discarded the wrapping and most of the smell disappeared.

Rafferty took the liver in his fingers. It was cold and glistening. Drool ran from his lips.

He tore into it, closing his eyes in bliss as the pungency hit his tongue.

No one would ever accept him for this. But right now, nothing else mattered.

A beam of light struck him out of nowhere. Rafferty's eyes flew open. He raised one arm instinctively, heard a man yell. A figure stood in the back entrance of the restaurant, but he was clothed in darkness behind the torch light.

Another light blazed. And then disappeared. The flash from a phone.

Rafferty leapt down from the bin, his mouth still full of half-chewed raw liver. He could feel the blood dribbling down his chin.

He sprinted off along the narrow back street, his feet slipping on rain-soaked cobbles, his heart lodged in his throat.

What the hell have I done?

They always said he was different. That he had the scourge of the Henderson family etched along his bones.

But now they had the proof.

CHAPTER TWENTY-NINE

When Haven and Meredith walked into the pub another meeting was in full swing. A man Haven recognised from the night before jerked an accusing thumb in his direction.

'This all started with *him*.' The emphasis on the last word came with so much derision that it was almost a weapon.

Haven took a step towards the group. A muscle twitched along his jaw. He was done with being nice.

But Meredith put her hand on his arm and he bit back his words.

'Sit down,' she said softly. 'Don't give them a reason to take their prejudice out on you. We both know there's something going on here, and they're desperate to pin the blame on someone.'

She was right, of course. They took up the seats in their usual spot. Haven scrunched two beer mats into a ball and stuffed them into an empty glass on the next table.

'I need to find Rafferty,' he said, his anger deflating as quickly as it had risen. His hair fell over his face as he leaned across the table. 'Sebastian was right. Rafferty *is* in trouble. I don't know how or what, but I'm fucking well going to find out.'

Meredith met his gaze. 'I'm going to tell you something now and I want you to listen without interrupting, because I'm not sure I'll get it all out if you do.'

There was something haunted in her eyes. The same look he'd seen earlier. A shadow that took away some of the light.

After she finished he steepled his fingertips under his chin and mulled over her words. 'So you're telling me Amelia and Grace knew about what you saw in the well. Are you sure?'

She nodded. 'Amelia tried to hide it. Said it was only the sun shining on the water. But Grace wouldn't look at me. She was scared, Haven.'

'Did you tell anyone?' He traced a groove on the tabletop with one finger, tried to absorb the chilling nature of her words.

'I was a little kid. Who was I going to tell? And anyway, I *knew* I shouldn't have been where I was, so I kept quiet.'

Meredith glanced over his shoulder. A smile broke on her lips. Rosa appeared and set two drinks in front of them. She had a cloth in her hand and began to wipe the tabletop even though it was clean.

'I don't like what I'm hearing over there.' Her gaze flicked in the direction of the group huddled by the fire. 'Be careful.'

'Are they threatening us?' Haven asked. If that was the case they were about to see just how pissed off he really was. If Meredith hadn't stopped him they would have found out already.

'No, not you,' Rosa said. She took two beer mats from her apron pocket and placed them on the table. *Playing for time.* 'It's the Hendersons.'

'They'd go after a boy and two older women?' His anger resurfaced, not the hot and feral kind, but the one that brooded in dark places, the one he sometimes turned on himself. He took a long draught of beer.

'They said they're done with living under their shadow. The collapsed grave, they blame that on them.' Rosa took a deep breath. Her next words caught in her throat. 'They wouldn't have dared when Sebastian was around. But now they see them as an easy target.'

'Rosa! Service here, please.' A shout from the bar where two men were waiting. She gave the table a final flourish and left.

Haven took another drink. It went down far too easily. 'This sounds like it could get dangerous.'

'Do not tell me that you don't want me involved.' Meredith's jaw tightened. 'I'm in this as much as you are. We stick together.'

Haven didn't miss the fact that she said we.

Part of him wanted to go it alone, as he always had, but another part really appreciated that she had his back. As partners went they were probably the oddest of couples, but he trusted her implicitly and trust was in short supply in this deplorable place.

'Okay.' He held up his hands. 'I'll come by tomorrow afternoon, to the house. You can show me the well.'

The door of the pub swung open and a man entered. A freezing blast of air followed him. He hurried across to the group and started talking to a heavily bearded man. The one who seemed to be in charge. The newcomer produced a phone and showed him something on it.

'What is it, Seth?' A woman in a chunky knit jumper leaned over to take a look at the screen. Now it was being passed around the whole group, and everyone's reaction was the same.

Shock.

Disgust.

Outrage.

'When did you take this?' Seth asked.

'About half an hour ago. I chased him but he was too quick for me. Slippery as a bloody eel.'

Multiple gazes wheeled towards them and this time Haven couldn't bow down. He stood, grabbed his bottle of beer and strode over to the fireside group. Tucker sat in the corner behind them, almost hidden by the shadow of the chimney breast. He met Haven's eyes, the slightest nod of his head.

'As I'm obviously part of what you don't like, how about filling me in instead of being passive aggressive?' Haven clenched his teeth. His throat ached with stifled words.

'Why'd you come here?' The woman in the chunky knit jumper threw the question towards him from her seat by the fire, her face flushed from the heat.

Haven thought about lying. *Screw it.* It didn't matter if they knew.

'I came to see Sebastian. He was my friend.'

No one offered any condolences.

'Then why did you stay?' said Seth. He leaned back in his seat, crossed his arms over his ample chest.

Haven flexed his fingers on his free hand. Counted to ten.

'Reverend Edwards offered me a job. As far as I know, that's not a crime.' He downed the last of his beer.

'That's not a crime,' the man with the phone said. 'But this? *This* is unnatural. Revolting.' Spittle flew from his lips. He thrust the screen under Haven's nose.

There, caught in the flashlight, was Rafferty Henderson. The photo was clear enough to see the blood smeared on his chin, a dark mass held in his hands.

But it wasn't only this that made Haven's heart flip over. It was the reflection in Rafferty's eyes. Not the normal red-eye in low-light conditions.

The retroreflector glow of an animal in the dark.

'Ha. Not so clever now, are you?' the woman said.

Everyone had turned to stare at him, their scrutiny like a flensing knife peeling back his layers, looking for his truth.

No one knew his truth.

Meredith appeared at his shoulder. She looked at the screen, her gasp of shock a quiet, painful inhalation.

'He's an abomination,' the woman by the fire said. 'Needs locking up.'

'Preach it, Anna.' Another voice. A low, harsh laugh.

Haven couldn't find the words to reply. His mind whirled with questions. He didn't think he'd ever get that image of Rafferty out of his mind.

He's not like other kids. Sebastian had told him this.

No shit, Sebastian. How about you could have told me how different?

Haven remembered the blood on Rafferty's sweatshirt.

What else didn't he know about Sebastian's younger brother? The brother Sebastian had asked him to help.

The mood of the group changed, the atmosphere shifting in a matter of seconds. Some of them stood, grabbed their coats. They pushed past him. He didn't have to ask where they were going.

He turned to Meredith, put his hand on her arm. 'Stay here. Talk to Rosa. Find out anything she hasn't told us. I think she knows more.' He lowered his voice. 'But she's scared.'

'Where are you going?' Meredith asked. But he could tell from the way her face had paled that she knew.

'I'm going to find Rafferty. Before they do. Because I don't know what they'll do to him if they get there first.'

Chapter Thirty

Rafferty ran like the hounds of hell were on his heels. More than once the slick cobbles sent him sprawling to his knees, but he was up and off again in moments.

This was why Amelia and Grace wanted him to stay hidden in the gatehouse. They knew that if he was let loose he would do something to fuck things up. People here didn't need a reason to hate him, but he had served them one up with his own bloody hands.

His burning muscles screamed for respite and he paused at the entrance to another alleyway. A light shone at the far end, raised voices echoing from the street.

'You check up by the corn exchange, he might have hidden inside.'

Rafferty pressed his knuckles against his teeth. They were coming for him.

He had to find his way to the church. From there he could cut across the fields to home.

Rafferty crept along the alley as the voices grew distant. With his back to the wall he peered around the edge. A taxi drove past and he flattened himself against the bricks. His swollen eye throbbed, his lip stinging with every facial movement. The shreds of liver felt as though they were slopping around in a sea of stomach juices. Misery coated his every thought.

He yearned for his brother's playful teasing and wanted to believe that Haven could help him, but he couldn't work Haven out. He seemed genuine, but Rafferty had zero experience in evaluating other people. And then there was the church—the instinctive fear of it overwhelmed him, something so deep he felt it twisting within his marrow.

He took a deep breath and, with his head down, turned onto the high street. They wouldn't expect him to be here walking along the same streets they trod. A grim smile touched his lips.

He kept to the shadows until the lychgate came into view, the smell of wet earth curling into his nostrils. The rain had slowed to a despondent drizzle. He hurried along the pathway, glancing over his shoulder more than once, but there was no angry pitchfork mob.

The lure of the open grave called to him in the dark. He gritted his teeth and ignored it. There were no lights in the annexe. Haven was either out or fast asleep.

Rafferty thrust his hands into the pockets of Haven's jacket, but there was no warmth to be found there.

A sound came to him as he walked up the pathway, as the mass of the crypt hulked in the dark.

He stopped. Looked around. Swept the wet hair from his face with the back of his hand.

The noise came again, this time closer. It sounded like something falling, like—his mind tried to find the right image—something crumbling, like shifting soil . . .

The paving stone under his feet shuddered. Movement in the corner of his eye. His jaw fell open. There, to the right of the path, the earth in front of a gravestone fell away, as though something had sucked it right into hell. He stood stock-still, but all he could hear now was the sound of tiny stones settling in the hole.

His legs gave way and Rafferty sank into a crouch, his linked hands covering his head. It was him. He'd caused this.

Not exactly true.

The voice settled upon him, fleeting and butterfly-soft.

Rafferty forced himself to stand, even though his legs felt as if the bones had been stripped away. He stumbled up the pathway with his hands over his ears. He couldn't stand the thought of hearing more graves sinking, of hearing that voice chipping away at his sanity.

He'd never felt more alone. Or more vulnerable.

Alternating waves of smouldering heat and intense cold wracked his body and there was a thirst in his throat that burned like acid. He fell to his knees by the crypt side, clutching his stomach. Then he lowered his head and lapped muddy water from a dip in the earth.

The drizzle intensified, in moments turning to angry rain that bounced from the waterlogged ground, pounded against his spine.

Rafferty splayed his hands against the crypt wall, used the structure to drag himself to his feet. He let it guide him around to the front. He would just take a little rest, close his eyes for a few seconds. He climbed the steps, each one a challenge, and reached for the door.

It opened and he stumbled inside. One moment where his eyes registered light, and then a hard shove against his upper back sent him sprawling to the ground, his cheek glancing down the rough stone wall.

Blooms of black flowers swelled in his vision.

Hands hauled him to his feet, then pushed him up against the wall. A forearm pressed to his throat. In his peripheral vision a lantern flickered. He could smell the oil burning.

Sorry, should have warned you about this. Just call it a rite of passage.

The voice in his head sounded almost apologetic.

There were three of them. Three of the boys from earlier. All in jeans and black hoodies.

'Come back for some more, puke boy?'

The ringleader stood before him, a lit cigarette dangling from his fingers.

They watched him like vultures waiting for something to die. One of the others unscrewed the lid from a bottle of vodka and took a long draught.

The pressure on Rafferty's throat lifted and he gasped for air, but then he was pulled forward, and almost instantaneously a rough hand in his hair jerked his head back. The bones at the top of his spine exploded in pain, the bottle forced against his lips. He tried to resist but they were stronger. And now the bottle was in his mouth, rattling against his teeth. The alcohol burned down his throat. Tears sprang into his eyes and their faces blurred. He couldn't breathe. His gag reflex—his instinct—kicked in and vodka spurted from his mouth, covering the boy with the cigarette.

'You little shit!'

A fist rammed into his stomach, wrested all the air from his lungs.

The sound of a zip unfastening filled the air.

No. No. Please no . . .

Hands dragged him to his knees, forced him prone against the damp stone floor. Grit dug into the ugly graze on his cheekbone. He struggled, tried to stand, but one of them held his ankles, the other his wrists in the small of his back.

Are you ready now? Remember this.

Warm liquid spattered onto the back of his neck. He turned his head, caught sight of a stream of urine in full flow. It flooded onto his face and he tried to turn away. But it was already burning in his eyes. Burning on his tongue.

They hauled him to his feet again, pushed him back against the crypt wall. The ringleader grabbed his jaw in one hand. Waved the cigarette close to his eyes.

'You're a fucked-up piece of nothing.' He hawked back and a gob of spit hit Rafferty's cheek. 'Do us all a favour and follow that brother of yours into hell.'

A spark flared in the hollow pit of Rafferty's gut.

He held the boy's gaze defiantly. 'I'll save a place for you.'

The boy tossed the cigarette onto the floor and pulled a blade from his pocket. It glinted in the lantern light.

'Maybe I'll carve out a piece of your flesh. They say Walsh did that. How do you think he stayed alive?' He dug the point into Rafferty's cheek. 'Or maybe I'll take out one of your fucked-up eyes. Human eyes don't glow in the dark. You're just a piece of shit wearing human skin.'

But it wasn't the threat that made Rafferty's blood ice, it was what he said about Irving Walsh.

Or maybe I'll come and find you when you sleep.

The voice seeped out of the stone around them. It sounded like Rafferty, but he hadn't opened his mouth.

The light in the lantern flickered behind the glass. It made shadows crawl across the crypt walls. Shadows that weren't created by the boys.

The hand around his jaw dropped. The boys shuffled back, their eyes darting around the crypt, all their machismo draining away. They edged towards the door.

Rafferty pulled his shoulders back. He wiped the urine from his face with the sleeve of Haven's sullied jacket.

'No more,' he said, and his eyes narrowed. 'Or I *will* find you. And there won't be anything left to bury.'

They ran. Rafferty heard their racing feet squelching through the waterlogged grass. Relief softened his limbs and he closed his eyes for a moment. Thought about what he'd said.

It was just to scare them, he told himself.

But another part of him wanted to look them in the eye before he tore out their throats and painted his skin with their blood.

CHAPTER THIRTY-ONE

One by one people left the pub, until there was only Meredith and an old man sitting in the corner, nursing an empty half-pint glass. He'd been here every night, as far as she could remember. A true old timer with grizzled stubble on his face and a flat cap pulled down over his eyes.

Maybe this was the only place where he ever felt less lonely. Meredith imagined him in a tiny house with no heating, making endless cups of tea with shaking hands.

Get a grip, Mere. She chastised her thoughts for wandering off in mawkish directions, blamed her mood on the unsettled atmosphere hanging heavy in the room even though the group had gone.

She wandered across to the bar and leant against it.

'What's with the old guy?'

Rosa clipped a new bottle into one of the optics and turned to Meredith.

'Oh, that's Tucker. He's part of the furniture. Comes here every day without fail and always sits in that seat. If anyone else ever takes it he just stands there and watches them until they move.' Rosa wiped her hands down her apron. 'He lets himself out when the fire's died down.'

Meredith chewed her bottom lip. If Tucker had lived here for so long he might know something.

'Get him another half pint, please, Rosa.'

Rosa opened her mouth to say something, then thought better of it. She took a glass and pulled another half pint. Meredith watched as the froth settled.

She felt Tucker's scrutiny as she walked across, even though his eyes were hidden beneath the peak of his cap and two bristly eyebrows. A stacked pyramid of beer mats sat before him on the table, one in his gnarled hands.

He reached for a small leather wallet and shook out a handful of loose change.

'It's okay,' Meredith said. 'I've got this.'

'I remember you,' he said, his voice stronger than he appeared.

Meredith fiddled with a pulled loop on her sleeve. She wasn't sure what to say.

'Why'd you come back?' He raised his face and the shadows hollowed out his cheeks.

She found that she didn't have an answer.

He took a sip of beer, froth coating his upper lip. 'You're clearing Walsh's old place.' It wasn't a question.

She nodded. Nothing escaped the village grapevine.

'Marie Claire,' he said. 'Look for Marie Claire.'

Meredith's lower jaw fell. She didn't know anyone by that name, but the way he was staring at her suggested that she take heed.

Time seemed to slow and it was only the phone ringing behind the bar that pulled her back into a vague reality, the vintage ringtone adding to her bafflement.

Rosa answered, twirling the coiled cable around one finger. There was something about the edge in her voice that made Meredith's skin tingle.

The barmaid placed the phone receiver back on the cradle. She looked at Meredith.

'They've spotted Rafferty, running over the top fields. Seth and Angus are trying to force him to turn back before he reaches the tarn.'

Nausea rose in Meredith's throat. She forced it down.

'He's just a boy,' she whispered. 'Why are they doing this?'

'Because he's a Henderson. Nothing else matters.' Rosa shook her head. 'They want me to spread the word.' Her upper lip curled in disgust.

Meredith pulled her phone from her pocket and rang Haven. She willed him to answer and when the call went to voicemail she clenched her teeth in frustration.

'You said the top fields? Laird Banyon's farm?'

Rosa nodded.

There were advantages to being brought up in this place. She knew the lay of the land.

Meredith grabbed her bag and coat. She paused at the door, one hand on the latch. 'If Haven comes back here, tell him where I've gone.'

He'd asked her to talk to Rosa but she couldn't stand back when she knew where Rafferty was, when an injustice was unfurling before her.

The last thing she saw before she went out into the pouring rain was Tucker stacking a final beer mat upon his cardboard house.

It tumbled to the floor as she closed the door behind her.

Meredith climbed into her car and stared out of the windscreen for a moment before starting the engine. She reversed and turned left onto the high street, the village soon lost behind her as she sped into the dark maw of the night.

She drove along the back roads, the ones barely wide enough for a single car, the gradient gradually increasing. Roads which zigged and zagged around fields that had been there for countless generations. Laird Banyon's farm stood on the shoulder of the hill, just below the basin of the tarn, acres of lush pasture and calm-eyed dairy cows. At least that was what she remembered.

Tall hedgerows obscured her view of the fields, broken by the occasional five-bar gate giving her little chance to catch a glimpse of what lay beyond. She knew the search party—for want of a better word—would be on foot. They'd be using local knowledge to inspect culverts and animal sheds, anywhere a boy might hide.

Rafferty must be terrified. But the image of him in the photo with blood smeared on his face, holding . . . she shook her head and refused to let that thought go further.

Meredith pulled in at the viewpoint on the curve of the hill. From here you could see the whole valley stretching out below and the village nestling in its palm. She climbed out of the car, her eyes scanning the darkness. Nothing moved within it.

She ran her fingers through her hair, paced around the car. The rain had dwindled to a freezing, miserable drizzle.

A shout travelled through the dark. She homed in on the direction it had come from, and there, a few fields away, she saw tiny, moving pinpricks of light.

Did that mean they had found him?

She yanked open the car door, dread weighting her limbs, sure that by the time she got there it would be too late.

The hair on the nape of her neck bristled. She turned slowly and stared into the dark.

Someone was there.

'Hey,' she called, praying it was someone from the search party taking a different route.

A breath of drizzle-laced wind lifted her hair from her face. She wet her lips with the tip of her tongue, her fingers closing over the edge of the car door.

And then something laughed in the dark. A harsh, mocking sound without a trace of humour.

The snap of a twig sent her heart rate into overdrive.

'Rafferty?'

This time she hoped with every ounce of her being that it wasn't him.

What if the villagers were right? What if something inherently evil lived in the blood of the Hendersons? What if Haven was trying to save something that shouldn't be saved?

She scrambled into the car and slammed the door, the thrum of the engine sweet music to her ears. Jamming the gear stick into reverse she swung around, small pebbles flying from the tyres.

She glanced in her rear-view mirror. In the white glow of the reversing lights stood a figure.

A boy, dressed in jeans and a T-shirt. A moment where his eyes met hers.

Meredith gasped, her foot stamping down on the accelerator. The car scrabbled for grip then launched onto the road like a racehorse exiting a starting gate.

But as she drove, her fingers white-knuckled on the steering wheel, she couldn't shake the way the boy's silver eyes had scorched their way into her mind.

CHAPTER THIRTY-TWO

Haven sat in the back of the flatbed farm truck as it lurched along the narrow lanes. His legs were braced against one side, his body tensed for each bone-shaking jolt. He'd given the driver an ultimatum as he stood in front of the truck parked on the high street, his palms splayed on the bonnet—give him a ride or run him over. The eyes staring back at him through the windscreen conveyed the impression they would prefer the latter if they could get away with it.

A bitter wind stung his face but at least the rain had slowed to a melancholy drizzle. The truck hit a pothole and Haven gritted his teeth as the vibration jarred up his spine. He had no real plan, apart from getting to Rafferty first. If he even was out here.

The search party was covering all bases: some on open ground, some in the village itself, some on all of the roads leading to and from this vile place.

It was a fucking witch hunt.

The image from the photograph had seared itself against his mind. There was so much he didn't know about Rafferty Henderson. *And let's face it, Haven, who the hell eats raw offal?* But then he remembered the boy he'd taken care of and his vulnerability. And Sebastian's final words. *Please help him.*

The truck swung off the road into a field. It slid sideways until the tyres grabbed traction on the waterlogged ground and

Haven braced himself.

It began to climb. He turned and watched the twin beams from the headlights bouncing through the dark. A startled doe darted in front of them, then was lost to the night. Haven narrowed his eyes. Up ahead, at the top of the hill, a light shone in a window. Diesel fumes engulfed him as the driver changed gears, and Haven pulled his bandana over his nose and mouth. As they drew closer, he could see the shapes of other vehicles, and people huddled around them.

The truck stopped and the man climbed out without giving him a backward glance. Haven jumped down onto the concrete farmyard, his back complaining bitterly over the rough ride. A group of people stood around another truck with an ordinance survey map spread out on its bonnet. The outline of a barn hulked in the dark.

Eyes wheeled towards him as he joined them. Their chill was colder than the night air.

'What's he doing here?' The woman from the pub glared in his direction. *Anna.* She wore a bright yellow cagoule over her jumper.

'Listen, I know Rafferty. He won't hide from me.' *A total lie.*

They looked him up and down. He refused to be cowed by their condescension, but now the danger he was in stroked along his nerve edges. He was severely outnumbered. And their hostility towards him pulsed in the frigid air.

'Haven.' A familiar voice came from the back of the group. Peter Edwards stepped forward. A weird kind of relief shot through Haven's veins. Maybe he wasn't quite alone.

'Peter,' Haven said, forcing a smile onto his lips. 'It makes sense what I'm saying, doesn't it?'

But Peter knew Haven had only just met Rafferty. He could bury Haven with one comment.

Haven held Peter's gaze. The older man looked away first before nodding.

There was a grumbling murmur and some dark glances, but at last Anna answered, 'I guess it does. You'll go with Boyd here.' She nodded at a heavyset man wiping moisture from his glasses.

'I go alone.' Haven emphasised each word. 'If Rafferty is out there, I'll find him.'

His tone suggested more confidence than he felt.

Part of him had thought about threatening them with police intervention. He had a phone, after all. But something stopped him. Did he really want any more attention focussed on the Hendersons? He thought about Meredith and hoped she was having more luck piecing together the puzzle. What she'd told him about the well squirmed in his mind like a maggot waiting to hatch.

'I need a torch,' Haven said. 'I'll go that way.' He pointed behind him. Dense woodland swaddled the edges of the field. He'd seen it from the truck as it lurched up the slope. His decision was pure gut instinct.

Anna jerked her thumb over her shoulder.

A box of heavy-duty rubber torches sat on the bonnet of a truck. Haven's lips tightened. This wasn't a sudden knee-jerk hunt. They'd been prepared for a long time.

He grabbed one and checked the light.

Now they all set off in different directions, in twos and threes, like spokes from a wheel hub.

Someone placed a hand on his shoulder and he turned to see Peter. 'Meet me here after you're done,' he said. 'I'll give you a ride back.'

Haven nodded. At least Peter didn't think he was a pariah.

He trudged across the field towards the trees, the scent of wet pine drifting from the dark. It wasn't long before the bottoms of his jeans were soaked through. If he spent any more time in this place he'd probably grow gills.

No fence acted as a barrier between the field and the woodland. One moment he was in open pasture and the next the gloom deepened and grass gave way to a soft carpet of pine needles. The light from his torch didn't reach very far.

You are deluding yourself, a small voice said. *He's not here.*

Rafferty had been brought up in this place. He would know every inch of it, every place to hide. Every secretive corner.

'Raff?' Haven called out, shortening the boy's name into something more familiar. As if that alone might persuade him to creep from the shadows.

A fox barked deep in the forest. It raised the hair along Haven's skin.

He stopped and turned in a slow circle, the torch light spinning with him. If he went in too deep here he'd lose his sense of direction, could end up going completely the wrong way.

Somewhere far to his left, another fluid stream of light as others from the search party probed through the trees. *Come to the spider, little fly.*

A noise erupted from the darkness. A rustle of vegetation. Haven wheeled, his torch poised. A flash of grey flank. He inhaled sharply as a young fallow doe sprinted into the undergrowth.

And then a scream echoed down towards him.

He took off towards it with his heart lodged in his throat. It didn't sound like Rafferty but he wasn't taking the chance. Vegetation tugged at his ankles. Low-hanging branches struck his face and shoulders. Never had he felt so cumbersome, so unwanted by an environment.

There wasn't another scream and he couldn't decide whether that was a good thing or not. The ground under his feet fell away and he pitched forwards, tumbling down a bracken-laced incline.

A dangling holly sucker caught him across the cheek, the sting radiating over his face. Then the shock of freezing water as his feet met a shallow brook.

With gritted teeth, Haven scrabbled up the opposite bank, the light from his torch a wild thing in his hands.

'Over here!' a voice called to him. He caught a flash of bright yellow up ahead.

Haven crashed into a small glade.

Anna lay on her back on the ground, a man cradling her head in his lap.

'We spread out,' he said to Haven, his eyes glazed with shock. 'She was only about twenty feet from me. I couldn't do anything.'

Haven crouched down. Anna's cagoule was torn open, the neck of her jumper shredded. Blood streamed from a wound above her collar bone, staining her neck crimson.

'What happened?' Haven asked. He put his hand on the man's shoulder but the man shrugged him off.

'It was that fucking animal,' he said, spittle flying from his lips. 'Came out of nowhere and attacked her.'

'Did he have a knife?' Haven asked. The wound didn't look clean enough for that.

'Hell, no,' the man said, his voice clogged with emotion. He swallowed before continuing. 'He bit her, I swear to God. I saw it with my own eyes. Tore a hole in her neck with his teeth.'

Haven wanted to believe the man was lying.

He studied the man's face. There was no trace of a lie there.

Haven stood, disbelief pouring iced water on his resolve. The full moon hung on the shoulder of the hill, pregnant with light, a slim silhouette painted against it.

Haven closed his eyes for a moment, and when he opened them again Rafferty Henderson was gone.

CHAPTER THIRTY-THREE

It was close to midnight when Meredith arrived back at the pub. The glow from the streetlights reflected in puddles, the rain-slick pavements dark and oily.

She let herself in and made her way up the stairs. It was a surreal feeling, being in a place that normally hummed with people, now empty apart from her own footsteps.

Her bones ached and she felt like she'd been on her feet for days. The room was just as she'd left it, although someone had been in to leave clean towels on her bed. Meredith pulled off her boots, massaged her aching toes.

She couldn't get the image of Rafferty out of her mind.

With a sigh she flopped back on the bed, looked up at the spiderweb cracks in the ceiling. At the village sketches from bygone days framed on the wall.

A gasp formed in her throat as a realisation filtered through her exhaustion.

She picked up her phone and tried Haven's number again, needing someone to talk this over with, but he didn't answer. She fired off a text.

The sensible Meredith who arrived here four days ago would have cleaned her teeth, cleansed her face, and tumbled into bed.

The new Meredith grabbed her car keys, pulled on her boots, and headed out into the night.

≈

She parked outside Walsh's house and grabbed her torch from the back of the car. The hulk of the house sat in the darkness, at one with the night.

All of her instincts were screaming at her to stop. To return in the daylight. She had an awful feeling that the house opened its eyes in the dark, let the memories of its long-dead sole occupant play amongst the rotting rooms, let them breathe. Because some things are too terrible to stay buried forever.

But she only needed a few minutes. Only had to grab one thing.

She forced her hand onto the door handle. Forced it to open the door.

The staircase loomed in her torch light, cobwebs strung out between the spindles.

With one foot on the bottom stair, she listened.

Nothing.

Sweat trickled down her spine even though she could see her breath ghosting in the dark.

She gritted her teeth and bolted up the staircase, her feet echoing on the bare treads. The door to the bedroom was shut.

She shouldered it open, pointed the torch beam at the wall above the bed. The light glinted off the frame of the painting.

This is crazy.

She wished Haven was here but he was roaming the night, frantically looking for Rafferty. Meredith clenched her fist, pressed it against her lips, and made a wish. Just like she had done all those summers ago. Maybe this time fate would listen.

She balanced the torch on the chair by the window, stole across to the bed, and climbed onto the mattress. The sheet of tissue she had laid out yesterday crinkled under her feet. As the mattress sank she rammed her elbow against the wall to keep her balance.

If this was a normal case, in a normal house, she would have slipped on protective gloves in case her fingerprints marred the painting. But nothing about this was normal. She closed her hands around the frame and tried to lift it.

It didn't move. She fumbled in the dark. The torch light didn't reach this far up the wall. Frustration forced a growl from her lips.

She yanked the painting. It came away from the wall suddenly, whatever was holding it there parting company with crumbling plaster.

The momentum sent her tumbling backwards. She hit the mattress with a jolt, cradling the painting to her chest. One corner of it speared into the soft flesh under her chin. An expletive left her lips.

Hurry, Mere, hurry. Urgency flooded through her veins.

She set the painting on the bed and grabbed the torch. Ran it over the name at the bottom of the frame.

Marie Claire.

Irving Walsh's ill-fated sailing ship.

The name Tucker had told her.

She flipped the painting over, expecting to see an aged canvas. Her eyes widened.

Stretched sackcloth lay across the back of the painting, the edges held in place by tiny tacks. There was a small hole in one corner where a moth had sampled the fabric.

Get in the car. Leave!

She thrust the thought away, her fingers already probing into the hole. The sackcloth gave easily, its old threads tired of holding the secret within.

There, in the back of the painting, was a sheaf of pages, held together by yellowed string.

On the front was a name, neatly inscribed in copperplate script.

Irving Walsh.

She took a shaky breath.

The edges of the paper were jagged, had been torn from a journal or a book. Had been hidden away because Irving Walsh never wanted anyone to read about the horror in the polar night. About what he'd done.

Meredith turned over the first page and began to read.

Downstairs, in the midnight gloom of the hallway, the front door closed softly.

Downstairs, in the midnight gloom of the hallway, the grandfather clock began to tick.

Chapter Thirty-Four

Haven climbed into Peter's car and watched the rest of the search party disappear in the wing mirror as the car pulled away.

He'd helped the guy, whose name was Nick, carry Anna back to the barn, had listened without hearing as Nick raged about Rafferty.

Waves of nausea flooded Haven's gullet and he had to keep swallowing to stop himself throwing up. Rafferty had attacked someone. Had torn a gash in her throat with his *teeth*. No wonder Sebastian hadn't gone into details. There are no words to describe that your little brother is a monster.

All kids can be monstrous, his inner voice whispered. Haven looked out of the window as the car lurched from the field onto the road. What he'd done had been monstrous too.

Was Rafferty Henderson some kind of hybrid vampire? The thought made his head spin. Haven closed his eyes as pain throbbed across his temple. All of his adult life he'd been searching for proof, searching for corroboration that the night in the warehouse wasn't some nightmarish one-off, and now it was possible that it had fallen into his grasp.

But Rafferty wasn't a fanged creature who dwelled in the dark and took human life. He was just a boy.

'Did you see anything?' Peter's voice interrupted his thoughts.

'It was pitch black,' Haven said, which was true, and stopped him having to lie. He wouldn't add to the lynch mob fever that had erupted when they saw what had happened to Anna.

He slipped his phone from his pocket and saw the missed calls from Meredith, read the text which made no sense at all.

Going to the house. Marie Claire. Tucker.

That was all it said. His brow creased and pain shot through his skull as the urgency in her words hit home.

Peter stopped at a junction and peered into the dark. 'They won't go to the gatehouse tonight. Seth has called an emergency meeting in the pub tomorrow morning.'

Haven glanced across and saw the way Peter's fingers were clenched on the steering wheel.

'Do you know something they don't?' Haven asked as the car swung left. Part of him wanted to grab Peter's arm, to make him spill what he knew. Frustrated anger bubbled under Haven's skin. He pressed his hands between his thighs.

'I'm not at liberty to say.' Peter paused and a silence expanded between them. The first of the village streetlights pressed out of the darkness. 'But I will tell you that Rafferty's past has been filled with trauma. I fear it has finally caught up to him.'

'Fuck it!' Haven threw his hands into the air, somehow got hold of the fury before it launched itself at Peter with no holds barred. 'Why does this place insist on keeping secrets? There's a boy's future at stake here.'

He nearly said life, but surely they wouldn't go that far?

Haven waited for Peter's reply, and as he did the hopelessness of Rafferty's situation settled like a stone fist in his gut.

Peter pulled up outside the lychgate. 'I'll drop you here. Try to get some sleep, Haven. And don't worry.'

Don't worry? He had to be fucking joking.

Haven climbed out of the car and watched it disappear around the corner to the vicarage. Exasperation was a live wire threaded through his veins. He grabbed hold of the gate and slammed it against its latch, his fingers white-knuckled on the wood.

With his heartbeat thundering in his ears he stopped and raised his face to the night sky, drizzle coating his heated skin. This wasn't helping. And it certainly wasn't helping Rafferty.

He pulled out his phone and shot off a quick text to Meredith, holding off ringing as it was gone midnight.

Call me as soon as you get up.

Haven walked under the lychgate and up the pathway, paused outside the church entrance. He looked up at the carved scrollwork above the door, at the imposing stone walls. He tapped his fingers against his thigh, then tried the handle on the door, just as he had done on his first night here.

It opened to him and a tight smile forced its way onto his lips.

The interior of the church lay in darkness, apart from the soft green glow of an exit sign to the right of the altar. Haven made his way up the aisle, his gaze on the stained-glass window dominating the end of the church. The pieces of crimson glass overpowered all the other colours.

Haven dropped to his knees. He didn't believe in the existence of one almighty power, not when he'd seen what he had. No god would have put Logan through that. The boy had lain in his own blood and waste on the cold, concrete floor and then, twenty-four hours later, he'd got up and staggered away.

Haven pressed his hands over his ears as a sound blasted from his memory. The scream from a throat that had been ripped apart, a scream that spoke of terror and unimaginable pain.

It ricocheted around Haven's head like a wayward bullet, finding all his tender places, rendering him immobile as the images played again and again.

Another scream came. But this time it was from his own lungs. He lowered his head and listened to it echo from the walls, until it finally sank into the stone.

He pushed himself up and raked his hands through his hair. His gaze fell on the vestry door.

The first day he'd met Peter, when Peter had invited him into the vestry for coffee, the man had a sheaf of papers in his hands. He'd flipped them over at one point. Not a true test of hiding something, but . . . Haven pressed his tongue against the inside of his cheek.

He tried the handle on the vestry door, sure that it would be locked, but the door squeaked open. He pushed it closed softly and brought out his phone. Flicked on the torch.

The desktop had been cleared of everything but an old Bible.

Haven pressed his lips together. He remembered Peter apologising for the mess. And now he'd been clearing up.

He went around the back of the desk and tried the drawer.

It was locked. He rattled it, hoping the lock would give, but it stayed firm. Irritation forced a growl from his throat and his eyes skimmed to a photo on the wall over the bookcase. Haven stole across and studied it. It was a photo of the crypt, or rather it was a photo of the inscription above the crypt before the weather had devoured its edges.

May God grant His mercy.

He exhaled slowly as the darkness in the vestry took on a different hue. Haven's gaze wheeled to the narrow, arched window. He put his hand on the stone sill and looked outside.

The vestry overlooked a small courtyard, bordered by tall stone walls—one with a postern gate—the side of the annexe at the rear.

For a few seconds, his mind couldn't comprehend what he was seeing.

Orange flames licked into the darkness, rising from the base of a hinged metal drum. The intense heat caused the air around it to haze.

A figure stood behind the drum, hidden by the flames.

Then it stepped into view.

Haven caught the gasp in his throat.

Peter.

And then the gasp stuttered from his lips.

One by one, Peter tore pages from a book and fed them into the fire. The book he had covertly covered when he was in the vestry with Haven. The flames devoured them instantly, paper residue dancing in the smoky air.

The radiance from the fire bathed his face in an unearthly glow but Haven couldn't see his eyes.

Haven watched as Peter threw the final page into the hungry flames, then grabbed a brush resting against the wall and slammed the hinged lid down onto the drum.

The flames died instantly. The light snuffed out. And the dark came rushing in like a wolf that had been kept at bay.

Haven sagged against the wall, his spine turning to jelly.

He knew instantly that what he'd been looking for was now ash on the wind.

Whatever secret Peter had kept was gone forever.

All he had wanted to do was find out more about Rafferty so he could help him. That the boy was in danger was a cold, hard fact. But what if the danger was Rafferty himself?

Haven was holding on to pure gut instinct. He had been instrumental in the death of one boy. He would not lose Rafferty to the same fate.

Please help him. And if you can't you'll know what to do.

He had an awful feeling that Sebastian had given him permission to carry out an execution.

CHAPTER THIRTY-FIVE

Rafferty ran. He didn't know where he was heading, knew he had to get out of the village, away from people. Amelia and Grace had been right. There was nothing for him here. No saviour. No redemption.

Pavement beneath his feet gave way to grass. The lights of the village faded, the horizon dotted with skeletal tree canopies silhouetted against the moon. The air was heavy with the earthy scent of petrichor, freezing drizzle coating his skin.

But it was the taunting humiliation from the boys that pounded in his skull.

Maybe I'll carve out a piece of your flesh.

It was all too much.

He was destined to live his life in the gatehouse, eventually alone, with the ghosts of the past in his shadow.

He ran towards the woods and stopped at the treeline, the brook singing softly in the dark. Hot tears stung his frozen cheeks. He swiped them away and his nose wrinkled in disgust at the stench of urine on his sleeve.

Rafferty lifted his head and sniffed the air. People had been here recently.

He slipped into the woodland and made his way along a track, veering off down a banking that led towards the brook, saw the water as a silver line in the dark. His feet sank ankle-deep in leaf mulch, and as he slid sideways a fallen tree trunk blocked his way. The trunk rested between two moss-covered boulders, and on the other side the brook cascaded over the side of a small wedge of rock, falling into a pool before meandering away into the night.

Rafferty scrabbled down to the pool's edge, tore off his jacket—*Haven's jacket*—and dipped his arms into the freezing water, rubbing his skin vigorously. It wasn't long before his fingers became numb, but he cupped his palms together and splashed water onto his face, onto his hair. Better freezing cold than stained.

He knelt there for a few moments with his head bowed, his eyes closed.

Part of him wanted to be home, safe in his bed, but another part was raging, a wild itch crawling in his veins. He had somehow crossed a line and nothing felt the same.

He raised his head, felt the trickle of frigid water running down his spine from his hair. His teeth started to chatter. An owl shrieked deep in the forest and his eyes flew open. Something hunting for food, as nature intended.

The dark water in the pool rippled softly, shafts of moonlight skimming across its surface, spearing through the bare branches. He stared at his reflection, at his pale skin.

For an instant he wasn't kneeling in the freezing dark, he was crouched behind a tree, his back pressed against the rough bark. And all he could smell was warm blood pulsing through succulent flesh.

His mouth watered. It was so tangible.

But it wasn't only that. It was the burning joy that came with it. The exhilaration he had felt the day he'd torn into the crow and devoured it raw. The day he had felt truly alive.

It was like a part of himself had split away, was hunting in the dark free from condemnation.

Is that too difficult to wrap your head around?

The voice that had haunted him for the past few days came again. The voice that he knew.

They took me from you.

'You're not real,' Rafferty whispered, gritting his teeth. 'You were an imaginary friend because I didn't have any real ones.'

Never imaginary, Raff, just part of you. A part they tore away. But I'm still here. I'll always be here.

'You're not real!' Rafferty plunged his hands into the water, cracking open his reflection. Ripples surged towards the edge of the pool, lapped against the rock in a frenzied dance.

He scrambled backwards, crablike, panic tunnelling his vision, hazy images floating untethered in his mind. He bit down on his tongue, found comfort in the taste of his own blood. Phantom fingers tightened around his throat.

What had they kept from me?

Rafferty clambered to his feet and backed away from the water. It was peaceful now, burbling softly as it ran into the night.

He turned and sped blindly through the trees. The cold wind ripped all feeling from his skin but he didn't care. Now he knew where he was heading and instinct pulled him towards it.

Home was a beacon in his mind but he bypassed the field that led to the gatehouse, skirting the hedgerow and darting into the woods he knew like the back of his hand.

The trees opened before him, silver trunks looming out of the dark.

He'd been here, just before Amelia screamed. Just before they found out their world had been hacked apart.

Stay away, they'd told him. *Stay away, the foundations are crumbling.*

He knew now that wasn't true. They had kept him away because they were trying to protect him from what he really was.

A monster. With a monster's blood in his veins.

He craved raw flesh, a craving that was only getting stronger with each passing day. He thought about the boys who had humiliated him, how the salt on their throats would explode against his taste buds before his teeth sank into their flesh and he tore it apart.

SHIP'S LOG (DECEMBER 1874)
CAPTAIN IRVING WALSH

I do not know what made me venture into the hull. I took a lantern, hung it from a rib, and tried not to think of the ice imprisoning my ship in its glacial grasp.

Hunger hollowed out my stomach. The rats had found the remains of the rations and all that was left were a few strips of salt pork and stale biscuit crumbs.

In the cramped cabin above me the only member of the crew left alive, Cartwright, tossed and turned in his hammock. I knew from the pallor of his face earlier it was only a matter of time before I was left alone in this frozen hell.

It was possible I was searching for medicinal compounds, but it was also possible some scrap of my brain knew something foul hulked in the belly of my ship.

I said before I believed the crew brought something back with them from the shore. That thought had only amplified with each passing night. With each horrific death.

Quite what I would do if faced with this foulness, I did not know.

Ice creaked in the frozen sea, and the sound vibrated in my chest.

The lantern swung slightly. Light skittered around the hull, creating shadows, then sent them skulking into the corners.

A mangy rat ran over my boot and I kicked out. It scurried beneath a tarpaulin. I lifted the corner and the stench of rot made my throat constrict.

Dead and dying rats lay in a nest about three feet wide, boards gnawed away around them. The rat I had seen peered up at me with dark, empty eyes. It dove into the nest, its teeth ripping into a kit latched onto a teat that gave no milk.

The kit squealed in agony and I dropped the tarpaulin, staggering backwards.

The rats were devouring each other.

Dear God, I am lost.

I saw it then, the thing I was looking for, and afterwards I fell to my hands and knees and wept.

It was encased in a block of ice through which I could see a shape that appeared to be human, although the bottom of the block was opaque and its limbs were obscured.

My first thought was that the crew had brought on board a hapless explorer, trapped in a frozen grave. But the shape bore no thick furs.

I stumbled back up to the deck, ignoring the throaty rumbles of the polar bears as they roamed the ice floes. I took a chisel from a chest of tools and returned to the hull, my focus entirely on the block of ice and what lay within.

A need arose in my veins, suffocating the gnawing ache of hunger.

I began to chip away at the ice. At the top of the block, where a concealed face lay.

Sweat ran down my brow into my eyes despite the frigid conditions, and behind me the few rats who were left alive scuttled away towards the steps.

I should have taken their heed.

When I at last forced my chisel through the final layer of compacted ice I saw that the head was bowed. All I could discern was dark, matted hair. It coiled around the face and shoulders. How long had this poor soul been wandering before death delivered mercy?

The thought took me to my knees and I collapsed onto the planks, sobs wracking my body.

You must remember that at this point I had lost all faith in myself and in God.

From above me came a cry. A harsh, shrill sound that drilled into my bones.

Cartwright.

I stood. Listened.

The lantern shifted.

Shadows played across the wooden ribs of the ship. In my despair I felt as if I was in the belly of a great beast.

The sound that came next is one that haunts my nightmares.

A sharp cracking. A splintering.

Something glacial-cold slithered over my shoulder and I was rooted to the spot. It took hold of my throat, wrapped itself around the back of my neck.

Muscle rippled along its length.

It turned me towards the ice block . . . and what I saw was not of this earth.

What held me in its grasp was a tentacle. They coiled around its skull, within its hair, a slowly moving mass of slithering that burned all reason from my mind.

The pressure on my throat increased and I thought surely this is when I die.

But that would have been the charitable option.

A smaller tentacle emerged, something with a narrower tip. Suckers pulsed along its length, opening and closing as if they were breathing.

It stroked across my lips and I wanted to scream but my throat was held fast.

A strange blue glow quivered through the ice, and where the tentacles touched me voltaic shock speared through my body.

Movement then, within the ice. Within the cavity I had opened.

The head of the creature tipped back slowly, slowly. The sharp snap of ice.

I could only stare. Lost in the terror unfolding before me. Powerless to fight.

Its face was marvellously human, though pale as death and exuding the texture of marble. A heart-shaped face with full lips and an almost pleasing countenance. But there was something askew about its features, something that jolted against the shreds of logic I so desperately clung to.

And then it opened its eyes and any beauty I had imagined fell away. They were perfectly round, the pupil as black as sin, the iris surrounding it a deep, fiery amber.

I had seen an eye like this before. On a tench I had pulled from a lake. My first fish.

The incongruous nature of those eyes in that face tipped my senses into oblivion.

I believe I may have laughed. I believe I almost welcomed the tentacle as it slid between my lips, the salt upon it exploding on my tongue.

I believed I was going to die. That all this was soon to be over.

But my nightmare was only beginning.

CHAPTER THIRTY-SIX

Meredith read the final sentence on the torn-out pages by the wavering light of her torch beam. Wavering because her hands wouldn't stop trembling.

She had meant to grab Walsh's words and run to the car, drive back to the pub and absorb them in the safety of her room.

But something made her stop. The urgent need to digest the words now, just in case they were swept away.

Irving Walsh had brought something back from his fated expedition. Something monstrous.

She went to the window, dragging the reluctant sash open a few inches, needing to feel the chill of the night in a room that felt as if all life had been sucked from it. Then she sat on the bed with the torch on her lap and tried to take in the unbelievable horror of it all.

And then she sensed it, the very human instinct of knowing that she wasn't alone.

Her tongue glued itself to the roof of her mouth.

She slipped the pages inside her jacket and zipped it up. Took the torch and crossed to the door. Sent the light along the pitch-black corridor.

There was a stench in the still air. Something brackish and sour. Like dead fish.

She remembered the sound of something dragging across the floor.

Her feet echoed on the bare floorboards, an ominous sound in an empty house, and her fingers tightened around the barrel of her torch. She peered over the banister to the gloom-drenched hallway below.

The front door was shut.

She knew she had left it open.

Panic fluttered in her throat. In her mind's eye she saw herself clattering down the stairs and pulling at the door. But it wouldn't open, and there was something in the shadows . . .

In her peripheral vision she thought she saw something shifting at the end of the corridor. Like a tongue probing from a dark, vicious mouth.

Meredith inhaled a long, shaky breath, told herself to stop letting her imagination run amuck.

A loud slam from the bedroom. Her heart skipped and she wheeled. The beam of her torch faded and she banged it against her hand, needing the little pathway of light like she needed air to breathe.

'Come on. Come on.' The plea fell into the callous dark.

Meredith pushed open the bedroom door with her shoulder and a fizz of relief bubbled through her. It was only the sash. It had fallen shut.

The torn pages from Walsh's diary crinkled inside her jacket. Pages he had hidden away because he didn't want anyone else to ever read them.

But how did Tucker know? Another question to add to the chaotic jumble in her head.

She squared her shoulders.

It was time to face Amelia and Grace. Tell them that she knew their secret.

Tomorrow?

Her lips cracked into a smile that held no mirth.

Don't put off for tomorrow things you can do today.

Her late mother's words came trickling back. Although if her mother knew what was going through Meredith's mind she would be turning in her grave.

She ran down the stairs and ripped open the box she had so carefully packed from the bedroom, tore into the tissue surrounding the knife and tucked it inside her jacket beside the pages. The feeling they belonged together made her scalp tighten against her skull.

Some part of her wanted to toss them both into the depths of the well.

She parked a little way down from the gatehouse, killed the engine, and sat drumming her fingers on her thighs.

'Bloody well go home, Mere.'

Her voice sounded strangled. Too high-pitched. Too full of fear. Her eyes flicked to the glove compartment where she'd stowed Walsh's pages.

She opened the car door and climbed out. Smoke hung in the air from the gatehouse chimney. A welcoming scent. She doubted that's what she would find.

Part of her wasn't surprised to see lights burning in the windows. Maybe they knew she was coming? *Stop it, Mere.*

With her heart in her throat she inched through the gates and marched up the pathway to the door. A wreath hung upon it. A circle of entwined willow, filled with pine cones and forest greenery.

Her knock against the wood sounded braver than she was.

Thirty seconds of waiting, her arms crossed over her chest, willing herself to stay her ground.

The door opened.

Amelia Henderson stood there. Decades older, grey threaded in her dark hair. But her eyes were unchanged.

'Meredith. What a pleasant surprise.'

No shock at the late hour. No astonishment at Meredith's sudden appearance.

Amelia closed the door behind her, and for the first time Meredith stood in the gatehouse. Embers glowed in a cast-iron hearth, a fringed lamp on a table cast wan shadows onto a threadbare rug, flowers drooped in a vase.

Another figure sat on the sofa in the near dark. Grace. The Shadow Girl.

'I found something.' Meredith launched into the crux of her visit. There was no need for small talk. All the women here knew that. But she couldn't stop herself adding a question that swelled like a pinprick of blood in her mind. 'How did you know I would be the one to clear the house?'

Amelia straightened a cushion, then rested her hands against the top of an armchair.

'How did I know?' A small, tight smile. 'The answer is simple: I didn't. Call it fate. It always knows what's for the best.'

'What did you find?' Grace, from the shadows.

'Something which explains exactly what you've been keeping a secret. Something Irving Walsh stashed away.'

'Tea, Grace.' Amelia burst into action. 'Where are my manners, eh? Please sit down, Meredith. I'm not sure what you think you've found.'

Meredith found herself complying like she always had. She sank into the armchair. The springs creaked beneath her.

Grace stood and crossed to the kitchen. The sound of water running.

'Did you know that they are searching for Rafferty tonight? Actually, not searching. Hunting.' Meredith changed the subject so she could prepare herself for Amelia's scrutiny.

A flicker of something that could be called pain flashed in Amelia's eyes.

'Someone saw him scavenging offal from a waste bin . . .' Meredith let her words trail off.

'He has special dietary requirements,' Amelia replied without missing a beat.

The kettle began to whistle, a harsh shriek that grated against Meredith's nerves.

'I can explain about Rafferty.' Amelia took a poker from the hearth side and stirred the embers. They flared into life.

Grace came from the kitchen with three mugs on a wicker tray.

There's nothing wrong here. Meredith told herself the lie as Grace pressed a mug of tea into her hands.

'He's never been able to stomach cooked meals, and his metabolism devours iron at such a vast rate that sometimes he craves foods others might find unappealing.' Amelia returned the poker to its stand. It clanged against the shovel. 'Surely I don't have to tell you that this family is blighted by things people find abhorrent. He eats raw food. That is his affliction.' She seated herself opposite Meredith.

The way Amelia described it made perfect sense. The weight lifted from Meredith's shoulders a little. She sipped her tea. It was hot and bitter and herbal.

'Now, what did you find in the house?' Amelia sat forward, her hands pressed together, fingers steepled under her chin.

'Oh, just some old papers. I'll bring them round tomorrow, if you'd like?'

She didn't want to tell Amelia anything. Not now.

It was one o'clock in the morning and she was hungry and exhausted, strung out on what she had read, what she had felt in the house. She curled her fingers around the mug, took another drink. At least it was hot.

'Are you going to tell her the other thing about Rafferty?' Grace's voice, but it seemed to come from far away.

'I don't think there's any need for that, Gracie.'

Meredith looked down into her tea, could feel Amelia's eyes on her, scraping away her layers. Her eyelids drooped, the warmth of the embers relaxing the stress from her muscles. A clock ticked loudly in a corner.

She grasped for the chair arm as her vision blurred. Her legs began to tremble. The mug fell from her hand and rolled under the chair. Her head lolled back.

Everything was swaying now as if she was on board a ship and the sea was angry. Meredith tried to speak but the dead weight of her tongue refused.

A shadow fell over her.

'Do you think I gave her too much?' Grace's voice. 'Little Meredith, all grown up and returned to us. It is a sign, isn't it?'

Meredith's vision hazed to black as the Shadow Girl's words chased her into the dark.

CHAPTER THIRTY-SEVEN

The full moon shone down into the well, bathing the stones and the surrounding ground in a milky glow. Rafferty sat with his legs dangling into the black hole. It was now or never. He had two choices: go home and face a life of rejection and loneliness, or climb down into a place he'd been warned not to go.

Just like the tarn.

A long shaft of absolute darkness lay beneath. And with the darkness came the unmistakable tang of brine.

He reached down with one foot and found a metal rung. Began to lower himself, rung by rung. But with each step the space between what he knew and the terrifying unknown dwindled. The fierce emotion that had driven him here began to wane. Fear drifted into the gap, making his skin crawl.

He had never been here, yet he felt that he knew it.

The water was close now. The chill from it dwelt inside each breath he took. He reached down with one foot.

And found nothing.

An empty space where a rung should be. He leaned back, stretched out his foot. An empty space that led somewhere.

One more step and he could trace the outline of a horizontal tunnel with his toe. Two more steps and his chest was level with the tunnel opening.

A trace of blue light flickered up ahead. He rubbed his eyes, sure it was just a trick of his jumbled mind, but the light was still there. He eased his body into the subterranean passage and crawled towards it. As he got closer he could see trails of it clinging to the tunnel surface like slime from a snail.

Rafferty reached his fingers towards the light, towards the bioluminescence, because that's what it was. He could see the veins on the back of his hands standing out. And there was something on the ground. He scooped up a handful and held it to the light. Moist tangles of seaweed. The briny smell was strong here in the enclosed space.

But seaweed wasn't natural in an underground tunnel and the coast was miles away. Did the tunnel run all the way to the sea?

Questions lined themselves up in his head like a domino run. He repeated them over and over so he didn't have to think what else might be down here.

The bioluminescence led him onwards. The tunnel ended sharply, and he had to grab for the sides as the ground fell away. A small chamber, hewn from the earth, layers of rock sprinkled with the blue light, ebbing and flowing like ocean stars. Rafferty's jaw dropped slightly at the savage beauty. He eased himself down into it, then clambered up a bank of rock at the other side where another, larger tunnel led from it. At least now he could walk upright. His feet tramped through curled clusters of seaweed, the scent becoming stronger the farther he went. The tunnel twisted, sometimes wider, sometimes so narrow he had to squeeze himself through the gap between its walls.

He had no idea how far he had walked or in what direction. He was suddenly very aware of the great weight above him, of his own insignificance. Of the very real fact he could be trapped down here. That he could freeze or starve to death. He longed for the company of the familiar voice.

Rafferty forced himself to focus.

There was something up ahead on the tunnel floor.

He ducked his head under an overhang of rock. Water splashed over his trainers as he focussed his eyes on the ground.

Something pale against the dark mat of seaweed.

He knew what it was before he crouched down to touch it, before he ran one finger across the rough, pitted surface. His breath caught in the back of his throat.

It was a bone. A human thigh bone, complete with a ball joint to the hip.

Maybe someone had died down here? But then, why was there only one bone?

He carried on for about twenty feet. The sound of rushing water drifted from up ahead. A few feet farther along it seeped through the earth ceiling, pooling on the ground underneath. He splashed through and rounded a corner. A gasp fell from his lips.

An immense cave lay before him, dotted with trails of the pulsing blue light, the air within so cold that every breath he took seemed to sear his lungs with a layer of ice. A steady stream of water tumbled down the back wall and disappeared into a narrow chasm at his left, funnelling into an underground river.

But all this wasn't what drew his attention. It was the bones littered over the ground, dozens and dozens of them. His gaze fell on the skulls with their sightless eyes. On the smaller skulls with rows of tiny milk teeth. All this on a bed of shells and seaweed and driftwood, as though the ocean itself wanted to claim them.

Rafferty stepped down into the chamber of horrors. His foot slipped as the carpet of shells and bones moved beneath him and he fell onto his knees, wincing as a sharp edge knifed through his jeans.

Something glinted, close to his fingertips. He hooked it out and stared at the brass handle.

A coffin handle.

He dropped it as if it had burst into flames. The splintered wood littered around him wasn't driftwood.

And then the full enormity made his heart freefall into his stomach.

The tunnel he had crawled along wasn't the only one. He'd seen another. Had looked down upon it as he knelt in the pouring rain.

The tunnel from the collapsed grave. And now he had found its end. He remembered the other graves he had heard shifting before the boys attacked him in the crypt.

But it wasn't the latter memory that made his skin feel like it had shrunk against his bones.

It was the fact that something had plundered the coffins, dragged the remains here, and left them like offerings.

CHAPTER THIRTY-EIGHT

Haven checked his phone for about the twentieth time as he walked down the stairs from his room.

Meredith hadn't rung him. Nothing since the text mentioning the house.

'One day you'll break a leg.'

The voice made his chin jerk up. His brow furrowed.

'Walking without looking where you're going,' Peter continued as he rummaged about in the cupboard at the bottom of the stairs.

Haven studied the man who had burned something he'd desperately wanted to see. A few moments of silence ticked between them.

'What time is the meeting?' Haven asked. 'If you don't mind, I want to go. I'll make up the time lost tomorrow.'

Peter stood and closed the cupboard door. 'I'm afraid it's already over. Seth called everyone and made it an early breakfast meeting. I didn't go, before you ask.'

'Fuck.' Haven didn't try to curb the expletive. He thrust his phone into his pocket and turned on Peter. 'You know I'm not going to stand back while they drag Rafferty out of his home, don't you?'

Peter brushed an imaginary piece of lint from his trousers. 'I do. I also know that you won't go to the police.'

'So you're saying it's me against them?' The lunacy of the idea filled his words with derision.

'Listen, Haven. I like you. You stand up for what you believe in.' A shadow passed over Peter's eyes. Something Haven recognised from looking in the mirror. Guilt.

'Should I feel special?' Haven's reply was petty, he knew it. But it made him feel better.

Peter cleared his throat. 'I could tell you to leave, but I know you won't. But I will tell you this, there's far more to Rafferty Henderson than meets the eye. Be careful.'

The warning hung in the air between them, before Peter gathered up a pile of hymn books and went into the church.

Haven suppressed a growl in his throat. Peter was somehow involved but was unable or unwilling to help him. So many fucking secrets in this place, tangled together like strands of barbed wire. If he wanted to unravel them he'd have to bleed.

His first stop was the pub. The front door was locked and he had to knock three times before it opened. Rosa ushered him in, one hand around a broom.

'I've come to see Meredith,' he said. 'Has she left yet?'

'She didn't come back last night.' Rosa bit the edge of her lip. 'I popped in when I started my shift to ask if she wanted breakfast, but the bed hadn't been slept in.'

Unease tripped across Haven's skin. He paced to the fireplace, a part of the room he'd never seen empty.

'Were you here?'

He didn't need to elaborate. She shook her head. Then turned away.

'I'm grappling in the dark here, Rosa, trying to work out what the hell is going on. Did Sebastian tell you anything that might help me?'

Rosa moved a chair from under a table and brushed out a crumpled crisp packet. She leant on the broom and met Haven's gaze.

'Sebastian and I were friends with benefits,' she said softly. 'No one knew. He came to me for comfort. We were both lonely.' She shrugged and tucked a strand of hair behind her ear. 'But he was a messed-up man with a fuckload of demons. One night I woke up to find him huddled in the corner muttering to himself, his hands covering his face.' She picked up the crisp packet and tossed it into a bucket. 'I didn't ask him to stay over often. I never quite knew where his mind was when he went to dark places.'

Haven nodded. His own thoughts swam in front of his eyes. How many times had he wondered where Sebastian's headspace was? He could recall numerous instances they were having an in-depth conversation and then, like a light switched off, Sebastian was there in body but not in mind.

'He was a good fuck,' she said. 'In case you were wondering why I put up with him.'

Haven lifted his hands. 'You'll get no judgement from me. I get far too much of that directed my way.'

He felt her scrutiny deepen. 'You're not who you pretend to be, are you?'

He was about to protest but let it slide. There were enough lies around here.

'Let's just say that I have my reasons.'

He checked his phone again. Meredith's absence gnawed against his nerve endings. He'd thought maybe she was pissed off with him for not answering her calls last night, but he knew she wasn't that shallow.

'Where's the house Meredith was packing up?' he asked, changing the subject. His mind had cartwheeled off into the vicinity of Meredith lying injured somewhere. He had to check.

And then he had to find Rafferty. The biting urgency of both scored along his bones.

'It's down Picket Lane,' she said. 'Turn right at the school then follow the lane until the end. You can't miss it. Wait here a minute.' She leaned the broom against a table and disappeared through the swing door to the kitchen. Haven surveyed the drinks behind the bar and wondered if it was too early to order one. Or two. The fact that things were skipping out of his reach far too quickly filled him with a gut-clenching dread.

Rosa reappeared and pressed a key fob into his hand. 'Take my car. It's around the back, the grey one. I'd go with you, but I need this job.'

He nodded his thanks and headed towards the door, paused as he opened it.

'What makes you think I can drive?'

She laughed. 'I told you, Haven. You're not who you appear to be. You just get top marks for acting.'

He ran to the back of the pub, through the cobbled alleyway where the dray horses used to deliver beer in huge oak barrels. The car sat with its nose against the wall. He unlocked it and climbed in, sliding the seat back as far as it would go before starting the engine and reversing out.

Haven wondered how a girl he hardly knew could see right through him. But the understanding was there at the back of his mind. The mask he wore, the mask he hid behind so he could drift in and out of the Goth community, was slipping. This place wanted to tear away his flesh and expose his vulnerabilities. It wanted to consume him.

He glanced in the rear-view mirror, caught sight of the ink decorating his skin, the barbed wire collar encircling his throat. An ever-present reminder of how fragile life was.

I'm coming soon, Raff. I'm coming soon.

CHAPTER THIRTY-NINE

Haven skidded to a stop outside the house. Meredith's car wasn't in the driveway. He wasn't sure if that was good or bad.

The door was unlocked. He went in.

In the room to his left were taped-up boxes. One had been torn open, sheets of discarded tissue hanging over the edge. Something was missing, had been removed quickly. A chill touched his skin.

He turned and stared into the gloom of the hallway. There was a stench about this place. Something brackish. He'd noticed it on Sebastian's coat sometimes.

Warped floorboards creaked under his boots as he crossed to the staircase. It was cloaked in shadows, the wan light from the doorway barely reaching it.

'How the fuck did you ever work here?' His voice spilled out, a question for Meredith that she couldn't answer.

The stairs groaned in protest as he went up, the musty scent of neglect rising from each of his dusty footprints. Haven paused on the landing. A door farther along on his left stood slightly ajar. He opened it cautiously.

An old bed. A gentleman's vanity stand. A chair. His eyes fell on the wall above the bed. There was a pale shape on the dirty plaster where something had once hung. A ghost painting.

And there it was, on the mattress, the back ripped open. Meredith had found something.

He flipped it over. A ship on a blue sea, its sails filled with wind. Not a particularly good painting; the depth perception seemed slightly off. He glanced down at the corner to see if the artist had left their name. They hadn't, but his eyes found something else.

Marie Claire. The fucking ship was *Marie Claire.*

Haven tugged out his phone and found Meredith's text, his heartbeat a wild thing pounding in his ears.

Going to the house. Marie Claire. Tucker.

He looked up and stared at the space on the wall where the painting had hung. What the hell had she found, and why was it hidden away?

Because this is where it started. As soon as the thought settled he felt the overwhelming truth of it.

Haven sprinted down the stairs, more than happy to leave the house behind. He sat with his fingers drumming on the steering wheel for a few moments. Agitation burned through him like a fever. There was so much he needed to do and he couldn't decide what was most important.

Finding Meredith. Finding Rafferty. Finding Tucker.

You could just leave.

He bowed his head and for a moment he wanted to act on the intense persuasion of the thought. It seemed so comforting. So easy. But then he'd spend the rest of his life wondering what had happened, flaying himself with his guilt, and he'd already done enough of that before coming here.

He started the engine, and, with a spray of gravel, drove out onto the lane.

It wasn't long before he came to the gatehouse. Sebastian had described its ostracised location numerous times. He drove past slowly, his gaze fixed on the place Sebastian had lived. The place Rafferty called home. An unassuming cottage, almost lost behind a bank of overgrown hedgerow.

He pulled into a lay-by a little farther up and backtracked on foot. Smoke curled from the gatehouse chimney.

Haven blew out a breath through his lips. He was used to skulking around in the dark. Daylight added another layer of wrongness. *Tucker's word.* He snapped his mind back into focus and skirted around the back of the house, glancing in windows, searching for one that was open. He came up empty.

Should he knock on the door? It was possible Rafferty was safe inside. His gut told him that wasn't true.

Urgency thrummed with the rhythm of his heart.

He stole around the side of the gatehouse. A flurry of movement in a chicken coop combined with hopeful squawking. No one came to the window.

Woodland flanked the gatehouse, stretching out as far as Haven could see, a pathway leading into it. He crept across, his boots sinking into soft, wet earth. But his were not the only marks.

Tyre tracks. A tight smile forced its way to his lips.

He followed them. When the pathway narrowed, broken branches and crushed ferns were the hallmarks that something had forced its way through.

Another secret spawned in this place. He wished he'd pressed Sebastian for more information but wishes weren't going to help him here.

With his boots caked in mud he squelched through carpets of sodden leaves, pushed his way through tangle after tangle of briar and bramble. At one point he tucked his hair under his jacket. The wayward thorns had already claimed far too many strands.

It was possible he was on a wild-goose chase, and he hated the thought he might be losing time following an ill-conceived idea. Soon the hourglass would be bottom heavy.

Rafferty and Meredith were missing. Was it a coincidence that they had disappeared together?

He thought back to last night and the wounds on Anna's neck. *No.* He shook his head sharply. He wouldn't let his thoughts drift there.

It made perfect sense why Sebastian had been so tight-lipped about certain aspects of his life. But he had begged Haven to help Rafferty. All the evidence pointed to the boy's guilt, but there must be something he wasn't getting.

He pushed a low-hanging pine branch to the side and it snapped back and slapped him against the cheek, rain spattering his face.

A low growl came from his throat. This fucking place was determined to drown him.

Haven stopped and pressed his fingers to his lips, grasped for a tendril of realisation as it floated across his mind.

A blackbird erupted from a nearby clump of bracken. It screeched past him, chittering its alarm, disappearing into a stand of taller trees. Haven's gaze tracked it, then swept back. Something had caught his eye. Something bright in the undergrowth.

He tramped towards it, cursing the thick vegetation. But the bright spot was like a beacon and he kept his eyes fixed upon it.

He came out into a small glade. A fan of pine branches lay on top of a faded green tarpaulin. One edge had been disturbed, maybe by animals, and what lay beneath was what Haven had seen.

He lifted the tarpaulin and hauled it to the side, but he knew what was underneath. Meredith's car. Despite the chill of the day sweat pooled in the small of his back. He half expected to find a body.

The door opened to his touch. There was nothing inside to suggest a struggle. He flicked the catch under the steering wheel and went around the back, opened the boot with dread singing through his veins. But all that met his gaze was the vacant space of a hire car. He leant against the boot with the heels of his hands on the rim and waited until his heart stopped racing.

Meredith had been here and someone had covered up her tracks.

He closed the boot and went back to the driver's door, scrabbled under the seat looking for clues, leaned across and did the same on the passenger side.

One more thing to check. He pressed the catch on the glove box and it clattered open. A loose page fluttered onto the rubber mat.

Haven picked it up with shaking fingers, pulled the rest of the pages from their resting place. Old paper. Faded ink. Words from a man long dead.

The man who had started the Henderson journey to hell.

CHAPTER FORTY

There was something down here. Something in the tunnels.

Rafferty let the full enormity of that realisation sink into his core. He stood with the eerie blue light pulsating around him, his feet rooted to the spot.

A sound drifted from the shadows. A splash of water. No, more than that. Something moving *through* water.

The thought ripped through his skull and finally his feet obeyed what his brain was howling at them to do. He scrambled backwards, bones rolling all around him, pitching him against the wall. A blast of pain as his shoulder took the full impact.

With his breath resounding in his ears he clambered up into the tunnel, his eyes wide and wild, all of his senses scorched with adrenaline.

He thought he heard the displacement of water again, but the cave was behind him now.

Something brushed along his arm, trickled to his elbow, and he wheeled. There was nothing there but the luminous, blue-edged dark. He raised his arm, saw blood dripping from his shoulder, a dark trail against his pale skin. Rafferty ran his fingers across the flow, then brought them to his lips, licking them clean. It was a small comfort.

Now he had stopped he couldn't hear the water anymore.

He tried to find a shred of logic. But common sense had little place when you were under the earth and the terrifying fear that you could lose your way was pounding into your skull.

The terrifying fear that you were being hunted.

He clasped his hands over his head and linked his fingers, his breathing loud and laboured.

All he had to do was follow the tunnel and climb back out of the well.

Up ahead, an overhang of rock, like an inverted arrowhead, clung to the roof. This wasn't the tunnel he had come through.

Rafferty's guts turned to liquid sludge. He forced his feet forwards.

Nothing made sense. There were no rational thoughts in his brain. Instinct took over.

The sound of moving water returned, the lap of it rhythmic and constant. He glanced down.

A sob left his throat.

The water was beneath him. Beneath the ground. And something was travelling through it, mirroring his progress.

This was what Amelia and Grace had been trying to protect him from. What Sebastian had known and kept a secret.

He stumbled on in the strange blue light, his feet slipping in patches of glistening seaweed. His chest tightened and he pressed his hand against it, felt the strong, racing beat of his heart.

Rafferty's world tipped off-kilter. For one moment he'd thought—

But he didn't have time to dwell on that because he could feel the flow of cold air against his skin. Cold, moving air.

His nerves began to tingle, the hairs on his arms rising to meet the energy thrumming through that air.

He followed the draught and found its source. A narrow passageway at ground level, burrowing its way through the rock. Hope burned like a flame in his heart. This might be a way out.

Rafferty dropped onto his front and edged his head and shoulders in first. Strands of seaweed trailed across his face. Gossamer threads of luminous blue lit his way.

Inch by inch, he pulled himself forwards. The cold draught licked against his face and it was this that kept him moving, even when he could feel the sheer weight of the rock pressing down against his spine.

He was crying now, silent tears streaming down his face.

The blue light flared twice. Then faded. The cold draught dropped like a stone.

In the pitch black a noise rolled towards him.

Something rising from deep water. He wasn't sure how he knew.

Because sometimes instinct rules over everything.

He heard it moving over the ground. Slowly, laboriously. A dragging of flesh.

White-hot hysteria flooded his veins. He tried to inhale but had forgotten how, and he was trapped, like a fly in a spider's lair, ripe and ready to devour. His throat closed up, cold sweat prickling through his pores, his heart pounding so fast it felt like it was going to shatter his ribs with its force.

He was going to die. Suffocate on his own fear. And no one would ever find his remains.

Whatever had climbed from the water was in front of him now.

A small cry left his lips. The helpless cry of a bird in a net.

Something wet touched his face. It trailed along his cheek and found the corner of his mouth, probing inside. Salt exploded on his taste buds and he gagged, the movement unclenching his throat. He took a ragged breath. Tried to pull away. Pressure against his skull as something wrapped around it.

He could feel it breathing against him and the stench of rotted meat filled his nostrils, filled every ounce of his being until he felt like this was all he had ever known.

A slithering under his T-shirt, curling its way under his arms, tightening around his waist. Small circles of flesh attached themselves to his skin. Multiple blazes of agony burned through him.

A tugging sensation.

He was lost now, caught in that space between hope and hopelessness, his life held in the grip of something that defied reason.

One last heave and he was free of the imprisonment of rock, his body bent like a pulled bow, his limbs dangling into air.

The suction on his skin released and feeling rushed in, caustic in its intensity. The ground came to meet him, the impact juddering along his spine. White sparks of light in his blind eyes.

Water dripped onto his skin. The weight of something looming in the pitch black.

The blue light rose gently from its sleep, dimly illuminating the walls of the chamber.

Rafferty Henderson was only slightly aware of this light, because his whole focus was on the soulless ichthyic eyes boring into his own.

Chapter Forty-One

When Peter Edwards came out of the church that morning there was already a crowd of people in the graveyard. He didn't need a degree in body language to see that they were angry. Angry *and* scared. A volatile mix.

Seth turned towards him and Peter inwardly groaned. He was not in the mood to be bombarded with questions he couldn't answer. That, added to what he'd done last night, made the smile he conjured for Seth more of a grimace. He could still taste ash on his tongue.

'Have you seen?' Seth pointed across the graveyard, his face pinched with cold. 'More of them, all like the first one. And not just old graves. Henry Roberts has gone, too, and we only put him in the ground four years ago.'

Peter let his eyes rest on the other figures swarming around between the graves. 'It's happened before. You know it's happened before.'

Seth's mouth was a thin, pale line. 'I don't need telling, Peter. I was here.'

'That was a very long time ago, Seth,' Peter said. 'But you know the earth here is liable to subsidence. The whole area sits on a cave system.'

Angus walked towards them, his hands gesticulating wildly. 'You need to come see this.'

Peter did not want to see whatever it was he was talking about, but he didn't really have an option. His mind was still on the journal he had destroyed.

He followed Seth up the pathway towards the crypt. Sweat pricked against the back of his neck.

Four gaping black holes disfigured the ground, like the shaft of an arrow with the crypt at its tip. Peter closed his eyes, willing this all to stop. He was tired, so very tired of keeping secrets.

He wondered where Haven was after their discussion earlier. Felt a twinge of regret he'd been caught up in all of this. A pang of guilt that he had been the one to persuade him to stay.

A chorus of people called his name and pulled him from his preoccupation. He looked at their expectant faces, at the veiled hope beneath the fear. They needed him to fix this. To say something that would alleviate the building panic. He could feel it in the air.

He held his hands aloft, palms up, as though he was standing in the pulpit.

'Now I don't think there's any reason to be alarmed.' There were multiple reasons to be alarmed. 'Yes, it's upsetting that our beloved have been disturbed in their eternal rest, but I'm sure this is purely a natural phenomenon. I will call in a geologist.' He hoped that last part would pour oil on troubled waters.

'A geologist?' Angus scoffed. 'You mean like Tucker? He doesn't know his arse from his elbow.'

'It's the Henderson curse,' someone at the back shouted. 'There'll be no rest for any of us until they're gone. And we all know it.'

There were mutterings of assent all around.

If this had been a few centuries ago Amelia and Grace would have been tarred as witches and driven out. Or something worse.

'And what about that Henderson boy?' Nick spoke from the edge of the crowd. 'What I saw him do. He's a monster.'

I did what I thought was right. The voices faded to a background murmur and he was a younger man, scribbling words in a journal by a light that flickered on and off with the rampaging storm. A testimony of the awful events he had presided over. But now those words were gone.

'Peter?' Seth's voice dragged him into the present. 'What are we going to do about this?'

We meant him, the man trusted to look after their mortal and immortal souls. The collective gaze turned his way.

'I'll contact a professional geologist today. And visit Amelia and Grace. Talk to Rafferty.'

'Talk? What good will talking do?' Nick's cheeks flushed crimson. 'That's not good enough. Not this time. We want them gone. We want all this finished.'

'Look, Peter.' Seth patted him on the shoulder. 'We know all about your no-violence ethics. Of giving people the benefit of the doubt. But this, it's gone too far.'

There were nods of approval and Peter felt the mood of the crowd shift from uneasy trepidation to a determined focus. He tried to find calming words, but the time for words was gone.

They began to disperse, making their way back towards the village. Their steps had purpose in them. He just hoped those steps would take them to the pub and they would lose the fire burning in their bellies.

He waited until the last person drifted away, then trudged up the hill. The open graves lay like black wounds in the earth.

The watery sun slipped behind a bank of grey clouds as Peter opened the door to the crypt. The smell of the stone assaulted his senses. This place had its own stench. He looked at the empty shelves where coffins had once rested and remembered the day

216

they had been removed. Remembered the small boy with the wide eyes in a too-pale face, clutching his brother's hand.

He had no idea then what he would be asked to do. If he had, he would have packed his bags and left without a backwards glance.

Saint Peter's was his church, and he'd taken a certain amount of ribbing from the locals when he first arrived. They said it was a good omen that a man of the cloth and his church carried the same name. He had to admit, back then pride had swelled in his chest for far too long.

Pride goeth before destruction, and a haughty spirit before a fall. Proverbs 16:18.

The perfect truth of the Bible verse wasn't lost on him.

But that was before the coffins were ripped from their rest, before he really understood the lengths Amelia and Grace would go to protect their own.

He might have burned his account of that night but he was part of it, whether he liked it or not, and his soul was tarnished with what he had done to Rafferty Henderson.

CHAPTER FORTY-TWO

Haven read the loose pages. Then he read them again. Waves of incredulity washed over him, but the solid truth was an anchor in its depths.

He turned his head in the direction of the gatehouse. At the secrets that lay within.

Haven climbed out of the car, tucking the pages inside his jacket pocket.

He trudged back through the woods, marched up to the front door, and knocked. The sound echoed within the house. He knocked again, peered through the downstairs window, saw only a small fire burning in the grate. No one came to the door. He tried the handle but the door was locked.

Haven stepped back and ran his tongue over his teeth. Either no one was there or they weren't answering. Not much he could do about either.

With a final frustrated bang on the door with the flat of his hand he admitted defeat and ran out to the lane. He drove back to the village with too much on his mind as the morning headed towards noon.

When he arrived back at the graveyard Tucker was waiting on the bench, a bag of stale bread on his knee. Pigeons strutted around him. They took flight as Haven walked over.

'You look like all the cares in the world are on your shoulders, boy. What's wrong?'

Haven sat beside the old man and rested his elbows on his knees, massaged his temples. Prayed for some kind of clarity.

'It's the knowing, isn't it?' Tucker said, folding the bag and stuffing it into his pocket.

Haven choked back a laugh. 'More like the not knowing. Feeling like the truth is one step ahead of me all the time.'

Tucker smacked his lips, his gaze settling on the crypt.

'Meredith is missing,' Haven blurted out. 'And I don't know what to do.' He studied Tucker's profile. Envied the old man's quiet presence. 'You told her about the house, about the *Marie Claire*.'

It wasn't an accusation, but steel hung on Haven's words.

Tucker nodded. 'That I did. I've always known about those pages.'

Haven unzipped his jacket and drew out Walsh's words. He thrust them towards Tucker.

'Can't see a thing without my glasses. Come home with me and I'll put the kettle on and I can have a read.'

'I haven't got time to drink tea.' Exasperation laced Haven's tone. 'People here are gunning for blood. I need to find Rafferty and Meredith.'

Tucker eased himself up using the arm of the bench.

'You need to look at the details, boy. Have all the facts before you blaze in. You're not thinking straight. You're not seeing.'

Something about the way Tucker looked at him pulled Haven back into the moment. Haven prided himself on noticing detail. Tiny incidental things could add up to facts that changed everything. Tucker knew about the pages. What else did he know?

Heads turned to watch them as they walked down the high street. Eyes drilled into Haven's back, judging him. *Here is a stranger. Everything is his fault.* This place was like living in the fucking Dark Ages.

Tucker turned down a narrow cobblestone alleyway and stopped outside of a weathered door. He unlocked it and ushered Haven inside a tiny scullery that led into a galley kitchen.

'Sit down. Don't mind the mess. I never do.' He took the kettle over to the tap and filled it.

Haven pulled out a chair and sat down at a table covered with an oilskin tablecloth. Detailed geographical drawings lined the walls. They were curled at the edges, yellowing, showing cross sections of terrain.

'What are those?' he asked as Tucker set the kettle on an ancient gas stove.

'They're of this place. Or, to be exact, beneath this place.'

'What's this part?' Haven stood and tapped his finger against a hollowed-out portion.

'That's the tarn, over on the hill.'

'And this?' He tapped the drawing again.

'The layers of rock and the water table. I used to be a geologist before they put me out to pasture. But now no one listens to an old fool like me. They say I ramble, that I should be off in a home where they feed me baby food and wipe my ass.'

Haven laughed, he couldn't help it. 'I get it. People judge you on what they think is right. Their own opinions. They don't ever stop to consider there might be other sides.' He paused then, realised he was talking about himself too.

Tucker grinned and patted his forefinger against his temple. 'Now you're thinking, boy.'

An easy silence passed between them as Tucker rummaged in a cupboard.

Haven closed his eyes. He had to focus, grab hold of the panic threatening to capsize his grip on reality. When he opened them,

Tucker slid a mug of tea across the table, followed it with a chocolate biscuit on a chipped china plate. Something about the gesture made a lump form in Haven's throat. He glanced away, registered something resting against the far wall that formed a question on his tongue.

'I don't think Rafferty Henderson attacked Anna.'

The question disintegrated as Haven's lips parted. 'I saw him, Tucker, in the woods. It was him.'

'You saw someone that looked like him.' Tucker's eyes held his as the old man slurped his tea.

Running footsteps sounded on the cobbles outside. A loud bang on the door.

Haven was up in an instant, putting himself between Tucker and whoever was outside. His fingers tingled with adrenaline.

'Haven!'

The voice outside belonged to Rosa. Haven flung open the door and she rushed in, her cheeks flushed with cold. She wasn't wearing a jacket. Distress lined her brow.

Haven guided her to the chair he'd just vacated and knelt in front of her.

'Tell me,' he said gently. 'Take it slowly.'

Tucker shuffled across. Haven felt the weight of the old man's hand on his shoulder.

Rosa closed her eyes. 'Okay.' A ripple in her throat as she swallowed. 'You need to get to the gatehouse. Now. Seth and Angus were talking in the bar. I overheard them saying they were heading over there.'

Haven looked up at Tucker.

'Go on, boy. Use your instincts. Remember what I told you.'

Haven strode to the door. He paused with his hand on the latch.

'One more thing.' Rosa twisted her hands together on her lap. 'They know Meredith is missing.'

It didn't take a degree in human nature to understand what conclusion they'd come up with.

I don't think Rafferty Henderson attacked Anna.

Tucker's words rang in his ears as he closed the door behind him.

CHAPTER FORTY-THREE

It was the bone-numbing cold that woke her. The cold combined with the slow drip of iced water onto her brow.

Meredith's eyes slowly opened, her lashes crusted with dried mucus. She raised herself up onto one elbow but her sense of balance was gone and she collapsed clumsily onto her side, the hard ground sending a shooting pain across her ribs.

Darkness surrounded her. But an eerie kind of dark, and she couldn't grasp what it was.

Her stomach heaved and a rush of watery vomit erupted from her throat.

Where was she?

Focus, Mere. For God's sake, focus.

She eased herself onto one hip. Her joints complained at the sudden pressure and she rocked to and fro to ease the ache while her brain fought to adjust. There was earth beneath her covered in a fine green algae, the surface slippery under her fingers. Something brushed against her cheek as she gingerly eased herself to her feet, swaying as her blood pressure dropped. A startled noise left her throat. But it was only a plant root sprouting from the wall.

The chamber she was in pulsed with some weird kind of bioluminescence. Trails of blue light spattered upon the rock.

The sound of running water came from somewhere close. And now she remembered what had happened, why her tongue felt heavy and swollen in her mouth.

Grace had drugged her.

She had gone to the gatehouse. She had asked about Rafferty.

The Henderson sisters were doing what they had always done. They had closed ranks to protect their own, no matter the consequences.

Meredith's hand went to her pocket. Her phone wasn't there. No one knew where she was. She realised with a pang of despair that getting out of here was entirely down to her.

I am under the ground.

The thought sliced through her and she had to curl her fingers into her palms, press her nails into the skin. Convince herself that she would be okay.

But she could barely move let alone start clambering over rocks, the after-effects of the tea leaving her with a hangover from hell.

Amelia and Grace had left her here for a reason, and that reason burned inside her skull. But she wouldn't surrender easily. Meredith Evans was as stubborn as the star sign she had been born under.

If they had brought her here there must be a way out. She took a deep breath and edged a few feet away from the wall, managed to stay upright. *So far, so good.*

The chamber she was in only had one opening. Very slowly she edged towards it, one tiny step at a time.

At least it's not pitch black. Small mercies, Mere. Small mercies.

By the time she entered the tunnel, her breath was heavy in her ears, and the real possibility she might die down here dragged its ragged claws across her resolve.

She had been wrong to come back to this place. Wrong to try to find the logic that would put to rest the nightmare from her past. What she had found only amped that nightmare up a thousand percent.

The discovery lay in the glove box of her car. She wondered if anyone would ever find Walsh's words, and if they did, would they simply toss them away?

Meredith paused and rested her shoulder against the wall.

A noise rolled towards her in the blue-edged dark. Footsteps.

'Hello!' Her voice reverberated from the walls. 'I'm down here.'

Slow, measured footsteps. Coming closer.

She peered into the gloom, sweat beading on her brow.

There was someone up ahead. She felt the density of them, watching. Caught the edge of a profile.

'Rafferty?'

An overwhelming relief made her legs tremble. He *must* know a way out.

'Almost. Some might say most definitely yes.'

Her lips pursed. None of what he said made sense. He took a step closer. Meredith studied the boy in front of her. She'd only seen him twice. Once, as he vaulted the gate into the field, and once, standing behind her car, his luminous eyes reflected in her rear-view mirror.

The image in the photo flooded her senses. His chin smeared with blood, the raw offal in his hands.

'Come on,' he said, beckoning with one arm. 'There's a way out through here.'

He vanished into the near dark and Meredith found herself stumbling after him, straining to hear his footsteps as they became fainter and fainter.

The tunnel twisted as she felt her way along its walls, the angle of the ground climbing. It was a good sign.

It opened up into the top of an immense chamber, a cathedral of rock, the blue light ebbing and flowing as if it was singing its own silent song. Water gushed down one wall, carving its way through the rock at its base. Droplets from the spray coated her face. She peered into the waterfall. Thought she could see a figure behind the veil. Rafferty?

A short, narrow ledge led to it, a steep drop at either side.

Meredith steeled herself, focussed her eyes on the wall of water and stepped onto the ledge. That moment of vertigo when instinct *knows* death is but a breath away—and then she was stepping down on the other side, passing through the soft spray at the edge of the waterfall.

'Rafferty!' She called his name but the rushing flow devoured it.

Meredith sank to the floor and buried her head in her hands.

Why had he deserted her?

A forlorn understanding settled upon her then. He had led her here for a reason. The same reason Amelia and Grace had abandoned her.

The knowledge she had pushed behind a stout door in her mind when she had found herself underground spilled out. Irving Walsh had brought something back with him from that Arctic expedition. Had trapped it here hoping it would die.

She'd glimpsed it in the water of the well all those years ago.

Something shifted in the darkness behind her.

Her brain shut down, roaring water thundering in her ears, her world tilting sideways.

The last sense to leave the body is hearing.

A weight dragging across the ground. A fleshy, wet weight. The same sound she had heard in the corridor of Walsh's house, although it was impossible it could have been there.

His sins are imprinted on this house.

A flash as bright as lightning. A brief intramural illumination discharged from a solid shape curled in the dark. Meredith registered a spine and the arch of ribs, the hollow eye sockets in a domed skull. But it was the bones extending from its pelvis that shattered her mind.

Awareness crushed the last shreds of hope from her heart as a tentacle snaked around her wrist and yanked her into the dark.

CHAPTER FORTY-FOUR

Rafferty opened his eyes. There was a small circle of light far above him. A bright light that hurt the back of his eyes and made them water. He swallowed, winced at the burn lining his tongue.

And then he remembered what had happened. It punched into him, hard and callous, and for a moment his mind faded to black. He cradled his belly, the internal bruising kindling a raw ache that took his breath away. The feel of something unfathomable still clung to his skin.

He tried to sit up and groaned—felt like he'd been catapulted against a wall at high speed. A shred of understanding unpeeled itself from the groggy mire in his mind—the circle of light was daylight. He was in a dry well—and despite the pain pounding through his body he dragged himself onto the ladder at the bottom, and rung by rung, hauled his way to the top.

Rafferty climbed out and knelt on the grass, digging his fingers into the soft earth. A grey and miserable sky greeted him but it was so beautiful to a boy who had thought he would die in the dark. Silent tears ran down his cheeks, but determination blossomed in their wake.

He hadn't dreamt the creature. He hadn't dreamt the chamber full of bones. And now he wanted answers.

He set off along the woodland track wearing the wounds of his ordeal, half limping, his clothing ripped, his hair a wild mass of tangles. Rafferty was well past cold now, his body temperature degrees lower than it should be.

A strange kind of hunger throbbed in his belly. A hunger that dipped its roots in thirst. It lay on his tongue, sharpened his senses to a dagger point. Rafferty wiped a trail of drool from the corner of his mouth. His head jerked up and his nostrils flared. He veered right, pushing through a stand of Scots pine, fallen cones littering the ground.

And there was the stream tumbling over small rocks as it made its way through the woods, clear and glacial cold. His foot slipped on a patch of sodden leaves and he skidded down to the stream's edge, his eyes fixed on a mound of wet fleece half in and half out of the water. It was a young lamb, its head floating in the current, one leg skewed at an awkward angle beneath it. Some predator had found it before him, had chewed a deep gash in its belly.

Rafferty splashed through the stream and knelt beside it. He fought with the desire running rampant in his veins, some part of him horrified beyond words at what he wanted to do. He dragged the lamb out of the water and cradled it in his lap, this dead thing that hadn't really had a chance to live.

A fly crawled out of the open wound and he gagged. But the smell of blood, of raw flesh, burned along his nerve endings. He pulled it towards his mouth, and before he knew what he was doing his tongue delved into the torn tissue and its taste exploded on his tongue. He lapped at the wound until there was no blood left on the surface, gnawed at the soft flesh around it, then he drove his fingers into the hole and found the ribcage, splitting it open with a snap of his wrist.

He knew he had overstepped a boundary, from the sanitised food neatly packed in the fridge, to feeding from the newly dead crow, to craving what other carnivores had already discarded.

But this was instinct, and he had no control over it.

He was soaked in blood and gore by the time he had eaten his fill, and the sun had moved round to pierce the branches of the pines that lay to the east.

Birds took flight as Rafferty stood, letting the carcass of the lamb slip back into the stream.

They knew a predator was in their midst.

Now his stomach was full and he turned towards home. He licked the blood from his fingers as he broke into an easy run, his feet knowing the way. A strange calm filled his mind, the kind of calm he didn't remember feeling before.

Took your time to embrace it, Raff.

And this time he smiled.

The smile was still on his lips when voices filtered through the trees. Only ramblers crossing a meadow, but he shrank back into the shadows and bypassed the track, keeping to the stream's eastern bank even though it was packed with dense overhanging foliage.

The wood smoke of home pulled him on. He came to the gatehouse at its rear, creeping around to the front hunched over, his hearing attuned to every sound. A strange car stood parked next to Amelia's. Raised voices came from the gatehouse. His gaze flicked to the open kitchen window, spider webs trailing from its base. It was never open.

If we're threatened, I'll open the kitchen window. Amelia's words from his childhood, words he never thought he would have to heed.

Two people speaking at the same time. A silence. Amelia's heated voice, arguing. His heart began to pound. A crash as something inside fell and shattered, Grace's cry of alarm.

Red mist clouded his vision. His hands curled into fists.

Rafferty took a deep breath and plunged through the door. It careered back against the wall and four faces turned in his

230

direction. Amelia knelt on the ground with Grace's arm around her shoulder. A vase lay in pieces on the fireside rug.

Two men circled the living room, pulling open drawers and scattering their contents. He could smell the sweat on their skin.

They wheeled to face him, expressions set in stone. Rafferty caught his reflection in the mirror on the wall. Blood-soaked, filthy and wet, his face bruised and battered, his eyes wild as a cornered animal.

'Where is she?' the bearded one asked him. 'Where's Meredith Evans?'

Rafferty recoiled from the anger scorching from the words. He shook his head, his hands held up in supplication.

'I don't know,' he said. 'I don't even know her.'

His gaze fell to Amelia. Her face as pale as bleached bone, her eyes rimmed with dark circles. Her lips formed a silent word.

Run.

Rafferty took a step backwards and his heart began to race.

He could see how it looked. A woman had gone missing. He was covered in blood.

The other man dived around the sofa and lunged at him with grasping hands. Rafferty spun out of the way, the man's fingers glancing across his shoulder.

'Rafferty, go!' Grace shouted, her voice breaking, and it was this and the fear wrapped in every syllable that gave his feet wings.

He sprinted down the path towards the car. Rafferty was a boy undone, his brain cartwheeling in overdrive and the flames of self-preservation, blind panic and overpowering fury ruling his limbs. Level with the passenger door, he glanced sideways, saw the figure inside, but it was too late to alter his trajectory. The door swung open and hit him full in the chest, sending him flying backwards onto the gravel. Dust filled his mouth as he tried to stand. And then a weight flung itself upon him and his wrists were pinned to the ground.

He looked up, tried to struggle free, but the weight was much heavier than he was.

'I don't know what kind of trick you pulled at the crypt. But no one threatens me.'

Spittle sprayed over Rafferty's cheek.

The face leering down at him was one he knew all too well.

CHAPTER FORTY-FIVE

Amelia gripped the edge of the Belfast sink in the kitchen until her knuckles screamed in agony. She had tried to stop the car leaving, had battered on the window with her fists, but the faces staring back at her showed no emotion. All apart from the boy in the rear seat. He'd given her the middle finger, his lips curled in disdain, laughed as Rafferty screamed in the boot.

Amelia had never wanted to hurt anyone as much as she wanted to hurt that boy.

It's payback, her inner voice chided. *Payback for what you did to Meredith.*

Amelia hung her head, exhaustion kneading into her muscles.

If only she hadn't been such a rational child. If only she hadn't demanded proof of everything. Why is the sky blue? Why do the seasons turn? Why do people hate us so much?

The questions had run through her veins like red-hot wires and when Meredith had tagged along with Alice on that long-ago summer it had seemed like she was a gift from the gods.

She wanted to be part of them, to be like Alice, to laugh and play under the summer sun, running free in the woods, telling each other stories. And Amelia had such stories to tell, brought up in a house where the sins of the past pulsed in every shadow. Ran in the blood of every male Henderson.

But still she needed proof. Maybe these things were just tales, passed down from generation to generation, gaining strength with each one? Maybe what befell the male line was just bad luck, bad genetics?

She wished Grace had stopped her, but of course she didn't, because when Amelia got a bee in her bonnet nothing could hold her back.

All of her life she had been told the tunnels and chambers that ran beneath their land and the village were dangerous. *Why? Why hadn't someone filled them in?* That there were things that defied reason. *What things?* That had to be left alone. *Why? Why are they dangerous?*

And in her mind, Amelia had come up with a plan, the first of many as she passed through her decades. And as with all plans, especially those birthed by childlike minds, she could see all the glorious ways it could work, could see how it would alter her life. She was right on the latter, but not in the way she had thought.

Amelia sighed and felt the weight she had carried all of her life press down upon her shoulders. She pulled out a chair and sat, her elbows on the scarred table, her head in her hands. The clock ticked in the living room; a lazy winter fly buzzed around the kitchen bin where the bloody wrappings of Rafferty's meals lay. She let herself drift back to that summer day.

Meredith hadn't wanted to go down the well, of course. But she was the youngest and the jammed bucket was the perfect excuse.

Amelia watched as the girl lowered herself, rung by rung. Could almost feel her fear rising up from the dank chill. She had seen the water ripple before Meredith did. Had held her breath as Meredith stretched out her foot . . .

Part of her wanted something to burst out of the water and drag the quaking girl away. She wanted—no, she *needed*—the absolute proof.

She saw something pale drifting in the water, saw the glistening tentacle uncoil as it broke the surface, but Meredith was slight and quick and agile. What could have been a meal emerged from the well in floods of tears.

Meredith marching up to their door last night, laying down her own gauntlet, was a gift. After Sebastian's betrayal, during Rafferty's coming of age. Amelia could sense him untethering and she wasn't sure if her heart could take it.

Giving Meredith to the tunnels was a circle completed. A sacrifice returned. They couldn't risk what she knew leaking out, even though Amelia felt as if this ship was sinking fast, water pouring in through boards long held together with fierce love and loyalty.

Her bones ached with weariness. Who could she go to now?

Grace came into the kitchen, the black-and-white photo clutched in her hand. The edges were curled, the image faded with time.

'It's our fault,' Grace said. 'We started this.' She looked down at the photo.

'We didn't have a choice, Gracie. You know that.' Amelia met her sister's level gaze. 'And besides, we didn't start this. Rafferty did.'

A noise outside made them raise their heads. The slamming of a car door. Amelia looked out of the window, saw a tall man striding up the path. Her brow furrowed. By the time she got to the door he was hammering against it.

She yanked it open and he almost fell in.

'Where's Rafferty?' he asked, pushing past her. 'I need to see him now.'

Agitation pulsed from him in waves.

Amelia straightened her shoulders. 'And who might you be?'

'Listen.' He held out his hands as though a book was splayed across them, pressed them together and brought them to his lips. 'My name is Haven. I knew Sebastian. I know about your family. Your secret. About what Walsh found. But right now my priority is Rafferty. I *have* to get him out of this place. There's a witch hunt going on and I'm fucking scared what they might do to him.'

'You're too late.' Grace's quiet voice from the kitchen doorway. 'They've already taken him. About half an hour ago.'

Haven gritted his teeth. He paced to an armchair and slammed the flat of his hand into a cushion. Drifts of small feathers fluttered into the air from the worn fabric.

Amelia threw down her own gauntlet. 'Why should we trust you, Haven? When everyone else wants us gone. Wants us dead.'

Haven paused. A small laugh from his throat. 'Because I know all this and haven't gone to the police. That would be the mark of a sane person and I'm so far from sane with all of this that I've lost the fucking map. Because Sebastian asked me to help Rafferty. And I think I'm the only one who can.'

Amelia flicked her gaze to her sister. Grace nodded.

'I want you to understand the danger. If you try to help him there's every possibility you will die.'

Amelia delivered this news as calmly as she could. If there was ever a time not to mince words, it was now.

Haven shrugged, snatched a floating feather from the air.

'There's a possibility I could get hit by lightning, but that's never stopped me walking in the rain.'

A smile tugged at Amelia's lips, despite the dread that lay curled in her stomach like a dead bird.

'There's one more thing,' she said. 'I hope you can swim.'

CHAPTER FORTY-SIX

The boot lid came down with a slam and Rafferty was plunged into darkness. It had happened so fast. The boy pinning him to the ground, his wrists tied behind his back with twine, the man with the beard heaving him into the car. It was all noise and chaos. Blood rushing around his head, drowning his thoughts. Amelia and Grace, their pleas falling on deaf ears.

The engine roared to life. Rafferty braced his legs against the boot side and tried to think.

Where were they taking him?

How strong was their level of hate?

His breath hitched in his throat as the car sped along the roads, the twists and turns of his mind mirroring the journey, creating horrifying conclusions he couldn't see a way back from. A change of terrain as the tyres went from a hard surface to something softer. The whine of the engine as it struggled.

At last they came to a halt. Doors opening. Footsteps on gravel. The slight rock of the car as the wind whistled around it.

The shred of logic left in his brain told him this meant he was somewhere remote. On higher ground.

The engine started again and the car moved off but only for a short distance. The sound of a heavy door clanging shut.

He turned his head, and even though he couldn't see anything in front of him he knew there was water nearby.

Time ticked on. Hours. Minutes. It meant nothing. He had only his own thoughts to keep him company. Cramps dug teeth into his muscles and he had to keep shifting around in the enclosed space, very aware that he could die here.

Now look where this has got you.

The voice came out of nowhere.

He laughed, a crazed, coarse sound.

'You're a delusion,' he spat out.

Silence.

Rafferty rocked to and fro and wished the voice would come back.

He was dozing when they returned. Images played behind his eyelids; he could sense the creature from the tunnels. Feel the slippery velvet of the tentacle as it slid across his skin, the sting as the suction cups took hold.

The image shifted and wavered as though water was cascading down upon it.

A shape lay on the ground, one hand resting palm-upwards, fingers curled like the petals of a rose. A woman's hand. And Rafferty knew in that moment that he was looking at Meredith Evans.

A loud bang on the boot lid tore him back to reality, the sound reverberating around his enclosed prison.

The engine started and the car moved off.

Maybe this was what they were going to do. Drive him from place to place. Leave him in the dark until he starved. This could be his coffin.

The car stopped, the engine idling. Voices outside. The boot flipped open. A torch beam shone directly in his face, and he screwed his eyes tight against the glare. Rough hands fastened a blindfold over his eyes.

'I know where Meredith is!' His head jerked from side to side, beseeching faces he couldn't see. 'I swear I didn't touch her.'

Hands on his body, hauling him out.

His legs gave way as they hit the ground, pins and needles shooting through his calves, through his bound wrists.

They dragged him away. Of course he struggled. Of course he knew it was hopeless.

He could smell wet earth, hear the creak of branches in the growing wind. Ozone on the air. And something else—something that made the hairs rise on the nape of his neck. A tingle ran across his skin, like the shiver of a dog when a fly brushes past.

'Let's get this over with,' said a woman's voice. A tight, emotionless voice. 'Before someone comes looking for him.'

'Are you sure?'

'Of course I'm sure. He tried to rip my throat out.'

Rafferty craned his head back and grimaced. Not at the words but because he was trying to catch a glimpse of where he was.

The movement caused the blindfold to slip slightly, a sliver of vision delivered to his darkness. A sob broke from his throat.

There on the hill, in the burgeoning dark, was the crypt.

And there before him was the closest of the collapsed graves to the Henderson family vault.

The first drops of rain spattered his face. Thunder rolled in the distance.

'Someone knows I'm here,' he said, clutching at any straw that came into his terrified mind.

'And who might that be?'

'Haven,' Rafferty said. 'Haven knows I'm here.'

He didn't see the woman look around the graveyard, her lips pursed. Didn't see her shrug as she stepped forward until she was inches from his face.

This close he could smell the wound on her neck, hidden behind an absorbent dressing, wondered what it would feel like to rupture the stitches and sink his teeth into that soft, bruised flesh. It would spill open to him like a ripe peach. His mouth began to water.

'You're a monster,' she hissed. 'I hope you rot in hell.'

Two hands grabbed his shoulders, a piece of scrunched-up cloth was rammed between his lips. A length of material pressed against his mouth, tied roughly behind his head.

Shackled. Blinded. Muted.

His eyes widened behind the cloth as a hand shoved him in the small of his back. They drove him forward until he teetered on the edge of the grave. The scent of the wet earth curled into his nostrils as he sensed the dark, gaping hole, his feet struggling for grip.

A hard push and Rafferty tumbled into the grave, all the breath driven from his lungs as he landed heavily on his stomach. A blinding skewer of pain as his cheekbone shattered. The blindfold slipped down over his nose.

He looked over his shoulder at the sky, at the first pinprick of stars, tried to scream through the gag. Desperate tears ran down his cheeks.

A clod of earth hit his back, followed by another and another. Wet, heavy earth raining down. Instinct zeroed in and he managed to drag his knees beneath him, strained to free his bound hands. But it was futile.

A muffled plea vibrated in his throat, silenced by the gag.

In the end he just shuffled to the end of the hole, pressed his spine into its cold embrace.

It was a very deep grave. They had made sure of it. And he knew that his disappearance would be smoothed over. *The boy ran away. Who could blame him?* Amelia and Grace would search for him, but in the end they would know the truth of what happened, what the villagers did.

They would always think he had murdered Meredith.

Haven would believe he had murdered Meredith. And it was this that Rafferty couldn't bear to dwell on.

Haven. All of his thoughts zoned in on the man he barely knew. The man Sebastian had confided in, the man who said he would help.

The earth came down heavier now, as though everyone above had claimed a shovel and was determined to bury him quickly. To bury their own sins.

It was pointless to struggle as the soil pinned his knees, his waist, his chest, against the grave side. All of his life he had been told to keep away from the water, but no one ever warned him about drowning in earth. Of suffocating, his last breaths gasped into a solid mass invading his nose and throat.

And now you suffer, said the voice. *You suffer like I did. Your turn to feel your life torn from you.*

There's a point beyond terror, where your mind unlatches itself from reality. Rafferty reached that point as the earth pressed tight against his throat.

Now you die.

CHAPTER FORTY-SEVEN

Haven drove back to the village breaking every speed limit on the way. His mind was teeming with images, with questions. Every junction and slowly moving car scraped away at the remaining shreds of his patience.

He needed to get back to Tucker, felt that the old man could answer some of his questions, but the overwhelming concern over what was happening to Rafferty made his skin feel like it was shrinking over his bones.

He pulled into a parking spot outside a newsagent, cutting up a van that was trying to back in. The driver flung his hands up, mouthed an obscenity. Haven ignored the desire to drag the guy out by his collar and slam him against his van.

He sprinted along the pavement, grateful that people moved out of his way, and wondered if they knew that a boy was in danger and were simply ignoring the fact because they didn't want to get their hands dirty, would say afterwards *oh, that's a shame* and carry on without another thought.

As he approached the cobbled lane where Tucker lived, Rosa turned onto the street, her shoulders hunched. She quickened her steps when she saw him, pointed to a nearby alleyway littered with fast food wrappings.

Haven slipped in after her.

She grabbed his arm and pulled him into a doorway. Her face was ashen, her lips almost the same colour as her skin.

'They took him,' Haven said, in answer to the silent question in her eyes.

Her throat rippled. 'I went back to the pub after you left, overheard Nick saying he'd seen Seth's car ploughing up the hill by Laird Banyon's place.' She paused, and a flash of anger flared in her eyes. 'He sounded so triumphant, Haven. Made me want to throw up.'

Haven chewed the edge of a thumbnail as Rosa's words formed dots across his visualisation. He tried to join them together. *Why would someone take a car up a muddy field when they had a truck?*

'Seth rarely uses his car.' Rosa's mouth twisted in thought. Then her jaw fell slightly and her hand tightened on his arm. 'They took the car because you can't hide anyone in a flatbed truck.'

A rush of exhilaration warmed his skin. He flung his arm around her shoulders, and she raised her face, her smile a little brighter.

'I'm going to check out Banyon's place. If Rafferty is there, I'll find him. Can you keep an eye on Tucker?'

She nodded. 'I'm guessing he'll be in the pub anyway. What makes you think he needs looking after?'

'Because he knows too much about Walsh and I don't want anyone getting to him if they know he's spoken to me.'

Rosa nodded. 'Give me your number.'

He read it out and she entered it into her phone.

'Have you heard anything from Meredith?' she asked.

He contemplated skimming over the truth, but fuck it. This place had too many secrets. His jaw tightened. 'I found her car in the woods. Someone tried to hide it.'

Rosa swore softly under her breath.

However you looked at it, it didn't seem hopeful.

'Did you see the drawings on Tucker's wall?' He changed the subject because he didn't want his mind dwelling on the awful possibility hovering above it. 'Can you tell me anything about the geology of this place?'

She pulled at a loose strand of hair. 'Well, it's in a valley, obviously. And there's the tarn up on the hill. We warn people about going up there though. It's like a big half egg, deep, really dangerous. The whole hillside is a series of chambers and tunnels, goes back to Roman times. We're five miles from the sea but people say smugglers stashed stuff there. The tunnels were used up until the last war, I think, but there are stories of people going down there and never coming back up. When I was a little girl one of the tunnels caved in and killed a scout master and three of his group. All the entrances were sealed up then.'

Could the collapsed graves have something to do with this? Why hadn't Peter mentioned it?

Haven remembered kneeling in the empty grave in the pouring rain and reaching into the dark, relived the image of Rafferty rocking to and fro by the same grave.

. . . there are stories of people going down there and never coming back up.

He remembered the loose pages, Irving Walsh's words imprinted on his mind.

Jesus Christ. Meredith was right. The creature from the *Marie Claire* wasn't just in the well, it was in the fucking tunnels.

Gooseflesh crept over his skin.

'Haven?'

Rosa jerked him out of the icy pit he had fallen into.

'Sorry, just thinking,' he said. He didn't have the words to tell her what had dawned on him, the sheer repellent horror of it. He dredged up a smile.

'I'll leave first,' he said, glancing towards the high street. 'I don't think being seen together is a good idea.'

'You're not my type either,' she said, her expression relaxing. It took a moment for him to catch on, and he arched an eyebrow. She laughed.

He could see why Sebastian had hooked up with her, and wondered with a pang of anguish if Sebastian and Rosa might have had a chance if his surname hadn't been Henderson.

Haven stole out onto the street, climbed into Rosa's car, and sped away.

Dark clouds brimmed on the horizon as Haven tucked the car against a hedgerow. It was asking for trouble driving up to the farm, a vehicle announcing his arrival far more than a single figure on foot. He doubted Rosa's little Toyota could negotiate the gradient anyway.

He slipped into the field and skirted the bottom hedgerow, making his way up the hill with the cover of the woodland on his right.

Curious sheep raised their heads as he crossed the field. A few scattered, running to the shelter of an old tin shack. He wondered if they could sense his agitation.

Cold nipped at his exposed skin as winter twilight hovered in the wings.

He approached the barn from the rear, clambering up a rocky slope, wincing as a few small stones clattered down the incline.

A stiff breeze tugged at his hair as he crept around the sides. The barn was constructed from corrugated metal panels bolted together. The door, when he came to it, was shut, padlocked with a hefty chain. There were no windows.

He resisted the urge to slam his palm against the metal. If Rafferty was inside, Haven couldn't get to him.

His gaze skimmed over the yard and the other outbuildings. There were no cars, only a tractor parked by a diesel pump. The farmhouse stood along a narrow track, piebald dairy cows grazing in the adjacent field.

Haven stole across the yard. He bit the inside of his cheek. Was Rafferty in the farmhouse? *No, if they thought he was dangerous they would keep him in the barn.*

He leaned his head to one side as the tension strung along his shoulders notched up another degree. A gust of wind buffeted him from behind and he turned. Through a bank of tall pine trees the pewter back of the tarn glinted in the fading light. A haze of white breath escaped his lips.

I hope you can swim. Amelia's words slapped him across the cheek.

He set off in the direction of the tarn, his focus on the line of water beyond the thin-boned trees. Another fear had latched onto the layers already lining his gut.

What if they had brought Rafferty here? *What if they were going to drown him?*

Chapter Forty-Eight

Rafferty took his last hitched breath as the earth rained down against his face.

It was a hard-won breath as the sodden earth pressed tight against his throat, his body immovable. And then darkness as his sight was taken, as all sense of hearing became dulled. Soil filled his ears, pressed against his tightly closed eyes. He tried to breathe again but there was no air in this nightmare realm.

Panic raged through him, hot and feral, the adrenaline in his veins telling him to run, to fight, but both were impossible. His lungs began to burn and he longed for the liquid embrace of water, something he'd never had.

But thoughts were gruelling now, his brain sluggish as the oxygen in his blood dwindled.

This is how all monsters should die.

He was beyond most coherent understanding when the tugging started. Beyond the comprehension his body was being dragged down through the wet soil, inch by inch.

Whatever held him was wrapped around his ankles, its grip tight and unyielding, the pressure bruising his flesh. And as it pulled him farther down into the earth, its hold slithered up his limbs. Now around his knees, his thighs.

His downward journey quickened, at some point his body going from his upright position to angled, then horizontal. But Rafferty wasn't aware of this because his heartbeat had stopped.

What pulled him from his grave knew nothing of cardiopulmonary resuscitation. Air was not its natural element, but it could exist on land for a short while and it understood his fundamental need at this point.

For now.

A moist tentacle probed between his lips, scooping out the soil in his mouth. Another penetrated his nostrils, sucking out the earth packed within. It was a delicate process for one who was used to delivering death, and blood did flow from Rafferty Henderson. It was perhaps a mercy he knew nothing of this, knew nothing of the tentacle sliding down his throat to drain the fragments of soil from his lungs, the sandpaper tongue that lapped the salt from his skin.

The creature took Rafferty's head between its hands, hands it rarely used, elongated fingers cradling his skull. A skull it could crush in an instant. It leaned over him, pressed a cold-lipped mouth against his, and exhaled.

But his body remained lifeless.

Another tentacle uncoiled from amidst the creature's hair. One as pink and glossy as a skinned rabbit. It probed beneath his T-shirt and wrapped around his chest, small suckers attaching to his skin.

A burst of electricity surged through it, its skeletal form visible for an instant through its flesh. Rafferty's body jolted at the rapid shock.

Again the creature tried, increasing the surge.

If this failed it would peel away his limbs and suck his tender organs out one by one.

It took all of four attempts for his chest to finally rise. It let the suckers fall away but kept on breathing for him until it felt Rafferty's throat constrict as he fought for his own breath. He spluttered and coughed, rolled onto his side instinctively and threw up a watery, soil-laced sludge.

His eyes opened. Sluggish, conscious thought erupted from the near-death he had hovered against. The linings of his throat and nose burned, each inhalation searing delicate tissue. Tears streamed down his face as tiny particles of soil watered from his eyes.

He'd been buried. The memory caught him, so real and so fresh it was as if a dagger was slowly gutting him. The tangible pain of it knifed through his body and he curled his arms around his knees, rocked to and fro as his mind tried to make sense of what had happened.

Gradually, his breathing settled into a regular pattern. His eyes flicked around his surroundings. That same bioluminescence from before lit the cavern he was in. Water glistened on its walls, the run-off gathering at the bottom and trickling into a pool sunk into the chamber floor. The air was heavy with the scent of brine, of the ocean.

The nape of his neck prickled, each tiny hair rising in unison.

He looked over his shoulder and found the creature sitting in the shadows, its ichthyic tail dipped into the pool. Small ripples fanned out from it.

He should have been afraid but he found that he wasn't. This was the second time it had saved him. Yet looking at its face was still something he was leery of, as if all the tentacles amidst its strands of ragged hair would rip him apart for the offence.

He stood, his hands using the cavern wall for leverage as his legs trembled. Slowly, he made his way towards the pool, finding it was easier to focus his attention there, to look at its quivering reflection.

His gaze travelled to a natural shelf in the cavern wall where two rock formations had merged eons ago. There, heaped on top of each other, were neatly stacked skulls, dozens of them, all sizes. On another shelf lay arched ribcages, another the curved cups of pelvic girdles.

This place was a gallery, a repository for remains. Something to look upon in contentment.

His jaw dropped as awareness bloomed in his ever-opening mind. The creature was the one who had created the tunnels, had made the graves collapse and ransacked the contents.

For food.

He could smell the creature keenly now that he was closer, could see the scaly membrane covering its powerful tail, the polar white iridescence flecked with arctic blue. As though it knew, the tail lashed the water once and Rafferty's heart shot into his throat. Very slowly he let his eyes track higher. The tail ended, merged into a pale-as-milk torso most definitely human, but Rafferty wasn't sure of its gender, if it had a gender at all. As if that really mattered.

His gaze fell to the water, at his reflection with the bioluminescence on the cavern roof surrounding his form, phosphorescent blue stars drowning beside him. The roar of the ocean filled his ears as if he had pressed a conch shell against them.

Hunger jolted through his frame, a savage urge that uncurled from his core, turned his senses into one unified probe for sustenance. He swallowed . . . thought about the flesh that had once clung to the lonely bones on the shelves, how alive it would make him feel to hunt and maim and devour.

'What am I?' he asked, his words echoing back from the rock walls. 'Why did you save me?'

The tentacles writhed upon the creature's head.

Careful, Raff, came the voice he knew. *What makes you think this one is on your side?*

He thought he heard a slow peal of mocking laughter rolling from the shadows, but when his gaze flicked across it was just an empty space.

A screech emitted from the creature. A harsh, shrill sound like all the seabirds of the ocean had all cried out at once. Rafferty clasped his hands over his ears but the sound was already ricocheting around his skull. His nose began to bleed.

The creature plunged into the pool. Water droplets sprayed against his face and Rafferty dropped to his knees.

A desperate fear spiked through him and he frantically searched for its form in the water's depths.

'Don't leave me.' It was a whisper that should have been a shout, but hope was a trapped moth battering itself against a window.

He couldn't face death for a third time.

Tentatively, he dipped his hand into the freezing pool. He wondered how deep it was and the childhood dread rose and impaled him, Sebastian's warning pulsing through his mind. He remembered going under and the stinging water in his eyes, greedily rushing up his nose and down his throat. The corroded bite of it all, the terror that came with it.

Now he could see the creature racing up from the pool depths, a sleek, fast form, its tail propelling it like a missile. It burst through the surface, water streaming from its body, its gaze settling on his face. He didn't have time to look away, didn't have time to react as it wrapped a tentacle around his waist and wrenched him into the water.

CHAPTER FORTY-NINE

Peter Edwards knelt in front of the altar, his hands clasped, his head bowed. He prayed for a clear mind. He prayed for deliverance. He prayed for forgiveness.

But he knew he did not deserve any of these things.

He had hidden in the vestry whilst members of his congregation buried Rafferty Henderson alive. Whatever the boy was, he did not deserve that. The weight of this guilt would plague him for the rest of his days.

Maybe it was all his fault anyway. If he hadn't been swayed by the sisters' persuasion . . . There was something in Rafferty that shouldn't be there. Maybe he had failed and it had taken him this long to admit it. Back then he'd been needled by the font incident, incensed by the desecration. He hadn't thought it through as he arrived at the gatehouse nine long years ago, was sure in some part of him it wouldn't even be necessary, that the sisters were only overreacting.

It was Sebastian who had opened the door, who led him up the creaking staircase to a room at the back of the gatehouse. Amelia stood at one side of the bed, Grace at the other, the small form of Rafferty between them, his eyes closed. His feet and hands were tied to each corner of the bed, thick ropes entwining his slim wrists and ankles. Alarm accelerated Peter's heartbeat. The boy was only six years old.

Candles lit the room on every surface, the scent of beeswax almost overpowering. A dark blue glass bottle sat on the nightstand. Peter's eyes flicked towards it.

'We've just given him something to calm him down,' Amelia said, by way of a greeting. 'To calm them both down.'

This was the moment Peter should have turned tail and run, the moment when he realised the sisters meant him to go through with this. He was very aware he had not sought permission from the bishop, that Rafferty had not been assessed by a psychiatrist and a physician. He had not performed a blessing on the gatehouse and all those that lived under its roof and had no experience with the craft of deliverance. He was playing with literal hellfire.

Sebastian closed the door to the bedroom and leaned against it, his face ashen.

Peter cleared his throat, uttered a prayer for the house. 'Visit this place, O Lord, we pray, and drive far from it the snares of the enemy; may your holy angels dwell with us and guard us in peace, and may your blessing be always upon us; through Jesus Christ our Lord. Amen.'

His words fell into a thick silence punctuated only by the tick of the clock on the wall.

Peter stood at the foot of the bed, all eyes upon him. If truth be told, he did not have the tools of redemption with him, only his faith, a bottle containing holy water, and his personal Bible. He raised his hand to deliver another prayer, and he felt it then, the presence of *something else* in the room. If he'd been asked he couldn't have explained it, he just knew by the way the skin on his scalp had tightened.

Rafferty stirred on the bed, his lips moving silently. Grace leaned over and pressed a damp cloth to his brow.

'Hurry, Peter,' Amelia said. 'He knows what we want to do.' The rope around Rafferty's wrists strained as he tried to sit up.

Did Amelia mean Rafferty or the other inside him?

'Help him, please.' Sebastian's urgent whisper from the corner.

A gust of wind hit the window and the glass rattled.

The candles flickered as one, then snuffed out, plunging the room into darkness.

The flare of a match as Amelia lit the closest candle, her shadow rising behind her on the wall.

Peter moved to Rafferty's side and knelt on the floor. Laid his hands over the boy's heart. He couldn't feel it beating and the bitter tang of fear flooded his mouth.

Grace took his hand and moved it across to the right side of Rafferty's chest. And there it was, the fast rhythmic *thud-thud* of a small boy's heart.

She met his astonished gaze, her eyes dark in the candle glow.

A small laugh fell from Rafferty's lips as they curled into a smile.

'Go away, little man. We don't want to play with you.'

Peter jerked his hand back and cradled it to his chest as though touching Rafferty had burned him. There was something at play here. Something unearthly.

An idea sprang to his mind, an idea that had no bearing on the church or its ideologies. This was a child he was dealing with.

'There is no we,' Peter said. 'Only Rafferty.'

The boy's tongue protruded over his lip, saliva glistening at its tip. His eyes flew open.

'There has always been we, right from the start.' It was a petulant voice now. His bottom lip jutted out.

Peter glanced across to Grace, a black-and-white photo clutched in her fingers.

'Only Rafferty,' Peter repeated. 'Only Rafferty. Only Rafferty.'

The boy began to thrash on the bed, limbs straining against the imprisonment of rope.

'No!' A screech came from him, a sound like chalk dragging across a blackboard. It made the fillings in Peter's teeth ache. 'No, I am here too!'

'And who are you?' Peter said, quite prepared for some demonic name, some utterance of an ancient tongue.

'Raphael, I'm Raphael.'

A gasp came from Grace, and Amelia put her hand on her sister's arm.

Peter wanted to ask more but the boy was agitated now and he knew he had to persevere.

'There is no Raphael, only Rafferty.'

The boy's head whipped from side to side, tension corded along his neck. His teeth were gritted, saliva foam bubbling on his lips.

'Amelia, please.' An entreaty from Grace.

'It's okay, Gracie. This is for Rafferty, you know that.'

A wail came from the boy's lips then, a sound of such distress that Sebastian rushed forward, tried to push Peter away.

'There is no Raphael—' But Peter did not have a chance to finish his sentence.

Rafferty's body contorted, his spine curving into a pulled bow. He hung there for what seemed like an impossibly long time, a time where Peter's knees were rooted to the hard floor, a time where he lost the ability for coherent thought. With a shudder Rafferty collapsed on the bed and Grace emitted a strangled sob. Blood ran from the boy's nose, a steady stream that followed the contour of his lips. His tongue snaked out, lapping at his own blood with a desperation Peter could almost smell. Small fingers curled into claws, the veins in his arms standing out. Sweat beaded on his brow, then ran into his eyes. They were dazed, the pupils fixed and dilated.

A cry left his lips. A soft cry with an exhalation of breath.

And then Rafferty Henderson stilled.

Chaos erupted. Grace flung herself to Rafferty's side, her fingers on his wrist, frantically searching for a pulse.

Peter stood and backed away, his hand over his mouth. His ill-conceived actions had murdered a child. His legs gave way and he sank to the floor, watching as Sebastian launched himself onto the bed, cradled his brother's head in his hands, whispering his name over and over.

But it was Amelia who stepped away from the bed, who looked into the shadows, a grim smile on her face.

'Go, now,' she whispered. 'Be at rest.'

The window flew open, crashing back against the wall, sending glass scattering into the night, the curtains sucked outward.

Grace threw her body over Rafferty's, tears staining her face. A trickle of blood ran from her nose and Peter found himself thinking it was like an echo from Rafferty, an echo she had taken within herself to share his pain.

His gaze fell to the discarded photo on the bed. An ultrasound photo.

A sound then, like something had inhaled all the air from the room, leaving only a vacuum. A shriek of wretchedness from deep in the woods.

Rafferty Henderson took a ragged breath as his heart began to beat.

CHAPTER FIFTY

Sheets of rain fell from the sky as Haven ran towards the tarn. The heavens had opened as soon as his thoughts had spun towards the body of water in front of him. As though it was trying to keep him away.

The deluge stung his eyes, plastered his hair to his face, soaked through his clothes as if they were paper. This place was out to drown him. This place was out to drown everything it considered a threat.

A north wind screamed down from the hills, skipping across the tarn, churning its surface, bending the stand of pines to its fury.

Questions pounded inside his skull. But there were no answers to be found in this impossible scenario he'd willingly wandered into.

There was barely any grip in the muddy field as he half ran, half stumbled his way across it. His boots sank, ankle-deep, and he had to drag each step from the quagmire, sludge weighting his feet, making it difficult to keep any kind of speed.

But he had to get to the tarn. *No one in their right minds will be out on a night like this.* But the villagers were not in possession of right minds, only ones blighted by the past.

A few days ago he would have laughed at the preposterous idea of normal, rational people drowning a boy intentionally because of some ingrained tale from over a hundred years ago. Now he knew they would do it in a heartbeat if it could stop whatever was going on. That they would sacrifice Rafferty then go back to living a totally ordinary life. If his body was ever discovered they'd throw up their hands in mock horror, put it down to the unsafe terrain and a boy driven by grief who didn't watch where he was going.

Thunder rumbled in the distance as he reached the edge of the tarn, the hills beyond cloaked by the dark and the driving rain. He ran west along its bank, the sound of his own breathing in his ears, his desperate heartbeat thudding in his chest.

Tucker's words about Rafferty filled the space between beats.

If it wasn't Rafferty who attacked Anna, who was it?

The evidence was undeniable. The day Haven had met him his sweatshirt was blood-soaked. The photo of Rafferty scavenging the waste from the butcher's bin. The attack on Anna where he'd been clearly identified. Meredith's disappearance.

Haven didn't want to dwell on these thoughts. Sebastian had said Rafferty wasn't as he seemed and once again Haven's exasperation flared. *Damn you, Sebastian, for not telling me more.* But soon shame doused that exasperation. Sebastian had thrown himself into a raging river because he'd been driven to the brink over something he couldn't see a way out of.

You're so fucking determined, Haven. So focussed. How do you do it? How do you not let the demons win?

The image was crystal clear in Haven's mind as he stumbled along the edge of the tarn, the unrest of the water in sync with his own turmoil. A bolt of lightning forked across the sky as though to imprint the message in Sebastian's words against Haven's skull.

Haven remembered saluting Sebastian with his beer bottle, the pleasant alcohol buzz fizzing through his veins. He'd taken it as a compliment, felt a glow of accomplishment, never realising it was this moment that Sebastian had earmarked him as Rafferty's saviour and begun his friend's savage decline.

The wind changed direction abruptly, lashing his soaking hair against his face. He swept it back and re-tied it, had an overwhelming desire to hack it all off because it was a front, a smokescreen to others, a way to fit in and observe from the shadows.

A harsh laugh left his lips. It turned out he didn't need to look in the alternative underground clubs for terrible things that defied logic, they were here, alive and kicking and starving, in a little pocket of rural England.

For fuck's sake, just hurry.

The thought drummed into his brain as he ran, as the thunder rolled over the invisible hills and the lightning came in staccato bursts of fire.

He was grateful for it though, as it lit up the shore in front of him, made him feel less alone. Made him realise that there was no angry mob here. Either he was too late or his hunch had been catastrophically wrong. He stopped, all the adrenaline in his limbs fizzling out. Despair turned its gaze upon him.

Another staccato burst imprinted itself on his retinas.

A craggy mound stood by the tarn's edge about a hundred feet away, glacial till left over from the Ice Age. For a split second, the outline of a figure against the mass.

Haven set off again, new focus in his veins. He reached the bottom of the mound. Stared up at the unwelcoming wall of rock. Ran his hand over the soaking, slippery surface.

He couldn't climb this. It would be suicidal.

And then, through the howl of the wind and the lashing of the rain, another sound met his ears. A forceful, rhythmic sound.

At first he thought he was imagining it, but as it continued he turned his face towards the source. It was coming from inside the mound.

He stumbled around the base, looking for an entrance, his hands blindly fumbling over the rock, using it as a guide. In the lee of an overhanging ledge, a small stream of light spilled out from a crevice.

Haven paused and listened. It was quieter here, away from the onslaught of weather. The sound came again. He eased himself into the narrow vertical crevice, the rock face taking him in its jaws. Sidestep by sidestep he wriggled through, afraid of what he might find at the other end.

Dread curled through his veins, insisting he was going to be too late. That the sound was someone tearing a hole in the rock to bury the lifeless body of Rafferty Henderson.

The noise stopped, and as Haven emerged from the crevice he was met by the swinging light of a lantern, a distorted face behind the glass.

'Help me, boy. I can't swing this like I used to.'

The figure behind the lantern was Tucker. Of all the people Haven had expected to meet, Tucker wasn't one of them. Haven's jaw opened, then closed, any words he wanted to say dissolved by surprise.

'Look lively, we can't stay up here all night and this needs to be done.'

At Tucker's feet lay the item Haven had seen resting against the old man's kitchen wall, the item that had been propped against the tree when Haven had jumped into the open grave. A pickaxe.

Tucker lowered the lantern to show a deep hole disappearing into the rock.

Haven crouched and stared into the dark chasm, stared up at Tucker.

'Before you ask, I haven't lost my marbles. This hole and me are old friends. I've bled in it. Sweated in it. Cried in it. We go back thirty years and I'm not about to give up on it now.'

'You've been digging for thirty years?' Haven heard the incredulous note on his own voice, but Tucker brushed it off.

'You know what Walsh brought back, boy. And I reckon you're savvy enough to know that it's still down there because it can't get out. Those drawings on my wall, I know them off by heart, and I know that this strata of rock is the only thing between the chambers under this place and a route to the ocean. Walsh knew what he was doing when he trapped it down here. He thought it would starve, but it's canny. It found a way to the churchyard, started taking bodies from the graves . . .'

Haven took the pickaxe in his hands as Tucker paused for breath. Answers began to fall into place. What he'd felt when he stretched his arm out into the tunnel as he knelt in the grave had been that creature. A violent shiver made his arms jerk. He gripped the pickaxe handle tighter.

'They took Rafferty,' he said. 'And I can't find him.'

Tucker's hand came to rest on his shoulder.

'I'm going to tell you something now and you have to promise me that you'll not run and try to fix this your way.'

Haven looked up at the old man, at the rain streaming down his face, dripping from his nose. He nodded.

'When I came up here I saw lights in the graveyard. Only a few, mind. They didn't want to attract attention. But I know the lay of the land and I know they were gathered around the collapsed grave nearest the crypt. I think Rafferty was with them.'

'Jesus.' Ice formed in Haven's veins. 'Those bastards buried him, didn't they?'

An overwhelming grief took the breath from Haven's lungs. He lowered his head, wanting to fall into the chasm and give himself to the darkness. For all of his efforts, he was too late. He wanted to tear someone apart for what they'd done.

'That they did. But I don't think he was dead when they did it.'

261

Haven didn't think it could get any worse. His mind couldn't comprehend the abject terror of it all. His own guilt was as sharp as the pickaxe blade, jabbing into his skull, reminding him of his own failures.

'All I can offer you, boy, is to not give up hope. There are things at play here that defy logic, you know that. If we can shatter that rock, give it a way out, it might yet save Rafferty.'

Haven gritted his teeth and lowered himself into the hole, the wan light from the lantern hardly piercing the dark.

He swung the pickaxe over his shoulder and sent all of his fury into the blow.

CHAPTER FIFTY-ONE

Candles burned on the hearth and mantel.

Dried herbs were sprinkled along each window sill and doorway; dill and parsley and oregano for protection. Bunches of dried lavender from the garden had been tied around each doorknob.

In front of the fire was a large copper bowl filled with salt water. It tied them to the sea, where it all began. Shells dotted the bottom: the fanned pink and white of a scallop, the inky blue of a common mussel, the straight lines of a pod razor. Shells the sisters had gathered from seashores they had trodden all of their lives, shells they had hidden away for a moment such as this. A moment they prayed would never come.

The Henderson women were pragmatic and unpretentious, and they had a deep respect for nature and the earth around them. How could they not, given the burden their name carried?

Grace stared out of the window into the blackness beyond. Hoping to see the mop-haired boy she loved so much.

'We knew it might have had consequences,' Amelia said softly, coming to stand by her sister's shoulder. 'But we did what we thought was right.' As always, Amelia blamed herself for any mistake. Any dropped stitch in the haunted fabric of their lives.

Nine years ago they had asked Peter Edwards to tear away the part of Rafferty that might have turned their sweet boy into the monster others thought he was, and they had nearly lost him in the process. Nine years where they had settled into a comfortable hum of living, or at least as comfortable as a Henderson could get.

'Come and sit,' Amelia said, taking Grace's hand.

They went to the fireside where the copper bowl glowed in the flickering flames. Rain drummed on the roof, splashed from the gutters.

Something still dwelled in the caverns and tunnels that ran like a labyrinth under the village. Something Irving Walsh had torn from its home. Something Amelia had only glimpsed. But you do not have to see a thing to know that it exists. They felt it as they walked in the rain by the tarn. Stared down into the black maw of the well. They grieved at its influence as one after another they lost the ones they loved.

Rafferty was the last, and they had both hoped he might be spared, some benevolent gesture from something that had toyed with their family so cruelly over the years. But it was not to be.

Unless.

Whatever was happening to Rafferty was out of their control. But they felt the horror of it unfurling innumerable legs under their skin. Felt the utter despair. The hellish terror of a world that had never treated him kindly, upping its remorseless game.

Rafferty wasn't a monster, despite what he ate. He was a victim. A victim of circumstance and a family who should have stopped breeding decades ago.

A gust of wind battered against the front of the house, making the curtains twitch in the draught. The candles on the mantel snuffed out. They both turned and watched the tendrils of smoke wafting from the spent wicks.

The water in the bowl began to tremble and the scent of the ocean rose from the gaps in the floorboards.

'It's time,' Amelia said.

The sisters rose and embraced each other. There were no tears, no words of sorrow. They both knew what they had to do.

The door creaked open and all they could see was the rain falling outside, a constant barrage of water from the heavens, as though the seas had taken hold of the sky.

They went out of the gatehouse, leaving the door wide open. They got into the car and drove along the narrow country lanes that skirted the village. They saw no one.

Amelia took the pebbled track that led up to the tarn. The car lurched over the slippery, uneven surface, tyres scrabbling for grip, the engine wailing in protest as Amelia forced it onwards.

The track ended at a gate and the sisters climbed out of the car. Sheets of rain battered against their faces, blinding them as they pushed forward against the wind, hand in hand.

In the distance was the tarn, and all their senses were tuned towards its glistening back.

They crossed over the field Haven had journeyed through, their feet sinking into the mire. It was a long and arduous pilgrimage for those who had decades in their bones.

But one thing the Henderson sisters did have was pure, unadulterated grit. They had one more card to play.

At last the mud gave way to patches of coarse grass pushing through shingle. The wind dropped and gave them a slight reprieve from the chilling cold. They pushed on through the line of tall pines, their feet crunching on brittle fallen cones.

The tarn lay before them, black and deep and brooding. Holding its secrets close. Holding the transgression of the blighted past.

If a chest can feel its heart shattering, they felt it then, an indescribable anguish that wanted to rant and scream and destroy. Fury that they had been unable to protect Rafferty from the consequences of his tarnished bloodline.

They had only one thing to offer on the slim chance he may be alive somewhere beneath the ground. Beneath the water.

Because that's where the creature had been torn from.

As it begins, so it ends.

Hand in hand they walked into the tarn, gasping as the arctic chill of the water wrapped around their knees, their chests, their throats.

A sacrifice from the sisters, a freely given offering to what dwelt here in the vain hope it might save the life of the boy they both so deeply loved.

A black-and-white photo floated on the surface of the water. A foetal ultrasound showing two tiny forms. Two tiny heartbeats. It was the only time anyone knew there was more than one, because on the next scan only one heartbeat blipped away on the machine.

A vanishing twin, they called it, the tissue absorbed by the remaining form. But Rafferty Henderson had devoured his twin in the womb purposefully, because his nature was shaped before he was.

CHAPTER FIFTY-TWO

Haven continued to swing the pickaxe even though the blisters on his palms had burst. He hung on to the sting as sweat ran into his eyes, telling himself that each blow was taking him closer to the tunnels. Tucker urged him on from above, the old man's voice becoming fainter as Haven dug deeper.

'What can you see?' Tucker shouted.

Haven paused, wiped his arm over his face. He took out his phone and angled the torch beam.

'Fucking rocks,' he said, and above him Tucker snorted.

'Do any of them look different?'

Haven crouched and focussed a little closer.

'There's a fracture hazing across the rock diagonally, then it slopes away.'

'Good, good,' Tucker said. 'You're closer now. That's a fault where two plates meet. Concentrate on that bit and you should break through.'

Haven swung the pickaxe again, the impact of the blade sending juddering stabs of pain through his arms and shoulders.

You are fucking insane, a small voice told him. *Digging a hole in a rock while Rafferty lies cold and dead in the ground.*

He knew damn well it didn't make sense, that if he tried to explain this to anyone they would think he was delusional. And maybe that's what people like Seth and Angus relied on. The impossibility of that information drifting off into the modern world.

Tucker is right. You know he's right.

Haven kept that at the front of his mind as he chipped away at the unforgiving rock.

He felt the structure of it change suddenly and with his next blow the fragments of rock didn't just fly around him; he heard the crumble of them beneath the ground.

'I think I'm close,' he yelled.

'Hold on, boy, I'm coming down.'

Haven turned and was about to tell the old man it was too dangerous but Tucker was already easing himself down the shaft Haven had dug, the lantern swinging on his arm.

'There's things I need to tell you before you go in,' Tucker said as his feet met the small space where Haven stood.

'Go in?' Haven's brows shot up. But really it wasn't up for discussion. He'd known he'd be going in the moment he picked up the axe.

Tucker thumped him gently on the chest. 'A bit of night and a bit of rain won't kill me, boy. I wish these legs were as young as yours, I'd be with you then. But this is all in your hands now.' Tears glinted in his eyes. 'No one bothers with me much. They think I'm a confused old sod with marbles for brains, but I got the best memory of anyone. I remember what my father told me, what my grandfather told me. But you? You got what I had and couldn't use, you got the will to try and save him and I reckon that fire in your veins needs an outlet before it burns you up.'

Haven wanted to tell Tucker to hurry, that every second counted, but something made him hold his tongue. That and the fact Tucker had exposed everything Haven had tried to hide.

'You know the Henderson curse is real. You knew Sebastian and no doubt he told you some things, but not everything mind, because no one could live with knowing everything. All you need to understand is that there's the Rafferty you know, and another one. One that was torn from him and has been biding its time.'

Haven blew out a breath. Just when he thought things couldn't get any more fucked up.

'You'll no doubt come across two boys that look like Rafferty down there. Two mirror twins. And there's only one way to tell them apart.'

'How do I know which one to trust?' Haven asked as a clap of thunder sounded right above their heads, so loud the vibration juddered through the rock.

Tucker shuffled forward and beckoned Haven to lower his head. He whispered against Haven's ear as though he was afraid that something might be listening.

Haven's eyes widened.

'You'll need to choose between them.'

'What are you going to do?' Haven shouldered the pickaxe again.

'I might have a little nap.' A grin warmed the old man's face.

Two heavy blows and the rock beneath Haven's feet crumbled away, leaving a yawning, dark crevice. He chipped away at it until he thought he could ease his body through. The scent of the ocean wafted up towards him.

'Here, take this.' Tucker thrust the lantern into his hand.

'You'll need it to get back down to the village.'

'I can wait 'til dawn, don't you worry. And besides, I can't go. I'm the Robin to your Batman and we all know Robin was the clever one.'

Haven laughed and squeezed Tucker's shoulder. His bones felt frail, as though with enough pressure they would shatter.

'When this is over I'm going back to yours and we're digging out that movie, okay?' Somehow he knew that Tucker would have a stack of VHS tapes cluttering up his living room.

Neither of them mentioned the heavy weight of the fact Haven might not ever see daylight again.

Haven hung the lantern on his arm and lowered his body through the crevice.

He slid on his side down a steep incline, small chips of rock raining down as momentum hurtled him into the dark. He kept his arm outstretched, praying that the lantern would survive the fall. His head bounced against an outcrop of rock, sending a burst of pain across his skull.

At last his feet hit something like level ground and he tumbled onto it. He lay on his back, his breath ragged in his ears, the brave light from the lantern hardly piercing the thick and brooding dark.

You're going to die, a small, insistent voice told him. Haven shrugged it off, not because he didn't believe it but because he knew he had to take the chance. He couldn't live with the guilt if he didn't try to find Rafferty. If another boy died because of him.

But he couldn't shake the knowledge that *something* else lived down here.

'No shit, Haven,' he said, just to hear his own voice.

He'd landed in a narrow tunnel with a low ceiling. Dust from the disturbed rock lined the back of his throat.

The sound of gushing water came from somewhere in the dark.

Had he opened up the tunnels like Tucker said? Or was that only vain hope?

Slowly, he crawled along on his hands and knees, moving the lantern every few feet. The impossible weight of what lay above him was a constant pricking across the raw edges of his nerves. Sweat dripped into his eyes despite the frigid air.

How the fuck do people do this for fun?

He was wondering that as he shoved the lantern a few more inches, aware of the ground dipping away as soon as he removed his hand. His fingers snatched into thin air as the lantern toppled.

The light went out. And darkness rushed in.

CHAPTER FIFTY-THREE

Rafferty was well used to terror at this point. But as he was yanked into the water, that terror became an all-encompassing spear, gutting him wide open. Instinct made him hold his breath as he spiralled deeper, the hold around his waist firm and unrelenting.

Memories scorched through his mind, memories of the time he fell in the tarn as a child, of going under and seeing the outside world through a watery veil, all he had known rapidly disappearing. He remembered the choking weight of water in his throat, burning his eyes, his limbs flailing uselessly. And then Sebastian hauling him out by his collar, his face as pale as bone.

'I told you about the water,' he shouted as Rafferty gasped and spluttered in his brother's grip. 'You must never go near the water!'

But there was no Sebastian to save him now, only a creature who was going to drown him. Who was probably going to eat him afterwards. Or during.

He stopped struggling and opened his mouth, felt the pop of the air bubbles escaping his nose.

Down and down until he could see the soft blue glow filtering through the water. A strange peace flowed through him. A moment of extreme calm as he decided to die.

The creature's face appeared in front of him, its hair floating like seaweed caught on the cusp of a wave. A tentacle wound around his chest, pulling him closer. Its mouth fell open.

Spiked canine teeth lined the front of its jaw.

For tearing flesh.

Large, flat molars at the back.

For grinding bone.

Its tongue unfurled from a fleshy pocket in the roof of its mouth.

He sobbed then and the water gushed into his throat and flooded his sinuses, sending a needle-sharp jab of agony through his skull.

Viscous lips pressed against his, a tongue probing between them. He felt the flick of its tip against his inner cheek and waited for the canines to tear him to pieces.

A strange vibration juddered along his gums, into the roots of his teeth. The tongue delved deeper and his gag reflex kicked in, but the creature's grip was as strong as an iron chain and he was powerless within it. The tongue slipped down his throat, and the sensation went with it.

A sharp ache behind his breastbone, tiny bubbles bursting somewhere inside. The violation of something alien within him.

The grip around his chest tightened, his ribs compressed to the point of breakage. An acute burning around them as though the skin had ruptured apart.

He felt himself slipping away, his body relaxing, his eyes closing. The water held him softly and he didn't have the energy to fight it.

The tongue withdrew. He felt it inch by inch as it dragged along the linings of his throat, as it licked across his teeth. As it lapped around his lips when it finally retreated.

A sound reached his ears and he forced his eyelids open. A pocket of sound that pulsed through the water. He glanced down and saw that it had let him go, that he was floating by himself.

Rafferty Henderson no longer felt like he was drowning. He no longer felt like he had to breathe.

The creature swam around him and he turned and followed its languid circling, his body moving easily in the water.

Part of his brain was a storm of confusion and disbelief, but another was euphoric in his newfound state. He expected to wake up in a cold sweat and find this was all the stuff of nightmares.

It swam away, its tail propelling it forward effortlessly. He could see each scale shimmering as it caught the bioluminescence, and the beauty of it prickled at the back of his eyes. A spurt of water flowed into his throat and he panicked, but found that he could expel it without thinking.

Don't go near the water, they all had warned him. *You don't know what it can do.*

And now he did know what it could do. He knew what the thing that lived within it could do.

He swam behind it, following that luminescent tail as it glided through narrow tunnels and chasms in the rock, his own movements clumsy at first but then refining.

Time lost all meaning. There was only the creature. Only the deep.

At last it stopped and pulled him up in a circle of shivering light onto a crag of rock. Hoisted him into the air.

His throat spasmed at the difference in environment. He took a breath, and then another, felt the flow of air down his throat. Forced himself to inhale and exhale as he had always done. His sodden clothes clung to his body and he wondered why he wasn't freezing cold.

But this, this thing that had happened to him, had surely choked away everything that was normal.

The creature had swum back to rest against a shelf of rock, half in and half out of the water. A light pulsed within its flesh. Rafferty could see the bones of its skeleton as the light quivered.

It raised one arm, the water streaming from it, and pointed with a long, curved finger. He turned and saw a shaft that wound upwards into the rock.

He scrambled to his feet and made his way across, his body reeling slightly. A splash behind him. He glanced over his shoulder. It had gone. But this time he wasn't afraid.

Rafferty edged along the shaft, the freezing rock face pressed against his body. It narrowed in places, barely wide enough for him to squeeze through, but he pushed on because the creature had told him to. His foot hit something and he heard it spin away into the dark. He followed the sound and crouched, his fingers finding something with a deadly tip.

The roar of rushing water drew him onwards.

It was the smell that reached him first. The smell of something newly dead. Of torn tissue open to the air, of coagulated blood. It crawled into his nostrils, drew him onwards. Rafferty edged towards it, to the place at the end of the shaft where the blue light ebbed and flowed.

He dropped to his knees and peered over a ledge. It was the chamber he had found before, although he had approached it from a different angle. The one with the broken coffins and the bones.

In the middle of the chamber floor was the reason for the smell. A woman, her chest ripped open, ribbons of flesh hanging from her ribcage. His eyes widened and he bit the inside of a finger to stop his cry of alarm.

Coffin handles gleamed in the flickering, blue-edged dark. But this woman had not come from a coffin. He knew that instinctively.

Yet it wasn't the woman Rafferty found himself staring at. By her side, sitting cross-legged, his hands covered in gore, was a hunched figure. The sound of chewing reached Rafferty's ears. The sound of crunching bone.

The figure raised its head and Rafferty's breath hitched in his throat.

A half grin met his gaze, a mouth with shreds of tissue caught between crimson-smeared teeth.

'Hello, Raff,' the figure said, licking a trickle of blood from a scarlet palm.

Rafferty froze, and the gasp he had tried so hard to withhold fell from his lips.

It was like someone had held up a mirror.

'Cat got your tongue, Raff?'

It was Rafferty's voice talking to him. He grabbed hold of the rock wall, disorientation making his head spin.

'Raphael?' The name he hadn't spoken for nine years croaked from his throat.

'You didn't fight for me.' The other boy's eyes darkened as he pointed a rib bone towards him. 'You owed me that, at least.'

Rafferty's mind skimmed backwards, fell over itself in its haste to find a shred of logic. It unearthed a long-buried image—he was lying on Amelia's bed, struggling to move, his tongue dry and heavy in his mouth, the light glinting from a blue bottle on the nightstand. He'd thought it was a nightmare.

'I was your brother, Raff. We could have grown up together. But oh no, your appetite kicked in so fucking early. So I had to settle for being a part of you. Your wariness about the church?

276

That was you remembering about us, about the one who tore me from you.'

Rafferty's legs gave way. He sank to the ground, cold rock seeping into his bones. His imaginary friend wasn't imaginary at all.

'Amelia and Grace decided I was bad for you, said I made you do bad things. So they told *him* and he made you reject me. I came here because I had nowhere else to go.'

'How did . . .'

'How did I get this?' Raphael gestured at himself. He paused and dug a finger into the cavity of the body by his side, plucked out a kidney, licked the bloody mucus from its purpled surface.

Rafferty's mouth watered. The horror of his instinct forced a whimper from his lips.

'I came here to hide. Found our mutual friend.' A bloody grin. 'Discovered it lived off bones and dead flesh. Discovered that weird energy within it. You could say it made me from the remains of the dead. You've read *Frankenstein*, right?'

Rafferty's head reeled. He took a step forwards.

Raphael slipped the kidney into his mouth, bit into its glutinous form. Coagulated blood ran down his chin. 'It's my turn to live now, Raff.'

Raphael rolled his shoulders back and studied the ravaged corpse. 'She so very nearly knew it all. Do you know the lengths Amelia and Grace went to just to protect you? This is their doing.' He jabbed a finger into the jutting rib cage and snapped off another bone.

'No.' Rafferty shook his head, then lifted his chin defiantly. 'They wouldn't.'

'They would and they did.' Raphael gnawed at the end of the bone. It shattered, the sharp sound echoing from the chamber walls.

'People die for you, Raff. In fact, right now Haven is well on his way to joining that tally.' Raphael stood and brushed a string of mucus from his fingers. His lips quirked into a smile. A smile that chilled Rafferty to the core. 'Let's see who can get to him first.'

CHAPTER FIFTY-FOUR

Haven bowed his head, felt the pound of his pulse in his temples. He was royally screwed.

Two options flickered through his mind: crawl backwards and wait at the bottom of the shaft until dawn, or continue and pray that somewhere along the line he would come across Rafferty. Or maybe the boy who looked like Rafferty.

What would Tucker do? Haven's lips set into a grim smile. There was no question what the old man would do. He set off along the tunnel, as blind as if someone had gouged out his eyes.

A sound rolled towards him, vibrating through the rock.

A lump formed in his throat and he swallowed it down.

'Rafferty?' The boy's name fell into the dark. Then silence.

Haven crawled onwards, the sting of the open blisters on his palms a constant reminder that he was still alive.

The air temperature dropped without warning. A soft splash up ahead. He focussed all of his attention on the nothing in front of him. Put one hand down, then the other, edging inch by inch, felinely fixated on what might be waiting. *Don't think about what you read. Don't think about those fucking words.*

He lifted one hand, put it down . . . a scream of protest from his shoulder as his palm continued its downward journey. He tried to offset his toppling balance but his weight carried him forward.

A moment of paralysing horror as he pitched headfirst into oblivion, arms and legs flailing as he plummeted.

His freefall ended abruptly as he hit the cushioning of water, breath driven from his lungs at the arctic cold, spinning and spinning in the coal-black dark.

He tried to kick out, instinct screaming at him to swim to the surface, to stop his hurtling descent, but there was some kind of current here and it only dragged him deeper.

Amidst the chaos and the fear a thought seared across his mind with serrated edges—this was how Sebastian spent his final moments.

Something touched his cheek and he grabbed for it. It was a length of seaweed and it wrapped itself around his wrist as though it was a sentient thing.

A faint blue glow came from deeper in the water, and even though the pressure against his ears made his skull feel like it wanted to explode Haven let himself be dragged down towards it.

Now he could see shelves of rock nestling in the glow, strands of seaweed floating languidly around them. He trod water for a moment and swept his hand through the light.

But he didn't have the time, or the breath, to wonder on this too much. He kicked out again and swam deeper, knowing there was no chance of making the surface again when he ran out of air. And that moment was rapidly approaching.

He pulled himself around a jutting ledge of rock and threw up his hands instinctively as a shape took form below him.

Something was embedded in a deep layer of silt on what must be the pool's bottom.

A slender, pale hand reached towards him, flakes of paint rising from its fingers.

Haven grabbed for it, the solidity anchoring the heartbeat of his panic.

He knew what it was, had seen it before on the painting. The figurehead from the *Marie Claire*, buried here like some kind of forlorn atonement.

Haven's sight began to blur, the crushing ache in his chest almost more than he could bear. Somewhere, on the way down, he had lost his hair tie and wayward strands floated around his face like the seaweed he had discarded moments ago.

He spun away, desperate to find a pocket of air—and was yanked sharply backwards. A net of pain across his scalp. Haven tried to turn and in his peripheral vision saw what was holding him. His hair had entangled itself around the broken laurel wreaths worn as a crown by the figurehead.

A wild despair knifed through him and he gasped, his lungs at bursting point. A stream of ice-cold water gushed into his nose and down his throat. He spluttered at the pain, his mouth widening in panic and the water invaded, hungrily.

Haven thrashed in the depths, watched over by the cold, dead eyes of Marie Claire.

A flicker of movement above him, a slick shape seen through vision turning to black.

Rafferty?

Haven hung on to his last shreds of consciousness. A flash of silver. His focus zeroed in on the knife clamped between the boy's teeth.

Rafferty was almost on him now. Haven couldn't understand how the boy wasn't struggling at this depth of water. *Unless . . .*

Unless this wasn't the Rafferty he knew.

I am going to die.

The boy was level with him now, his eyes beseeching Haven with some kind of silent plea Haven didn't understand. Rafferty took the knife in his hand and Haven flailed his arms, trying to knock it away with the dying threads of his strength.

Rafferty pulled him close, one hand wrapped around Haven's shoulders. The hand with the knife drifted behind Haven's back. Haven prepared himself for the brutal blow, for the sight of his blood blooming into the water.

But instead the pain came in waves across his skull. His head craned backwards. A sudden release. A lightening.

Then Rafferty's mouth against his own, the taste of salt, the water in his throat being sucked away. Haven clung to the slight frame holding him, felt death open its jaws and wait with hooded eyes.

A certain kind of self-preservation kicked in as this reasoning settled. A certain spurt of energy that filled his veins with fire.

It scorched through him and he kicked out, letting Rafferty guide him. Sometimes the boy pulled his lips away and bubbles escaped his nostrils, but then the kiss came again and Haven let himself believe that he would live, even though he didn't understand how any of this was possible.

There was darkness, then patches of light, then more darkness, and finally the pale blue glow welcomed them into a tunnel. An acute dizziness took hold at the difference in the water pressure. At one point he blacked out, and when he came to they were swimming upwards.

They broke through the water's surface and Haven took a gulp of blessed air. His sinuses screamed in pain as water streamed from his nose. He dragged himself up onto a rocky ledge, coughing and spluttering. His lungs felt like someone had set them alight.

Rafferty watched him from the water, the strange blue light on the cavern walls casting an eerie glow across the plains of his face.

'How . . . ?' Haven started to say, but his throat wasn't ready for words and he hacked out another mouthful of water.

His gaze locked with Rafferty's and he wondered . . . but this had to be him, right? Otherwise why would he have bothered to save him from drowning?

The water behind the boy started to ripple but it didn't seem to bother him.

Haven watched as a pale mass mushroomed beneath the surface. He wanted to hide behind his hands but his limbs were frozen.

And then a shape burst through behind Rafferty, rising half out of the water like a whale in motion. Haven caught a glimpse of a chalk-white face, of features that at first looked human but were arranged slightly out of kilter. He felt like he was staring at something in a hall of mirrors. The mouth was too large, too wide, and the eyes too round, too protruding.

And its hair was made of streaming water and seaweed and things that writhed.

Tentacles. They were fucking tentacles.

If Haven's lungs could have, they would have screamed, but all he managed was a moan of absolute terror.

The creature slipped an arm around Rafferty's waist and in the blink of an eye, they were both lost in the water's depths.

Chapter Fifty-Five

Tucker waited by the breach in the rock. He was angry at himself for not being able to help Haven. *An ageing body is a millstone when the mind is still as sharp as cut glass.* But he knew his anger was a futile thing. It was time to pass on the torch. If Haven failed, so be it.

He dozed for a while, his chin drooping towards his chest, and it was the first rays of dawn breaking through the cloud-heavy sky that woke him.

He'd taken a great chance unloading what he knew, unloading what he thought he would take to his own grave. Part of him had hoped that his sons would take up his gauntlet, but they were modern men and his talk of superstition and things brought back from the deep only caused them to pat him on the shoulder and exchange glances with each other over the top of his head.

It had taken him over half of his lifetime to pull it all together, and parts of that time he had sometimes wondered if he was losing his sanity, that maybe he was on a fool's errand to hell.

But when the Henderson women took the bones from the crypt and he heard whispers Peter Edwards had been seen at the cottage soon after, it only fanned the flames of his obsession further.

His great-grandmother had possessed the knowing, just as Tucker did, but his was rusted from lack of use. Some may have called her witch back then, but never to her face, for she was a formidable woman. He thought about her, and the Henderson sisters. It was always the women who bore the brunt of the failures of men.

She knew what had happened on that godforsaken expedition, knew that what Walsh brought back remained alive beneath the ground in the waterlogged tunnels that once led to the sea. But no one would believe a woman of her lesser standing, so she told her stories to her sons and made them promise they would do the same. Until it ended.

Her recollections still lived within him and sometimes Tucker dreamed of her standing on a windswept shore, her shawl clutched around her shoulders, but when he followed her gaze it was always turned towards the tarn.

And now he had told a complete stranger what he had buried in his heart for decades.

He'd seen in Haven a fragment of himself, a desire to uncover the truth no matter how painful, how strange it could be. And knowing that Haven had ties with Sebastian only cemented Tucker's reasoning. Sebastian Henderson was—Tucker checked his thoughts, *had been*—a powder keg waiting for a fuse. His forays into the village, his disappearances for days on end, as though he could ever outrun his fate. Or his name.

But Tucker knew he loved Rafferty. Maybe it was the return of the Other that had flipped his final switches. Or Rafferty's growing appetite.

No one took any notice of an old man. Especially youth as it surrendered to its instincts.

Tucker's stomach grumbled and part of him wished he was ambling around his kitchen, setting a kettle to boil on the stove. Slathering butter on a slice of fresh bread.

The beginnings of a chill crept along his bones. *I'm a stupid old fool*, he thought. *Staying out here all night in the rain.*

Tucker needed to go meet his maker with the knowledge that he'd at least freed what was imprisoned beneath the ground, that he had somehow broken the hold it had on the Henderson name. But longing for something didn't mean that it would happen.

The ramblings of an unhinged mind, some would say.

Maybe he should shut his eyes again for a minute? Just until Haven came back . . .

He muted the nagging ache that told him that maybe he'd never see Haven again, glanced at the leaden sky and wished the sun would shine to warm his bones.

But just as he was about to drift off he sensed he wasn't alone.

Part of him understood this was coming. That was the problem of having the knowing. It sometimes showed you things you'd rather not see.

He heard something breathing in the dark maw of the crevice. The scent of brine came with it. Movement as a figure climbed into the wan daylight.

Tucker opened his eyes and stared into those that looked like they belonged to Rafferty Henderson. They were glazed, the pupils dilated. A thin line of drool dripped down his chin.

Every line on the blood-smeared face looked like Rafferty, down to the smattering of freckles across his nose. Even the damp hair swept in the same tousled waves.

But what had he expected?

The boy inclined his head and looked up at Tucker.

'Are you him?' Tucker asked, as his heart rate rocketed.

A moment where Tucker felt himself examined, probed, like a corpse on a slab.

'I'm who I'm meant to be.'

No one, not even the old, are truly prepared for death.

CHAPTER FIFTY-SIX

Haven sat for a long time in the near dark. He watched the pale blue light play across his skin. Shivered as his sodden clothes clung to his frame.

Let his mind wander back over what had happened—he had been a fragment away from dying, could still taste the sour tang of it on the back of his tongue. And then Rafferty had saved his life. Rafferty had breathed life *into* him.

And what had he seen in the water? It defied all logic, made him want to rip the image from his consciousness, bleach it away into oblivion. Haven lowered his head, clasped his hands around his skull. It was too much to absorb, even for someone who had already seen the impossible.

Another kind of dread dripped down his spine. He had no idea how to get out of this place. His own insignificance thrummed in time with his pounding heart.

'Rafferty!'

Haven's voice echoed around the rocks. He could hear his own desperation laced within it.

Slowly, he got to his feet, managed to tamp down the rampage of panic threatening to choke him. Rafferty had left the knife; whether on purpose or not Haven didn't know. He crouched and picked it up. Hefted the weight in his hands.

It was old, the handle inlaid with something that could be ivory, could be bone, but the blade glinted in the ebb and flow of the light, a wicked wink that calmed Haven's shattered nerves.

It was something to hang on to.

He inched along the ledge, bowed his head, and ducked into the narrow tunnel that led from it.

The scent of brine hung heavy in the air, the occasional strand of seaweed clinging to his boots.

He focussed on what he knew. Water can force itself into virtually anything. The ocean had found a way in. Found a way to reclaim what belonged to it. Tucker's words came back to him: *If we can shatter that rock, give it a way out, it might yet save Rafferty.*

It was a slim chance but it was something. And he still wasn't sure if the boy who saved him had been Rafferty. What if it was the other one, playing with him, drawing out his fear like a cat taunting a mouse before it ripped out its innards?

A sound reached his ears and he paused, lifting his head to try to locate it.

The rush of water.

He felt his way along the tunnel, grim determination aching in his jaw. This was where he was meant to be, the near-constant rain and soakings all leading to this moment.

Haven latched onto this port in his raging storm. He quickened his steps, followed the tunnel as it twisted and turned, almost stumbled as the floor fell away to nothing. His hand anchored around a spur of jagged rock.

There, in a cavern so tall that Haven could barely see its ceiling, was the source of the water. But it wasn't that which caught his attention. It was the bones and shattered coffins strewn along the ground. A figure knelt by a body.

Rafferty?

Haven clambered down into the charnel pit, fragments of rock grinding into the raw flesh of his palms.

He didn't want to go closer, but he had to. Anguish tore through him without mercy.

Her face was turned towards the wall but Haven could see part of her skull was crushed, brain matter glistening in the eerie blue light, strands of silver hair coated in crimson. Her body cavity lay open. Ravaged. He bent over and threw up, the bile burning his throat. He knew that this harrowing image would hitch against the one from the warehouse and follow him all the days of his life. The people he had failed.

He forced his gaze back, crouched and held her curled hand in his. It felt like cold marble against his smarting skin.

He glanced across to Rafferty, saw the tear stains on his cheeks, water dripping from his wet fringe. Saw the injuries on his face from the beating. Haven placed his free hand against the back of Rafferty's bowed head.

'It's my fault,' the boy said. 'All of this is my fault.'

Haven wanted to shoulder that blame, because if he'd answered her phone calls she might still be alive. But Meredith hadn't waited for his help; maybe she hadn't really needed it. She had been on her own voyage and they had passed like ships in the night.

'Did she fall?' Haven asked, although as soon as the words left his lips he discounted them. His eyes flicked to the toes of her boots. The leather was scuffed, shreds of it blistering the surface.

She had been dragged here by something. Dragged here by something and eaten.

Haven laid Meredith's hand gently on the floor. He let his arm drift across Rafferty's shoulder and pulled him close, resting his chin on the top of Rafferty's head. He could feel the racing beat of the boy's heart, smell the salt in his hair.

'They buried me alive,' Rafferty sobbed, his voice muffled as Haven hugged him close. Rafferty lifted his chin and gazed into Haven's eyes, his shoulders shaking. 'I know it sounds crazy but there's another one of me here. Another one who'll try and twist your mind, trick you into believing that he's me. I don't know how to fight him. Please help me.'

The vulnerability in the boy's tone tore strips from Haven's heart.

'You know I'll help you,' he said. 'Come here.' He pulled Rafferty close again and whispered an invocation to any god who would hear him.

Then he slid the knife from his sleeve and plunged it into Rafferty's back, the blade slicing cleanly through yielding flesh, penetrating the boy's heart. Bright, frothy blood gushed over Haven's fingers.

If you can't save him, you'll know what to do.

Haven held on to Rafferty as the boy sank to the ground, as blood bubbled from the corners of his mouth. As his eyes began to dim, but not before fury blackened them.

Numbness blossomed through Haven's body, taking control of his limbs. He had played his card on the secret whispered to him by an old man who everyone thought was crazy.

Had played his card because his gut instinct screamed at him that this was right. But however he looked at it, he had the blood of another boy on his hands. And he wasn't sure he'd ever be able to come back from that.

Chapter Fifty-Seven

ONE MONTH LATER

The midnight sky was alive with radiance as the Northern Lights ebbed and flowed within, as though it held some celestial ocean of its own. Curtains of neon green and deep violet, threaded through with bands of pink. A constantly changing ballet of mesmerising colour.

It was an awe-inspiring sight, but no one in the small car winding its way down the isolated track to the remote Scottish coastline found it beautiful. Except, perhaps, for one.

Rosa sat behind the wheel, her hands tightly clenched upon it, as the car gamely navigated the uneven terrain. The seat next to her was empty. Tucker said his bones wouldn't like the long trip, and besides, they didn't need him now.

Haven would always need him, because without his insight, his knowledge, things could have played out very differently. It was Tucker Rafferty had gone to, bewildered and traumatised when his terrifying encounter in the tunnels finally struck home. After saving Haven's life. Although Tucker had said the appearance damn well nearly stopped his old heart for good.

That's when it began. The change.

Of all the horrors Haven had witnessed this was the most heart-wrenching to suffer.

291

He glanced out of the window, one arm around the slight form at his side. Haven had always wanted to see the Northern Lights but now that they were here he knew that they would always remind him of what was going to happen next.

Rafferty stirred and lifted his head, his gaze towards the illumination. Towards the ocean.

The sharp tang of salt water rose from his hair.

Haven had talked with Rosa on the long drive north. Talked again about how he had known the boy by Meredith's side wasn't Rafferty, despite his pleas. Despite the injuries on his face. It was the heartbeat, Haven had said. The heartbeat at the left-hand side of his chest. Rafferty's was on the right, situs inversus mirroring his organs, as it had mirrored so many other things.

Tucker knew. Had known on the day he barged into Haven's room and ran his hand over Rafferty's chest. Had whispered his secret to Haven as they stood in the rain-drenched dark with the foreboding waters of the tarn as their witness.

The car lurched to a halt as the track ended abruptly. Now all that lay before them was a narrow expanse of shell-dotted sand and the ocean, the ethereal lights reflected from its surface. As if the churning water and heavens had joined forces to create something both deadly and beautiful.

The symbolism knifed through Haven's gut.

Rafferty pushed open the door. A freezing gust of wind blasted in but he didn't seem to feel it.

Haven wanted more time. Rosa turned to face him and he saw the tears in her eyes. He fought back his own as he followed Rafferty onto the sand. The roar of the ocean made words impossible so he concentrated on keeping in step with the boy at his side, their feet sinking ankle-deep into the cold sand.

Waves crashed against the shore, leaving small shells and clumps of seaweed in their wake. The wild sea gives and the wild sea takes.

But above the roar came another sound. A sound that pierced Haven in such a way he felt it vibrate within his marrow. Haunting. Melodic. The cry of the last albatross. Or maybe the cry of something that had finally gained its freedom.

A shaky breath left Haven's lips as the wind tangled his hair around his face. It was still a surprise to feel its shortened length.

'You don't have to do this,' he said. 'We can find a way.'

The boy turned to him, the lights casting an eerie glow across the plains of his face. Spray dotted his cheeks, dried salt on his lips. The retroreflection of his eyes glowed moon–silver.

Rafferty's chin trembled. His eyes flicked to Haven's. 'You know I do. I can't live a life here with what I am. With what my instincts drive me to do. You've seen it . . .' The boy's voice tailed off.

The constant need for water. The constant need to consume. The chains around his feet and hands that Haven had secured each night. The agonising cries that made sleep impossible for both of them. Scouring the woods for small creatures to trap, to bring back, to leave the room before Rafferty tore them apart.

'How long before I get caught? Before I kill someone? Before someone kills me for what I am?

Haven didn't have an answer. He offered the only thing he could. 'We can go someplace new. I'll keep you safe.'

But Haven knew existing as they had done over the past month would one day shatter both of them.

Rafferty placed his hand on Haven's arm. 'No one can keep me safe. I can't promise that one night I won't break free, that you won't find me standing at the base of your bed. That I won't see you as anything else but my next meal.' He shook his head, distress contorting his features. His fingers tightened for a moment.

The soaring cry came again as the lights danced over a rock at the far edge of the bay. Waiting there was what had dwelt in the

293

tunnels, its tail dipped into the ocean, its hair a Medusa tangle around its face. Haven glanced away. He had a feeling that if he looked for too long he might lose the last of his sanity. As if it knew, a burst of electric current illumed its bones.

It was finally free, but saving Rafferty's life had come with a price.

Rafferty kicked off his boots and walked to the water's edge. His feet sank into the soft sand as the ocean tasted him for the first time.

'I need to go now,' he whispered, his voice whipped away by the wind. But Haven caught it. He reached out and grabbed hold of Rafferty's hand, pulled the boy into a fierce embrace. Kissed his brow and tried to make the moments last. They clung to each other as the dazzling lights turned from green to gold, washing over their forms.

Letting Rafferty go was the hardest thing Haven had ever done. When Sebastian had begged him to help, Haven knew that this outcome had never been in his friend's plan. That what he meant was to destroy Rafferty if he couldn't save him.

But Haven had already destroyed the other side of him.

This? This was right, even though every fibre of Haven's body screamed in dissent.

We all came from the ocean. We all return when it is our time.

Rafferty tugged off his jumper. His T-shirt.

Haven tried not to look at the three diagonal lines slashed into his ribcage. At the gaping pink tissue glistening along each defined lip. At the glimmering, blue-edged scales along his spine.

He watched as the boy strode into the ocean. Up to his knees. To his waist. He peeled off his jeans, let the waves carry them back to the shore.

A sob broke in Haven's throat and he walked out until the sea churned around his knees. The water was so cold it took his breath away and soon his teeth were chattering, forcing him back to the shore. The dark water had no need of him.

People were not meant to wade out into the ocean and survive in its depths. Just like people were not supposed to lie on a warehouse floor with their throats ripped open, then get up and walk away.

Haven thought of Logan, the boy he had wronged so many years ago, as he watched Rafferty let the ocean take his weight, as he bobbed like a cork in its embrace.

The creature shrieked then, a primeval sound of triumph that echoed across the rolling water. It was out there, waiting for the boy with Irving Walsh's blood in his veins. And maybe that was okay, although in the grand scheme of things the horror of it scraped along Haven's bones and he would wear those scars for the rest of his life.

All he had wanted was to save Rafferty, to somehow even the guilt-wracked scorecard in his heart. To atone. But this wasn't ever about him. He realised that now.

All of his life Rafferty Henderson had other people exercising control over him, making choices they thought were for the best.

His final choice was his own.

But as Rafferty swam out into the deep, merciless ocean, and Haven watched until there was nothing left to see, the thought came to him that maybe second chances on the life you had was how it was meant to be.

EPILOGUE

In the musty dark of the room Irving Walsh once slept in, a painting lies forgotten on a stained mattress. Face down, its back ripped open, exposing torn sackcloth and a mildewed, half-eaten frame. Movement from one corner as a deathwatch beetle scurries along an edge.

Under the bed, the same beetle has chewed its way along a length of floorboard. Through the masticated wood, a corner of a piece of folded parchment is barely visible, tucked away by a man who did not wish these particular words to ever see the light of day, for it condemned him to eternal perdition.

But yet, he could not destroy the evidence of his sins, and he lived with the depravity of his actions until the night his devils gathered around his bed and stole his last breath.

SHIP'S LOG (DECEMBER 1874)
CAPTAIN IRVING WALSH

I awoke sprawled on the filthy floor. Pain seared through my fingertips and when I focussed my eyes I found the mangy rat with its teeth sunk into my middle finger. Its black, beady eyes held no soul in the flickering light of the lantern.

And then I remembered the creature. I spun, staggering to my feet, the rat scurrying into the shadows. My throat burned as though I had imbibed a potion made from hellfire itself.

Had I dreamt this nightmare?

But no, it was still there, its head bowed as if asleep, those awful tentacles coiled around its face.

Burn it, a small voice said, and I laughed, the sound hoarse and forlorn. If I burned this monstrosity, burned my ship to embers, I was sealing my own death warrant, for I would not survive out on the ice in the jaws of the polar night.

It will not matter, the voice whispered again. You are a dead man walking.

Unless . . .

Above me, in the cruel dark, a low moan filtered down through the frigid air. Cartwright. He lived still.

Ice cracked behind me as the creature stirred.

I climbed the rickety stairs, the stench of blood and waste rising from each tread, my steps leading me to his meagre cabin. I could smell him, smell the disease as it corrupted his body, smell the rancid sweat coating his skin.

A thin line of drool ran from my lips.

I pushed open the door, hunger rising in my gut, unfolding itself limb by limb, obliterating any other thought but survival. It flooded my mouth with its need and I welcomed its controlling caress.

My knife was in my belt. I withdrew it, the bone handle heavy and comforting in my hand.

Three steps took me to Cartwright's side. His eyes fluttered open, bright with fever, but I saw something else swimming in their depths. A terrible, haunting fear.

I had to end his suffering. It was the only humane thing to do.

But I did not do that.

297

I lowered my head, lifted his sullied shirt, ran my tongue over his trembling belly. His blood sang to me, hot and honeyed, his flesh soft and warm and enticing.

Here the words become scrawled, ink smeared across the cursive, words scratched out and replaced, gaps between the letters as a mind fought to unburden its terrible truth before these last rushed lines were penned.

As I dug the tip of the knife into the bottom of his ribcage, as I parted the skin, the blade effortless in its duty, exposing the fragrant, pink meat of him, the lantern flickered then faded. The shadows in the corners of the cramped space rushed to enfold me as a shriek echoed from the depths of the hull.

I knew then that it had claimed my soul, but I gave it freely, because the morals of man mean nothing when death stares you in the eye.

Did you enjoy this book? You can make a big difference.

When it comes to getting attention for my books, reviews are the most powerful tools. Much as I'd like to take out full page advertisements or put posters on buses, I don't have the financial muscle of a big publisher.

But I do have something those publishers would love to get their hands on.

A committed and loyal group of readers.

Honest reviews of my books help bring them to the attention of other readers and helps me to continue to create stories for you to fall in love with. If you've enjoyed reading this book I would be very grateful if you could leave a review (it can be as short as you like).

ACKNOWLEDGEMENTS

A book starts with the writer, but there are so many other people who nurture it through its growth from seed to flower. My grateful thanks to my wonderful editor, Rae Oestreich, who helped shape it into the tale in your hands. To the first eyes on this story and for that all important first critique, Nicole Eigener and Shane Douglas Keene. Eternally grateful for the love and support. To Sarina Langer and my beta crew who received an early draft of this and waded through with comments and suggestions – Coy Hall, G.R. Thomas, Josh Radwell, and Lisa Niblock. To Kealan Patrick Burke and Elderlemon Design for my haunting cover creation. To Platform House Publishing for beautiful interior design. You are all absolute stars.

Thank you to my friends and loyal supporters on Twitter and the #bookstagram community on Instagram, for showing me the human side of social media. Writing is a solitary craft but I am never alone with your constant loyalty and encouragement.

And to those who discover my books through other sources—welcome, and my warmest thanks.

ABOUT THE AUTHOR

Beverley Lee is the bestselling author of the Gabriel Davenport vampire suspense series (*The Making of Gabriel Davenport, A Shining in the Shadows* and *The Purity of Crimson*) the grief/gothic horror, *The Ruin of Delicate Things*, and the isolation/folk horror, *The House of Little Bones*. Her shorter fiction has been included in works from Cemetery Gates Media, Kandisha Press and Off Limits Press. In thrall to the written word from an early age, especially the darker side of fiction, she believes that the very best story is the one you have to tell. Supporting fellow authors is also her passion and she is actively involved in social media and writers' groups.

You can visit her online at *www.beverleylee.com* (where you'll find a free dark and twisted short story download) or on Instagram (@theconstantvoice) and Twitter (@constantvoice).

CPSIA information can be obtained
at www.ICGtesting.com
Printed in the USA
LVHW040003180323
741890LV00005B/62

9 780993 549069